# Eva 2:

## FIRST LADY OF SIN

# *Eva 2:*

## FIRST LADY OF SIN

### by

# Storm

Eva First Lady of Sin Part 2. Copyright © by Storm. All rights reserved. Printed in the United States of America. No part of this book may be used or reproduced in any manner whatsoever without written permission except in the case of brief quotations embodied in critical articles or reviews. For information, address Melodrama Publishing, P.O. Box 522, Bellport, NY 11713.

www.melodramapublishing.com

Library of Congress Control Number: 2007910290
ISBN-13: 978-1934157114
ISBN-10: 1934157112
First Edition: September 2008
10 9 8 7 6 5 4 3 2 1

# ACKNOWLEDGMENTS

I thank God for his infinite wisdom, unwavering patience, and unconditional acceptance. Who else, but the Almighty, could keep this STORM RIZING from self-destruction when so many roads got rough?

I'd like to thank *Lace & Melodrama Publishing* for giving me another opportunity to regift my literary gifts. I'm sure working with me on this third book was . . . interesting. Especially you, Lace. Thank you for another opportunity to bestow my special blend of eroticism and witticism upon the literate world and for suffering through my endless questions and emails, again.

**Mr. K.** Dare I say it? Gasp!! Might there be a chance to redeem ourselves? Thank you to my better half in fighting crime on a daily . . . all over Philly. The streets are safer when the nights were sweaty . . .
All in a day's work . . . vests, duty belts, cold, hard steel & fixed sight, seventeen rounds . . .

Thank you to my sons who put up with my absences, and my love, often from afar for the last five years. I love you for believing in my attempts to improve our lives. Thank you for allowing me to bring my work home and miss Tuesday game night 'cause *Eva & Nadia* wouldn't act right! My love for you knows no bounds. Smooches ; - )

**Meat Man,** (Why am I saying this again?) Let's try getting out of high school, dude, please. Summer school is hot for a reason. Okay? Hmm, let me think. It's eight PM; is your cell phone off again?

**D Oven,** let's work on that handwriting, okay? And, stop missing the school bus! No more Nintendo DS game cheats. Let's try to practice that violin . . . for a few minutes at least. Dang!!

**Kev,** don't forget to give out shout-outs when you're at the Olympic trials for track and the NFL Draft. Remember, we knew you way back when…Oak Lane Wildcats and cold Saturday mornings…

And please, gentlemen, . . . LOTION . . .'cause ASH is still not attractive!
RatBoy & WildBoy, Callory & Baddy, Maad & Janae, ya'll got a part in the tale of the Ghetto Daycare starring Mick, babysitter extraordinaire.

Thanks to my family—Whetstone, Bowens—PA & NJ, Phillips, Davis, Willis, Johnson, Vadel - NJ, Holt, Hayes, Cook – KY & NC for conversing with my Dell Wyle E. Coyote laptop instead of me since October 2005. On the cruise to Hawaii and Nags Head, when I was supposed to be coming up with ideas about our next venture: I swear I was paying attention . . . and subliminally putting forth my thoughts and suggestions.

To my label-mates at Melodrama—Endy, Lace, Jacki, Kiki, Linda: keep doing your thang, ladies! Keep striving for that *Essence* Best Seller List.

To Trina Bellamy & Tory Hagains for being the best and honest friends for so many years. Ya'll kept it real for so long. Thanks for putting up with those late night phone calls and early morning text messages.

Thanks Dina Pullen outta Philly, hair stylist extraordinaire, who keeps me gorgeous when I can catch her. Answer your damned cell phone!

Thanks to all my 'EVA' & 'DEN' readers who supported me, bought the book, shared it with friends, spread the word and showed up to book signing to show some luv!!

To my Myspace.com friends who visit the site, read my crazy blogs and leave STORM & EVA the best messages. Keep showing luv!!

Ms. Toni—reppin the Midwest—& Lady Scorpio outta NYC . . . my IM (LMFAOROTF) partner . . . thanks for everything. Endy, keep pushing out the hits and I swear, I will respond to those emails!!

Thanks to the readers who emailed me to let me know what they thought about EVA's sexual drama and non-stop foolishness! And to my readers who thought Nadia was a blindfolded mess in DEN OF SIN, please keep me on track with your thoughts and emails!!

Thanks to RAWSISTAZ, OOSA, APOOO, Asante Books, Black & Nobel Books, Horizon Books, Borders, Walden's and all the other book stores and websites for supporting STORM. Thanks for the opportunity to regift my literary gifts.

JayeGrey, you are my muse and without you, there would be no Storm.

Thank you, from the bottom of my heart, to everyone else who gave a damn and believed I had this book in me. Thanks to the many Urban & Suburban readers for supporting books written by, you for you when they thought we couldn't do it.

Thanks to all who gave a literary damn. Thanks to everyone who has shared a kind or descriptive word for STORM, Eva, Den of Sin & Eva2. I hope you enjoy the wild, backstabbing ride.

To the readers who still love to hate Eva...Email me and let me know! Hit me up at *stormrizing1@yahoo.com* & myspace.com/storm-phillyauthor to find out what's real with this STORM-rizing.

If I've forgotten anyone, please charge it to my head and not my heart. If you know me and are still waiting for a return text or call... you're not alone.

~ Please keep in mind that Eva2 is *FICTION* and simply a figment of my wild, erotic imagination. Let's all practice safe sex and strap it up every time. ~

I know you'll enjoy Eva2—tale of passion with a twist.

Much Luv,

# PROLOGUE

*Eva*

**5:45 PM - Wedding Day**

The organist played the wedding march as I glided down the aisle on the arm of Aunt Mirabelle. At the altar I could see Brand waiting for me, looking like my knight and savior. I didn't care what happened after today. I was getting married, and that was all that mattered.

I tried not to look at Mavis, dressed in full regalia, looking like an actual minister. For once, I tried to muster some feelings of respect and gratitude. Never mind, too much work on my day. Let her marry me so I could be done with her for good.

I caught Evan's eye as I slowly marched down the aisle. As Brand's best man, he stood next to the groom, looking good as shit! Calm down, Eva, get your thoughts together. Okay, but I knew he was not giving me the eye and doing his best lip-licking LL impersonation.

Damn, those lips felt good on my clit.

I tried to avoid Shawn's eyes, but her gaze caught my eye and had me stumbling. She ran her hand over her breasts, making slow, lazy circles around her nipples. She knew everyone's eyes would be on the bride. Saucy wench. I knew what she was signifying, and my clit jumped again.

Damn, those lips felt good on my clit.

I caught Taylor's eye as I continued my march. She looked stricken, caught somewhere between a smile and a grimace. Then she glanced at Shawn and caught the last finger lap over her breasts. She immediately looked into the crowd and I saw her gaze fix on one particular individual. I was sure she didn't realize that Shawn was signifying to me, her best friend.

Had I really fucked three people from my wedding party?

Aunt Mirabelle and I reached the end of the runner that had been laid out for my march. We stopped at the altar, where she wiped a tear and handed me over to Brand. I wanted to kiss him right then, the crowd be damned! Didn't they understand what this day meant to me? Didn't they know all that I had gone through to get this man here? Forget them. This day was all about me.

Mavis stepped forward and joined my hand with Brand's.

"Ladies and gentlemen, we are gathered here today to join this man and woman in holy matrimony. I digress for a short moment, as this is a particularly special day for my family and me. This beautiful young woman is my daughter, Evangeline Arianna LoDolce, and I couldn't be happier or more proud to join Evangeline with Brandon on this day."

I watched Taylor's eyes narrow and peer into the crowd. Maybe Shawn wasn't flirting with me and there was someone else out there. Despite this being the part of this day I'd lived for, I was dying to turn around and see what had caught Taylor's attention. .

"Our loving couple has written their own vows, and will recite them as a symbol of their love and commitment to one another. Brandon, we will start with you. You may begin."

Brand turned to me, still holding my hand. We'd been practicing our wedding vows in between arguments over the last few months. We knew the ceremony was thrown together and perhaps a little non-traditional, so we wanted to make it as special as possible.

"Eva, in the presence of God and these, our friends, I take thee to be my wife, promising with divine assistance to be unto thee a loving and faithful husband, so long as we both shall live. I will be yours in times of plenty and want, in times of sickness and in times of health, in times of joy and in times of sorrow, in times of failure and in times of triumph. I promise to cherish and respect you, to care for and protect you, to encourage and stay with you, for all eternity."

Mavis beamed at Brand like he was her star pupil. I almost expected her to kiss him for me.

"Evangeline, you may begin."

My heart was beating and I hoped I made Brand as proud of me as I was of him. His vows were so honest, and filled with such emotion! I cleared my throat and took a deep breath.

"Brand, in the presence of God and these, our friends, I take thee to be my husband, promising with divine assistance to be unto thee a loving and faithful wife, so long as we both shall live."

There was a rustle and a burst of murmuring from the crowd. Taylor's face turned white and her eyes threatened to pop out of her head. The entire wedding party stood motionless and stared behind us, and a flash of anger surged through me toward the person trying to steal my glow on my day.

I wasn't having it, nor would I give that attempted usurper the pleasure and acknowledgement of interrupting my wedding ceremony. I raised my voice and continued without missing a beat.

"I will be yours in times of plenty and want, in times of sickness and in times of health, in times of joy and in times of sorrow, in times of failure and in times of triumph. I promise to cherish and respect you, to care and protect you, to encourage and stay with you for all eternity."

At this point, Evan stepped forward. He seemed to stare right through us, his fists clenched and a murderous look in his eyes. Brand turned around, still holding my hand, and followed Evan's eyes as Evan walked past us to meet this unseen foe.

I still did not turn around to validate or acknowledge this intruder.

Evan reached the stranger first and I could hear him confront the unknown person.

"What's up, brotha? I don't think you belong here. This is a private ceremony, and you weren't invited by Eva or Brand."

I knew that this was a tame approach for Evan, compared to the lively and colorful language he used on a regular basis.

"Eva." It was unnaturally quiet in the sanctuary. Completely non-plussed and at an absolute refusal to stop my wedding, I tuned out the voice.

"Eva." I could hear the emotional voice behind me. No. This was not happening. I wouldn't admit to myself that Bryce was standing behind me, calling my name at MY wedding to Brand.

"You can't be here to marry Brand, after all you've told me about him! Eva, how are you about to marry Brand, when you accepted my engagement ring two days ago?"

Brand took a step away from me, his eyes full of hurt and confusion.

"Eva, turn around and tell me what the fuck is going on." Bryce sounded as if he was near tears.

I stood motionless, afraid to turn around and meet Bryce's gaze.

"I know you're not marrying this nigga, after what you told me he did to you. He ruined your fuckin' life, Eva, and you're giving him your entire life to continue to mess up!" Bryce was now trying to get past Evan. "Eva, we've been together for almost a year. You took my ring and promised that you would marry me two days ago."

Brand looked at me like he didn't know who I was. "Eva, who the fuck is this clown, comin' in here, talkin' about you was about to marry him? I know you ain't that fuckin' stupid."

I heard fabric rustling and knew, without looking, that the verbal confrontation between Bryce and Evan had escalated to the physical. I heard a shout from the crowd, then the sounds of fists meeting skin.

Brand released my hand and sucker-punched Bryce, catching him off guard. Stunned, Bryce caught Evan's foot to his ribs on the way down. Brand and Evan attacked him, taking turns kicking him as he tried uselessly to defend himself.

Brand was out of breath and breathing hard. "Pussy, I should kill you, comin' in here like that. Fuck makes you think you could come in here and talk to my girl like that?"

Evan stood to the side with a sly grin on his face.

I heard Bethany make a noise, and then she was quiet. I couldn't turn around to see what had happened to her.

Brand was cursing, calling me names, and kicking Bryce like a maniac. He truly looked as if he intended to kill Bryce right there on the floor in Mavis's church.

The wedding guests started rapidly dispersing.

"He's got a gun!" someone shouted, and pandemonium broke out. People were jumping over pews and knocking over slower guests in an attempt to reach the sanctuary doors.

Taylor ran to stop Brand from kicking Bryce. "Evan, why are you just standing there? Stop Brand before he kills him! Do something! Somebody help me!" She grabbed Brand, only to be pulled away by Evan.

Mavis stood immobile at the altar, first whispering and then shouting. "Evangeline, what have you done?" she screamed. "The blood of Jesus! Evangeline, I taught you better than this. The blood of Jesus! Evangeline, what have you done? The blood of Jesus!"

It was enough of a reprieve for Bryce to stagger to his feet. Then Evan was all over him again. Bryce traded punches with Evan and hit

Taylor in the process. Brand was immediately back in the fray, cursing Bryce for hitting Taylor.

Taylor was now in the mix, looking like a super lightweight. Evan delivered kidney shots to Bryce's midsection. As Bryce bent over from the pain, Taylor pimp-slapped him upside the head.

I had to do something. I put out a hand to assist someone. I didn't know what to do. I could hear Mavis moaning and wailing in the background. Her words were alternately indecipherable and then crystal clear.

"The blood of Jesus!"

Bryce was bleeding everywhere. Evan had a cut on his eye and Brand had blood running from his mouth. Taylor kept bitch-slapping and kicking Bryce after Brand and Evan hit him. She mainly stayed on the outside, but managed to get in a few punches.

I felt a hand on my shoulder and whirled around to defend myself. Shawn's body was molded against mine, and her other hand, hidden from view, caressed my ass. I felt my clit jump as I tried to forget the feel of her lips on me.

"Now that you won't be marrying Brand, you can return my calls and we can spend some time together. I want to make you cum like I did before. You remember, don't you?" She kissed my open mouth and stepped toward the fight to grab Taylor.

I looked behind me. Brighton was kneeling over an unconscious Bethany, who'd fainted after the first couple of blows. Poor thing.

"The blood of Jesus!"

Wayland and his younger brother Winston climbed over people and pews and broke up the fight, pulling Brand and Evan off Bryce.

Bryce fought against Winston as he was pulled down the aisle.

"I love you, Eva! It didn't have to happen like this." He coughed up blood through swollen and busted lips. "You know where to find me when you have had enough of that nut-ass nigga you about to marry." To Brand, he said, "Brand, we can do this again when it's just you and me. I'ma see you again on the bricks." Winston hauled Bryce out of the sanctuary and into the street.

"The blood of Jesus!"

Brand walked over to me, standing in the exact same spot that I had been standing just moments ago, speaking my vows. He laughed in my face.

"You is a tramp-ass whore, Eva. That's why I always treated you like one. I'm not even surprised that some nigga came in here at my wedding to kick my ass over you." He spit out a mouthful of blood. "I told you to marry that trick-ass-nigga you was fuckin' with."

He turned around and motioned Evan to follow. Evan wiped blood from his nose and blew me a kiss as he followed Brand out of the sanctuary.

Brighton had roused Bethany, who was now sitting on the floor.

"Bright, what happened? Where's Brand? Eva, is that blood?"

Bright went out after Brand, bumping my shoulder and arm as he passed, pushing me forward. "You better watch your back, bitch."

Oh, God. Brighton fought women like they were men.

"The blood of Jesus!"

Taylor and Shawn had disappeared. I was sure Shawn was somewhere tending to Taylor's wounds.

In the end, I didn't have Brand or Bryce.

I was still standing in the same spot, clutching my wedding bouquet and wearing my wedding dress. A few nosey guests stood on the pews, whispering amongst themselves, waiting to see what would happen next.

As I realized that the rest of my wedding would not take place and my world faded to black, I could still hear Mavis shouting, "The blood of Jesus!"

## Four months before the wedding

"Eva, I gotta go to this job interview on Tuesday afternoon," Taylor informed me. "I need you to drop Shawna off at her doctor's appointment, and I'll pick her up after I get this damned job."

I almost choked on my Honey Nut Cheerios, and had to jump up to keep one from going down the wrong pipe. "What? You've got to be kidding me, Tee." Now that I wasn't choking, I laughed. "You? A job? Yeah, right. Who's gonna hire you, and to do what?" Taylor had been at a junior college for like five years.

"Look, trick, I ain't askin' for no comments from the peanut gallery. Since ya nosy ass had to ask: I have an interview at a juvenile detention facility in Norristown at two-thirty, and I can't do both."

"Okay. If they hire you, I'll make sure no kid of mine ever goes there." I couldn't help myself and laughed again. When I heard Taylor gear up to start in on me again, I quickly added, "All right. I'll take her. You just get a damned job so you can take care of your girlfriend, 'cause she ain't gonna keep letting you fuck her for free."

"Whatever. Just 'cause you gotta pay for your pussy, don't put that shit on me. You gotta work that pussy, don't let that pussy work you. Anyway, just get Shawna where she needs to be by four-thirty and if you can't make it, call one of us, and I'll see what I can do."

"Alright, Tee, just get off my back."

" Shawn, it's Eva. I'm around the corner. Are you ready?" I was on my cell phone, late to picking Shawn up from Taylor's house. I felt like slapping Taylor for having me play limousine driver to her girlfriend.

"I'll be just a few more minutes, Eva. Just come in for a minute. I left the door open. I'm so sorry; I promise I won't take long."

"Shawn, I'm already running late, can't you move any faster?"

"I promise. Just come in for a few minutes."

"All right, I'm parking now." I could have slapped the shit outta Shawn and Taylor. I was thinking that we'd never make her appointment and Taylor would surely blame this on me, somehow. I got inside and sat on the arm of the couch, listening to Shawn walk around upstairs.

"Eva, do me a favor, please? Can you get this for me?" Shawn appeared in the living room, shirtless, and holding her bra together in the back. I looked at her pretty face, her D cups hanging out of the bottom of her bra, and my clit awakened, hard and ready.

Her nipples were hard and I watched her breasts, swinging loosely in her unhooked bra. Was it my imagination, or did she just strike a pose in the doorway? I must have been trippin'. With every step and saunter, her breasts fell farther from the cups.

I sat there, dumbfounded and mesmerized.

Shawn stood before me and bent to give me a hug. My arms hung limply at my sides, daring me to reach out. I didn't trust myself to touch her when my clit was responding like a live missile, ready to destroy.

Her hands stroked my hair and her head turned as she placed a kiss on my cheek. My hands stayed in place but my head responded of its own accord and I met her kiss halfway. Her mouth settled on mine in a light, quick kiss. She stepped away from me, looking, hands on her hips, her head cocked to the side.

Her hands found my clit through my jeans. She stroked my pussy, moaning as I pulled her breasts free and sucked her nipples into my mouth, one at a time. Shawn was stroking my clit, drawing sighs from me as I was caught up in the sight and sounds of my lips drinking in her lush cleavage.

Then she was crouched before me, her hands pulling at my jeans. Something inside my head screamed, "Stop her!" But my hips went along with my jeans, in accordance with her movements to rid me of them. Her lips were on my clitoris before my pants were completely down. Shawn's small, pink tongue disappeared into my swollen lips, locking onto my clit, sucking it softly. I barely had the opportunity to grind my hips into her face when I lost control and exploded on her tongue.

She continued to suck softly and I rolled into another orgasm, smothering her as I pulled her face-forward into my vagina, screaming as a third ripped through me. I pulled her up before I busted again and kissed her lips. Although no woman had ever brought me to a multiple orgasm, I didn't have time to cherish the moment; Taylor was creeping into my thoughts.

I remained in place, my head hung low, wondering what I was doing kissing Shawn in Taylor's house. And then her breasts were completely bare, in my face, her nipples a dark rose against caramel skin, hard and smooth. Pushing her breasts together, she used her fingers to guide them to my lips, opened, ready to receive. I pushed her hands aside, roughly grabbed her breasts in my hands, and rolled my tongue around the areolas.

Thoughts of Taylor and Brand threatened to break into my conscience and my hands roamed over her breasts, down her flat stomach, and into her thong, slick from wetness. I don't know when she unbuttoned her jeans, but her pussy lips were pushing against her thong, enabling me to rub in between her lips, pushing my middle finger into her pussy, feeling her warm wetness. I sucked her nipples hard, finger-fucking her until I heard her gasp and push against my hand, languishing in her pussy. "Come for me." I managed this as I moved from the right nipple to the left, inching slowly back and forth.

I allowed the thought of Taylor gushing about Shawn's preference of being finger-fucked while having her pussy eaten. I used my mouth, fingers, and hands to please her, patiently awaiting the luscious sounds Shawn emitted for Taylor when I was on the phone.

"Come for me, Shawn." I pulled her face down and kissed her lips, darting my tongue in and out of her mouth, sucking her lips and licking her teeth. I felt her responding to my sexual assault. I grabbed her hair from behind and yanked her head back, pushing her down farther on my finger inside of her.

I heard her muffle a scream and say, "Taylor."

I drew her nipples into my mouth to escalate the sensations of her orgasm and rode her waves, caressing her body as I told myself that I didn't care what I was doing.

Shawn made it to her doctor's appointment on time—she'd called ahead and told them she'd be more than half an hour late, so they scheduled her for a later appointment. What a crafty and beautiful wench.

After such idiotic behavior, I went to Brand and told him that I needed to postpone our nuptials for a little while. I couldn't bring myself to give him a specific time, so I copped out with "a little while." He accepted it a little too easily, but at the time, I had no choice.

The next evening, I drove to Bryce's house in Chalfont, PA and returned his ring, telling him that I needed some time alone to figure out my life; I never bothered to call him back.

Now I had to constantly remind myself: *You are getting married, Eva. Brand will marry you. You will be the newest Mrs. DeLoache and you will live happily ever after. Forget about the past and put aside any negative thoughts.*

I was finally marrying Brand. Our wedding was only four months away.

# CHAPTER 1

*Eva*

**The Present**

"The blood of Jesus!"

I awoke from my dream, literally screaming at Mavis to shut the fuck up! Then I realized that I was in bed alone, and that my mother was not screaming in my bedroom. I put my hand over my beating heart and closed my eyes, offering up a silent prayer. My God, a minute ago I was in the middle of a nightmare where my boyfriend, Bryce, crashed my wedding to my fiancé, Brand.

This was the second time I'd had this particular dream.

The last time was the night before my original wedding date to Brand. I had to cancel that wedding. I had to. Two weeks before the actual wedding date, I took a station break from Brand and attempted to get my libido in check. I was literally fucking everything that moved.

Surprisingly, or not so surprisingly, Brand took the news rather well. Way too well, honestly, since I was canceling the wedding so close to the actual date. Bastard. He probably had his own shit going on, and that was why he wasn't too damned upset.

I had been running wild on Brand since his surprise proposal at Pod, an Asian fusion restaurant in the University City section of Philadelphia, almost two years ago. After years of putting up with bullshit from Brand, after he gave me herpes and I got close to forgiving him, I was ecstatic when he finally asked me to marry him. For some reason, though, I couldn't seem to keep my legs closed, and I was fucking everything in sight—male and female.

During what was supposed to be only a six-month engagement, I fucked Shawna, the live-in girlfriend of my best friend, Taylor. I still didn't know how that happened. Honestly, I banished those memories from my thoughts as soon as the forbidden tryst was over. I told myself that I had a wedding to plan, and I moved on.

I had to force myself to face Taylor from that day forward, and not allow the guilt to eat a hole in my esophagus. Memories would creep in when I wasn't focused and vigilant in focusing on forgetting.

Then Shawn started calling at odd hours of the day and night. I never answered her calls, as that would have been an admission of the guilt I kept locked away. Shawn was Taylor's girlfriend and somehow, I managed to stick my tongue in her pussy at Taylor's house, and I still wasn't sure how all that came about.

However, I often used the memories of Shawn's tight, creamy pussy and stupendous cunnilingus to bring myself to orgasms when I felt moments of sexual weakness.

Please, let's not forget that I fucked Bryce on a daily—all over the place. Damn. That man, with his tall, strong, chocolate self. Fine. Really. Now y'all know I couldn't leave him completely alone. I performed stupendous, award-winning fellatio in the parking lot at the Willow Grove Mall, and then I called myself being good and stopped letting him physically stick his dick in my pussy. Not the tongue, though.

Then Bryce proposed to me two days before my original wedding date, and I accepted his ring. Yeah, I had two fiancés for a brief period and I loved it. Please, don't even trip. Men do it all the damn time, scandalously cavorting with various women, and no one cares. Hell, women know it and go for it anyway.

And that, ladies and gentlemen, was the reason that I postponed my original wedding to Brand, the love of my life.

I had to. I was out of my mind and out of control.

I had to. I was sexually uninhibited and reckless.

I was about to play myself out of the best and worst thing that had ever happened to me. I needed to regroup.

Honestly, though, I thought Brand was relieved that he got more time to do him before I shackled that ass to mine for eternity. Shortly thereafter, I dumped Bryce, too, and dropped out of his life for good. Oh, well.

So now, two years after Brand originally proposed to me, we were back on track to get married. *Breathe deeply, Eva,* I told myself. I was marrying Brand. Maybe not today, but soon. The wedding had not taken place. It was just a dream. Bryce had not crashed my wedding and ruined my chances to be with Brand forever.

I pulled my knees toward my chest and rested my forehead on my folded arms. I was having a conscience attack, as I usually did when my sinful past came to mind. Try as I might, I could not undo my past transgressions. I couldn't seem to stop doing everything that violated the Ten Commandments. Damn it! My mother and her fake Christian ranting constantly interrupted my thoughts. Damn it, I had nothing to be ashamed of, so I forced my mind away from the ruined wedding of my dreams.

My six-thirty AM alarm sounded, blasting Philly's Power 99 FM and Kanye West's "Good Life." My right hand shot out and slapped the snooze button to quiet the unwelcome noise. In the next instant, my cell phone rang on the pillow next to me, blasting Alicia Keys's "No One." My left hand shot out to silence the irritating ring. I flipped open the phone and then smiled for the first time.

It was a text from Brand. I MISS YOU MRS. DELOACHE. He knew that I couldn't wait to become his wife and latch on to the DeLoache surname, so he often called me Mrs. DeLoache to make me happy. He may not have known that he was my meal ticket to a life of luxury and bliss, but men never needed to know everything. Besides, they just couldn't handle the truth. Never again would I have to worry about shelter, sustenance, or how I would maintain.

He'd been sweet over the last few weeks, trying to erase the strain and tension between us. I was already over the fact that he'd been acting like an asshole for the last few months. Honestly, though, short of homicide, there was nothing that he could do to dissuade me from wanting to marry him.

*"The blood of Jesus!"*

I sneaked a quick look around my bedroom, finding it empty, of course. Maybe I needed a Valium or something, because I swore I heard Mavis right next to me. I looked around my room again, half expecting to see her in my personal space. I wouldn't have been surprised to see a church group in the shadows, praying for the soul Mavis claimed I lost after my first bout with fornication.

Damn Mavis! She was determined to ruin my special day. It was bad enough that she was presiding over my wedding, uninvited. Who cared that she was an associate pastor at some church? I couldn't believe she had managed to ingratiate herself into my momentous day, anyway. She was barely my mother! I'd left her house at sixteen, prepared to become a homeless vagrant—anything to avoid being under her tyrannical care one minute longer. If it hadn't been for Aunt Mirabelle . . .

*Calm down, Eva. Slow down. Breathe.* I needed to let Mavis's negative image and words ease from my mind, like raindrops falling from leaves in the garden. This negativity was what she wanted for me. She wanted me to second-guess myself. She wanted me to believe that this wedding would not take place. She wanted me to believe that my marriage would never last.

My body was tense and shaking as I forced myself to banish Mavis from my mind. The day I had looked forward to for the last two years was here, a day that I had looked forward to ever since Brand asked me to marry him. I still remember that day like it was yesterday.

# CHAPTER 2

*Taylor*

I couldn't believe Eva's simple ass! If she wasn't caught up in some vicious drama shit, she wasn't fucking breathing. How could she take the chance of blowing her engagement with Brand, over some bullshit like fucking Bryce right after the engagement? She was one simple bitch. She needed to be happy that nigga was finally marrying her. I swore if she wasn't my best friend, I'd whip her ass and take her man. At least she was finally getting married to Brand, and I damned sure hoped that she didn't do anything stupid to fuck shit up this time.

Don't get me wrong; Brand wasn't shit half the time. Truly he wasn't. When Eva finally told me that he gave her herpes, I offered to slice dat nigga for her. Then later, when she was breaking up with him for it, the nigga had the nerve to tell her he slept with like sixteen chicks during their relationship, the first time they were together. Yeah, the first time, 'cause they'd been together and then broken up more times than Destiny's Child.

I swear, niggas ain't shit.

But, I guessed he figured he'd make up for all that dumb shit. I mean, Eva had the biggest goddamned rock on her finger that I'd ever seen. No, a diamond couldn't make up for having a disease that he didn't tell her he had until she contracted it from him. But, yeah, that rock was definitely saying something.

I damn sure didn't want to be in Brand's corner, but Eva was making it damned hard to be in hers when she kept doing dumb shit, time after time.

Then she was fucking Bryce damn near every day before the first wedding date! But, naw, it wasn't Bryce. It was Eva. The bitch knew she was wrong 'cause she had only been engaged to Brand for a few hours when she went out with Bryce and fucked him! Okay, she claimed they used protection, but the condom supposedly broke. Why invite drama into your life?

I swear, I was talking major drama in this child's life. If you wanted to fuck your ex, fine, that was okay with me. But Bryce wasn't even really Eva's ex-boyfriend. More like her ex-sometimes-sex-partner. And you don't fuck your ex-*anything* on the night you get engaged to somebody else.

Okay, so I was trying to explain all this to Shawna, my girlfriend (yes, my actual girlfriend—like I eat pussy and everything) how Eva slept with Bryce the night before Brand asked her to marry him. She slept with him again the very next night, which was the same day of their engagement. Who knew who else Eva had fucked in the months before the original wedding date? And now, the wedding was soon approaching again. I just wasn't sure if Eva and Brand were going to make it.

"I swear, Shawna, Eva's fuckin' crazy." I had her tits in my hands while we were lyin' on our bed in my house. We were face to face and I couldn't keep myself from stoppin' my sentences mid-stream to lick her hard nipples. I swear, I couldn't keep my hands off this fine-ass chick.

"She acts like she wants to be happy and have a man who will be honest and faithful to her; and when she gets Brand to propose to her, she acts like she's lost her fuckin' mind and goes off with Bryce the day before *and* the day after Brand proposed to her."

Shawna was squirming at all the right intervals as my mouth worked on that cream-colored flesh. In between pants and during my sexual attack on her body, she managed to ask, "Why would she have sex with Bryce the same day Brand asked her to marry him?" My middle finger found her clit and my fingers started an exploration project of their own.

"That's my point. She claimed that's what she wanted, but then she took off her ring to go out with Bryce. I don't know what the hell was wrong with her." My lips were now roaming around Shawna's face, finding her lips, her ears, and then back down to her breasts. Such a delightful treat at my disposal.

Shawna was too busy appreciating my foreplay to respond to my comments.

"But she wouldn't be Eva if she wasn't fuckin' somebody. I know that sounds fucked up, but this is what she does. If she ain't fuckin' up her own life and relationships, she fuckin' up somebody else's shit."

My fingers fit so nicely into Shawna's creamy pussy. My exploring fingers hit gold inside her love nest and I latched onto her left tit. One of us turned and then I wasn't sure who did what, but we were sixty-nining and her legs were clamped around my head. I was doin' my best to move into her snatch, lips first.

I could hear Shawna moaning, begging, and pleading with soft words for me to end this delicious torture. My pleasure, ma'am. When I felt the familiar short breaths and heard the panting, I knew she was close. I slid further into her body, licking and sucking as I ate my way to her orgasm.

Her delightful tongue eased me into a mini-orgasm shortly after she was finished with her first. It was okay. She made sure I got mine. Plus, my satisfaction was a small piece of our sex life. It was really all about Shawn, and she knew it. Knowing that tight, smooth body belonged to me and was at my disposal was enough to get me off most times. My real pleasure came with her pleasure.

My talented tongue licked her to another orgasm, and only when she was damn near crying, pushing at my head and trying to get away from me, did I finally stop. I was a chick and I had some sympathy for her. I knew how intense and irritated the clit could feel after vigorous cunnilingus.

Sated and beautiful, we were again lying on the bed. Just as before, my hands roamed her chest, pinching and licking as I went along. If this chick wasn't a dime piece, I didn't know who was.

I continued talking as if there hadn't been a fifteen-minute lapse of oral sex extraordinaire. "You know how they are. Eva and Brand break up to make up all the time, and enjoy themselves immensely in between gettin' back together."

My lovely Shawna had finally caught her breath.

"So, wait, didn't you tell me that Eva went to Bryce's walk-through of his new house and then fucked him all over the house afterward? I'm missing something. If Eva was with Brand and he was going to propose to her, why was she out fucking Bryce at all?"

My lips kept finding her nipples.

"Girl, you know Eva. She don't need no damned reason to be fuckin'. But they weren't really together then. They'd been spending time together, but Eva thought that Brand didn't pay her enough attention, and when he wasn't available, she ran to Bryce. You know, in her defense, Eva had no idea that Brand would propose to her at the same restaurant that she'd eaten at with Bryce the night before."

Her nipples were hard again. My mouth kept finding her tasty body parts.

"Look, all I know is that Eva went to dinner with Bryce one night, saw his new house, told him about the disease Brand had given her, and fucked Bryce senseless in about four rooms inside his new house."

*Sheeit, do all women taste like this?* I wondered.

"Then the very next night, Brand took her to dinner at the same restaurant and surprised her by asking her to marry him. I don't know how she went on a date with Bryce later that same night. I figure the bitch lost her mind, took off her engagement ring, and went to Bryce's for one last fuck."

*How come she always smells so good?*

"Tell me where you want my lips, Shawna."

*Would Congress let me marry this girl?*

"Taylor, stay focused. You never told me this part. What happened after that?"

*Should I fuck her again now, or just wait?*

"Nothin'."

*Shit, I was all distracted.*

She slapped at my hands, which were roaming her svelte curves.

"Damn it, Taylor, keep your paws to yourself. What do you mean, 'Nothin'?' Something had to happen." She paused to kiss my lips, 'cause she knew that was what I liked. "If you don't start talking, Taylor, I'm putting my clothes back on."

Her words brought me up short and slowed down my bullshit.

But it didn't stop me. I crawled over her body and lay flat on her back, my hands cupped around her tits. My mouth found its way to her neck. I felt her body tense. She knew where I was going. It was where she wanted me to go. She forgot about our conversation and arched her back. Her ass dug into my clit and I suddenly wished I had a penis, wondering how that sweet-ass pussy would feel around my hard-ass dick.

Now she wasn't too interested in my running dialogue.

Shawna wanted my tongue on her and in her. She knew what she wanted and she knew what I would give her.

But she would have to wait.

My tongue left a wet trail across her shoulders.

"So, anyway, Eva's runnin' around, fuckin' Bryce and God only knows who else. Then Bryce asked her to marry him during her engagement to Brand, and she said yes! The bitch was crazy and had apparently lost her mind. So she's got Brand's ring and then she had Bryce's ring, too. I swear, for the life of me, I don't understand Eva at all."

My left hand was lower, moving in tandem with my lips on her back.

I could hear her breath catch as my fingers probed her wetness from the front. My lips met her ass at the same time. I felt her body stiffen and smiled.

I bit one ass cheek and moved to the other. This time I sucked hard, bruising her light flesh and branding my territory. I offered a silent sorry for my aberrant behavior and covered the darkening blemish with light kisses around and over her warm, sweet-smelling skin. My tongue made lazy circles over each soft mound, in between, up and down her crack. I knew what she wanted.

"Of course, now she claims she's faithful and a changed chick. Yeah, right. She can't help but be Eva. And where there's Eva, there's sex, drama, niggas, and bitches."

My tongue reclaimed its rightful place on Shawna's luscious ass. She arched her back, her butt level with my face. She was ready for what I had in mind for that sexy ass.

I felt her hand pulling my fingers upward. Her lips caught two of my fingers in her mouth and she started sucking softly, then vigorously. She was alternately drawing my fingers into her mouth, parting them with her tongue, sending sparks shooting through my clit.

My tongue found the tiny hole in between her pulsing cheeks, licked gently, then harder, mimicking her sucking motions. Her ass was moving up and down off the mattress, granting me further access to her anus. Using my free hand, wet from her juicy pussy, I pushed Shawn onto her knees.

My mouth never lost contact with her body, and as she moved up, my mouth dipped lower and caught her swollen lips in my mouth. One hand in her mouth, and the other massaging her clitoris, I ate her pussy from behind, just the way she liked.

My jaws tired, hand cramping, I wondered if she was taking her time purposely, unwilling to desert her favorite position. I sighed when she screamed out, calling my name only as she could, so sweetly, as she came with a shudder.

I stayed where I was, nose stuck in her pussy as I waited for her fine ass to finish cumming. She released my fingers and crawled around to face me. I was sure that I was shiny with perspiration and sweet-smelling pussy juice. I'd have to remember to ask her later.

Her kiss didn't catch me off guard or surprise me anymore. I responded to her soft, seeking kiss as she sucked my tongue, licked my cheeks, and ate her pussy off my face.

She was just getting started. I leaned back and pulled her with me. Now I was ready. Her oral game may have been tighter than mine, and that was saying something.

She fell on me, laughing and kissing me, her fingers already in my panties, running her fingers through my slickness. She straddled me, staring into my face after she released my mouth from captivity.

Nose to nose, she stared at me.

"You know I love it when you do that to me, don't you? I know you know. You think you slick. I guess you want me to do you back now, huh? You lucky ya ass is cute and you eat my pussy like it's your last meal."

She was moving down my body, dragging my panties off as she went. "Tell ya bitch what you want her to do to you."

Instead, I showed her.

# CHAPTER 3

*Eva*

A s I lounged in our bed, I willed myself to get up and get a move on the day. I thought back to the night Brand asked me to marry him. For obvious reasons, I remembered that particular night vividly and played it through my mind often. Mostly it came in dreams at night and during the day.

*January 2007—The Proposal*

*"Yes, Brand, of course I'll marry you." Brand leapt to his feet, gripping me in a bear hug and then bowing graciously to the cheers and jeers from fellow diners. A hundred thoughts flashed through my mind as I stood there lost in his embrace. Suddenly I was ecstatic and I felt tears in my eyes. I was looking through blurred, teary vision at the three-carat, marquise diamond ring Brand had presented to me and placed on my left ring finger.*

*I was suddenly relieved, feeling my burdens lift off me and fly from my mind. I was kissing Brand, holding his head, gently sucking his tongue, oblivious to the crowd and noise. My hand made its way down his stomach (rock hard) and dipped between his legs, stoking his penis (rock hard). I felt his jerk of surprise, but I knew what I was doing.*

*I was letting Brand, my man, know that I was ready for him whenever, wherever. Damn, were the other diners still clapping and cheering? I guessed I should let him go now. But why should I? Did these people know what I* had been through? What we had been through? Did they know that I deserved this man? This moment?

And then, that quickly, the doubts entered my thoughts, and for a second, I was scared to death. So much of our past flashed through my mind—all of the doubt and distrust, the other women, and the herpes we shared. I was trying to be happy. I really was. I was trying not to turn this into a sappy-ass moment where my tears of joy were really tears of sadness and misfortune. Why wasn't I ecstatic? I would be, damn it. I would make this work. Brand and I would make this happen.

After our standing ovation from the patrons and wait staff, Brand and I left the Pod. We practically ran to the parking garage and jumped into the Range when the attendant drove down the ramp. After a short drive, we pulled over onto Kelly Drive where Brand buried his face in my breasts, hugging me around the waist. I was so turned on. I kept looking at my left hand, staring at the diamond winking in the streetlights. The ring was making me horny. The thought of showing off this diamond every day, everywhere was turning me on.

Brand kept thanking me and telling me that he loved me.

"I'll make it all up to you, Eva, I swear. I want to make you forget everything I ever did to you." I saw tears in his eyes as he moved up to kiss me softly. "Do you forgive me? Will you let me make this up to you?" Brand was practically in my lap, kissing my face. "More than you know, I love you, Evangeline LoDolce. Wait. That is your name, isn't it? Ouch! Don't hit me! I'm just playing, Eva DeLoache."

"I know you love me, Brand. I want you to love me forever. I'm not letting you get away from me this time. You hear what I'm telling you?" My ring continued to wink at me. "I got something good for you tonight, Mr. DeLoache.

"Why don't you tell me what you got for me, Mrs. DeLoache? You got something for your future husband who had the best jeweler on Jeweler's Row make this ring that looks like some man loves the shit outta you?" Brand's voice was suddenly serious and just above a whisper. His mouth moved closer to mine and I could feel his breath inside my mouth. He was breathing hard and his hands moved up my thighs, finding their home in between my legs. He asked me again, "What you got for me, Eva?"

It was too much. The proposal. The ring. The size of the winking diamond. The engagement. Brand's hands in between my legs and on my breasts. His lips were on top of mine, but not quite kissing me, just lingering closely, teasingly. I forgot that we were in public and that cops from the Ninety-second Police District cruised this area almost hourly.

Slowly, deliberately, I used my left hand to guide Brand's head down as I unbuttoned my shirt with the right. No bra—these beautiful breasts were meant to be seen. I moved forward in my seat, pressing my clit into his hand, grinding my hips on the leather seat.

Oh, I knew where I was now. Brand's lips were on my nipples, biting, tugging. His hands had worked their way into my panties, rubbing my slick clit. Eyes closed, moving to an unknown rhythm, senses overloaded, I came quickly on the leather seat of the Range while parked on Kelly Drive.

Brand held my breasts in his hands, sucking and moaning as he worked one nipple and then the other. He caught my moans in his mouth, licking at the tears that flowed from my eyes. I pushed Brand away as I caught my breath, feeling my wetness flow from me, and told Brand to get me home. Quickly.

He drove home rather quickly, as per my request. We got to Brand's newly leased house in Chestnut Hill and ran up the stairs. We tried to move quietly through the house so as not to awaken the butler. We were probably fooling ourselves as he saw and heard everything anyway. We tiptoed and kissed while holding hands, Brand dragging me along when my mother popped into my head.

I could see her as clearly as I could hear her in my mind, sneering in my face, but not too close lest my sinful ways leap from my pores into her pristine, Christian body. I could hear her voice, blazing with fury.

"Evangeline Arianna LoDolce, your whorish and devilish ways will be the death of you! You shun goodness and godliness in favor of the flesh. Men and their dangling members will not save you from YOUR destruction when HE comes!"

God, why now? Why was I thinking about Mavis now, during the happiest moment of my short life? Since I was four years old she'd been spouting off the same pseudo-Christian bullshit. Mavis and her Bible thumping were the reasons I had moved from her home when I was sixteen years old.

Brand felt the hesitation in my body as he continued to lead me up the stairs.

"Eva, what, you cheatin' me out of mine? Come on, baby. You're going to be Mrs. Brandon DeLoache, need I remind you?" Brand stopped at the top step and pulled me to him. Feeling my resistance, he was suddenly serious and insistent. "What's up, Eva? What's going on?"

I was silent. How did I say, As I was planning to rock your world, leaving you breathless and weak, my mother crept into my thoughts, making me feel like a whore? Where was Mavis when I was sucking Bryce's dick dry, in that empty house, the night before? Why now?

I shook off Mavis. I was here, she wasn't. I was here with the man who loved me and had just asked me to marry him. How dare that fake Christian hypocrite impede upon my wondrous night? I didn't even answer Brand's question. Instead, I kissed him lovingly, allowing my passion and tenderness to answer for me.

To further remove Mavis' image from my thoughts, I continued to kiss Brand and then slowly kneeled on the step in front of him. I wanted him to feel powerful. I would be his personal whore from now on, starting tonight. I pulled down his pants and boxers, allowing his penis to rub into my mouth and nose, and through my hair. With one hand holding my head and the other gripping *the carved, copper banister, Brand worked himself into my mouth and into an orgasm that threatened to knock us both down the steps.*

*I was going to be Mrs. Eva DeLoache!*

Then everything got crazy. I got hornier and couldn't stop screwing around. I continued to have senseless, mind-blowing sex with Bryce right up until the initial wedding date. I couldn't seem to help myself. I think I knew, deep down inside, that I would never marry Bryce, but I accepted his ring and deluded myself into thinking that I could pull off having two fiancés.

I had been counting down the months, then weeks, then days before the momentous wedding that would bind me to Brand and the DeLoache money forever.

Mavis threatened to overtake my mind and thoughts again, so I chased her image away and settled in to dream of my future with Brand. Sometimes those thoughts scared me. I wondered why I thought so negatively at times. Were these thoughts a foreshadowing of drama and dumb shit on the horizon?

My initial plans to get Brand into our wedding bed within six months after our engagement didn't pan out. For maybe not-so-obvious reasons, I wanted to get married right away. I wanted to wrap him up and get him off the market as soon as possible. Brand asked me to marry him in January 2007, and I had our wedding date set for the summer of that same year.

Yet there we were now, almost two years later, and I had exactly four more months until our wedding took place. I'd remained busy, of course. Trust me that I'd kept myself amused and immersed in extracurricular activities.

But enough of that. I needed to prepare for my fairytale wedding.

I had waited long enough.

# CHAPTER 4

*Taylor*

I still couldn't believe that Eva and Brand were about to get married. I swear it seemed like last week that she told me about that bastard giving her herpes. God, it seemed like she went buck wild after she found out. I wasn't even sure I could keep up with all of the names of the guys Eva slept with, and it was all his fault. He should have been honest and up front with her from the start, and taken his chances that she'd be willing to continue to see him, knowing he had herpes. He had ruined her fucking life.

I thought back to the day I met Eva at the Community College of Philadelphia (CCP), and the day I introduced Eva to Brand. I never explained to Eva how I knew Brand or why I was so willing to introduce her to him. Maybe I should have told her then.

It was funny now, but Eva and I hated each other at first sight. We'd only seen each other from across the cafeteria or a classroom, but that was enough for us. I misjudged Eva, assuming that she was a stuck-up, mulatto, I-think-I'm-cute type of bitch. Now, of course, we laughed about it, often reminiscing about the memories of the months of hating each other before we became friends.

As I half-listened to Shawna murmur directions to the restaurant, I flashed back to my first face-to-face meeting with Eva.

*We were standing in the school bookstore line for over two hours when*

I started the initial conversation. Eva, to her credit, had been ignoring my ass for two hours, pretending like she didn't know I was standing there. But I had been quiet and bored for too damned long and had to say something to somebody. My undiagnosed ADHD was kicking in, big time.

"Which classes are you taking this semester?" I asked, after pushing Eva's shoulder to get her attention. I didn't allow her to answer before I continued. "Why don't you look at my schedule for this semester, and see if you have any of these books I need for my classes? I'm not trying to owe CCP my firstborn child from textbook debt." I laughed at my own joke.

In true Eva form, she looked me up and down before offering a dismissive, "No thanks. I'm taking five advanced classes this semester. And you?"

"Oh, well, I'm taking two classes this semester. You know, just enough to keep the student loan people at bay and hold on to my deferments." Up close, I could see that Eva was prettier than she appeared to be from across the classroom or cafeteria.

"Pretty much what I thought," Eva uttered with disinterest. She offered no further comment.

But somehow, over the next forty-five minutes, we discussed life, love, and our future goals. We were giggling like schoolgirls when we finally reached the bookstore cashier.

Eva, who needed textbooks for a full course load of advanced classes and labs, almost fell the fuck out when she saw her total on the cash register. Broke-ass honey was $55 short of the total. I swear she checked every pocket five or six times, lookin' for money she knew wasn't there. I kind of laughed at her until she looked like she was about to break down and start that female-ass crying.

I knew her proud ass wasn't going to ask me for the money—and I had plenty of it, thanks to student grants, which seemed to be providing me with a lifetime of free money. I walked over to Eva, who was still standing at the register with four classes' worth of books in her hands.

*"Don't sweat it, Eva. With this book stipend they give me, I could probably pay for my books, your books, and books for half the students here. And I don't have to pay back one red cent."* I flashed a grin and tried to act nonchalant, 'cause I knew she felt like she was at a soup kitchen, asking for handouts. *"Just pay me back when you get it, okay?"*

*I finally got her to accept the small loan and we left—she, excited about her upcoming classes, and me, looking forward to my next refund so I could buy new clothes. After three hellish hours in that line, we got to be pretty cool and she asked me for my cell number so she could lock it in hers.*

Eva never had the chance to repay the money, although she did try. By then, Eva was my ace and I couldn't take something from her that she didn't have. Plus, the government was footing my entire bill, and I planned to take them for all they were worth. I was only too happy to share my loot with my new best friend.

Then there was that damned Brand. How was I going to explain to Eva how I really knew Brand, and about our past?

# CHAPTER 5

I suddenly jumped, literally, when Shawna's voice interrupted my thoughts of the past.

"Are you okay, baby?" Shawna asked as she jolted me back into real time when she grabbed my hand. "You are aware that you just made a left turn on a red light, aren't you?" She laughed at my baffled expression. "You, sexy, were gone miles from here." She leaned over to kiss my ear and whispered that we were going the wrong way.

I smiled in response and lifted her hand to kiss her palm. No, I was not aware that I had made an illegal left turn on red, and for a minute, I had forgotten that I was in the car with Shawna, driving to Center City to our favorite restaurant. I looked up to focus on the intersection and noticed that I had actually had run the red light.

"What's up, Taylor? What's on your mind?" Shawna was concerned because my silence in her presence was unusual. Her concern was also warranted because my hands, usually up her shirt, massaging one or both of her breasts, were solely on the steering wheel.

"Nothing much. I'm sorry, sexy. My mind is on everything but driving." I smiled in a silent apology and attempted to focus on the road as I drove down Spring Garden Street. "I was just thinking about something that Eva told me a little while back." I looked for a place to make a U-turn so we were not late for the reservation she had made.

I didn't feel like talking about what was on my mind, but I felt guilty 'cause I had been ignoring Shawna for most of the ride.

"I was thinking about Eva and Brand. It seems like just yesterday that she told me Brand gave her herpes and the next thing I know, he asked her to marry him."

"Herpes?" Shawna almost shrieked out the word and I looked at her like she was crazy. Or maybe a little too hyped. "What? Are you serious? Brand gave her herpes? When?"

Oops. Damn, I forgot that she didn't know, and I was supposed to be keeping Eva's secret. Oh, well. It was only Shawna, so I played it off.

"Shawna, I know I mentioned that before. I must have told you when my tongue was buried somewhere below your Mason-Dixon Line. You only hear what you want to hear when I'm down there."

"And Eva's still going to marry Brand, after he did that to her?"

"Hey, look, that's their mess. What's done is done. They seem to be okay with it, so why should I complain? I'm just trying to make sure Eva's ready to marry him this time."

"Why do you sound worried about it all? Are they breaking up as usual?" Shawna had yet to meet Brand, but she felt like she knew him from my non-stop conversations about him and Eva.

"No, not specifically, but something's off. Something doesn't feel right. I don't know what it is, but never mind. I want to concentrate on us."

Shawna let out a small sigh. "Well, it's about time. I've been sitting here for ten minutes, wondering where your thoughts were, 'cause they surely ain't been on me." Shawna, usually the quiet one who let me take the lead, turned down the radio. She actually turned off Jim Jones' "Ballin'."

"Taylor, what are we doing? I mean us. What's going on with us?"

Shawna looked frustrated, I guess 'cause I hadn't been talking to her while I was driving. "What are we doing, Taylor?"

Because I had been daydreaming about Eva and her drama, and ignoring her for more than a few, I gave her my undivided attention for the rest of the trip but I didn't say much.

Once we parked, she got out of the passenger seat and walked around the car to me. She kissed me and grabbed my hand as we walked into the restaurant. I was tripping because we were out in public, together, holding hands, our business all in the street for anybody to see. I mean, Shawna was a dime-piece, don't get me wrong. But she was a female and I was a female, and we were holding hands, walking down the street.

Shawna was the first chick I'd been with this way. I mean, I thought women were attractive before, but never enough to fuck one with regularity. Our relationship, honestly, up until this point, had been only sexual and that was fine with me. I couldn't believe that we had been seeing each other, off and on, _____ two y____

But there we were.

The Rose Tattoo was our fav____ restaurant in downtown Philadelphia. We were supposed to be c____ebrating our two-year anniversary or something, whatever she called it. Waiting for the host to get our seats, I grabbed Shawna and pulled her to m____

I leaned her back up against me a____ my arms around her waist. I mean, fuck it, we were just walking down the street like two faggots in Boystown. I felt her lean into me.

"Taylor, what are you doing?" she asked.

I kissed her ear. "I'm sorry, Shawnee," I whispered. "I guess I could be doing better than this on our anniversary." She had been planning this dinner for weeks, and had been looking forward to this night. Hugging her sexy ass from behind, I was wondering what I was doing, in public, at the Rose Tattoo, kissing my main chick on her ear.

But whatever. Right here, right now with Shawna, I was feeling good and for a minute, I didn't care what people thought. We stood there with Shawna leaned up against me like I was her man, waiting for our seats. I was sure people were staring at the spectacle we must have made—two fine-ass chicks all hugged up in public. Fuck them. Shawna's game was tight as shit, and fuck whoever couldn't understand that.

For this anniversary thing, she had reserved a second-floor table that looked down on the kitchen and large bar area. This was considered their private table and it had these fake trees and plants on both sides. The table was off to the side and only the waiters had access to it. The waiter held Shawna's chair and I was checking out that onion as she sat her fine ass in the chair.

"What are we drinkin', Shawnee? Get me whatever you get."

I watched her read the menu. *What am I doing here with this pretty chick?* I wondered. Shawna was beautiful, and I wondered how we got to this point when neither of us was looking for a relationship, and damn sure not with someone of the same sex.

The waiter interrupted my thoughts as I was giving Shawna the evil eye as she ordered my favorite drink—champagne and Chambord. The bitch was gonna hit my pockets hard as shit tonight. I wondered what the fuck I had done wrong, 'cause she was definitely sticking it to me.

That was all right. I was gonna let her have this one. I was planning on getting that ass drunk anyway. Shawna didn't know it, but she would enjoy it later, 'cause I had plans for her fine ass later tonight.

Shawn started in again as soon as the waiter disappeared.

"So, what are we doing, Taylor? What are we doing here together? How did we get to this point?" The questions weren't necessarily specific, but I understood that she was hinting about us fucking around almost exclusively.

Technically, we were two straight women in a semi-committed, homosexual relationship. We had been seeing each other for two years, but most of that was sexual, and mostly when she stayed with me when she got tired of living with her parents. I didn't know what Shawna was looking for. I wasn't sure what I had to offer, or what I was offering, if anything.

"Taylor, what are we doing here? Not literally here, in this restaurant, but here, together, with each other?" Shawna asked again. She sighed in exasperation. "What are we going to do? I have to tell my mother something, because I can't keep telling her that I just happen to spend the night at your house every night. Plus, how am I going to explain a baby and no father?"

The waiter interrupted with two flutes of champagne and a double shot of Chambord. It gave me a minute to think about her questions and what she was getting at. This pretty young thing had me talking about getting a sperm donor for a baby. She even had me rethinking my friendship with Eva sometimes. Eva did take up a lot of my time.

I wanted to answer her questions. I just needed to think about them first. For some reason, I wanted to please Shawna like I had never wanted to please anybody before. I had only fucked with men before her, and I already knew what they wanted—sex, silence, and food.

With Shawna, I was a little lost. I didn't know what we were doing, other than having some seriously fierce sex, and wasn't that enough? I hadn't given this thing much thought, and definitely not about its longevity.

She told me she loved me, and I, in turn, ate the shit outta her pussy whenever the desire struck. I made her cum in three languages and four hemispheres. I thought that was enough. I really liked this girl and she obviously loved me. I just didn't know what to do with her.

And then, because I still didn't have a response, I lifted my glass in a toast.

"To Shawnee, my fine sex kitten. I'mma eat the shit outta your pussy in"— I glanced at my stainless steel Movado—"in approximately a hundred and eighty minutes. You better drink up all this expensive champagne, 'cause I'mma make your ass pay when I get you home. You think your ass is slick," I added. "You gone pay me in pussy for this expensive shit." I tapped my glass to hers and then gestured. "Your turn, cutie."

"You didn't answer my question, Taylor, but I'll let you slide for now. I probably let your pretty ass get away with too much, but you got this one." She raised her glass in toast and crossed her eyes in my direction.

"I'll make this toast to you, Taylor, my first girlfriend. You are the first woman I've ever cared for this way, and I think I'm in love with you. I don't know what we're doing, Taylor, but I'm loving it. I love spending time with you, and I love the intimacy we share. You are my friend, my lover, and you definitely know how to give a girl multiple orgasms. That, I'll definitely toast to!"

# CHAPTER 6

*Eva*

Brand and I were in love. I mean, what was the difference, really? We engaged in fine dining, had stupendous sex, went to the movies, and fought as we always did. There was no difference, really.

Well, my diamond still winked at me on a daily basis and I was more than used to it now, as well as the reaction from everyone who saw it.

Talking about being the perfect fiancé! Brand was showing his true colors and his commitment flags were waving splendidly, indeed. He was patient, attentive, loving, and extra giving. He gave me a new car and a monthly allowance for clothes and other personal necessities now that I represented him and would be the new Mrs. DeLoache.

I, too, was being the perfect fiancée. I lived with Brand at the DeLoache home in Chestnut Hill and took full advantage of the live-in butler when I was too lazy to cook, fetch my own hot tea, or wash my own clothes. Brand's money helped me through graduate school without having to worry about getting my hair done or my eyebrows growing wild. I hadn't slept with anyone else since we decided to postpone the wedding.

But enough of that.

Brand and I would be together forever. The thought was stimulating and intoxicating, and I had waited long enough to become a wife.

I was only eighteen credits away from getting my master's degree in social work (MSW), and I was getting married in four short months. What more could a girl ask for?

I thought about my upcoming graduation from Temple University's Social Work Program. It took me sixteen months, including a full roster through the summer, but I accomplished my goal. I also constantly thought of the financial freedom a college degree would bring me in addition to the DeLoache wealth. I had been poor and had no desire to go back there. I knew what it was like to want *things* and not be able to afford them. I knew what it was like to be envious of others and I would *not* go back there.

Sometimes I wondered why I had even bothered to go back to school.

An MSW was my meal ticket into a six-figure income in addition to and in case Brand started being his usual asshole self. I loved Brand with everything that I was capable of, but a man, at the end of his hard dick, was still a man. I wasn't putting all my hopes into one man who may or may not have been willing to aid me in realizing my dreams of living the fabulous life.

I sent a stack of résumés to area mental health agencies within the week. I was applying for the position of as a behavioral specialist consultant, but I would take mobile therapist position if necessary. A BSC position paid an hourly wage of forty-five dollars, whereas an MT earned thirty-two dollars per hour.

I was done with meager case manager and therapeutic staff support positions that paid nineteen dollars per hour; very little money compared to a BSC or MT. If I sat in another elementary or middle school with another ADHD kid whose mother didn't want him and failed to teach manners or the ABCs, I'd kill someone—likely a client or two.

I had done my time. I put in the hard work.

I had put up with their moms, dirty, bad-mouthed kids, and their conniving siblings long enough. I was tired of driving to and from school, to their low-income houses and taking them to Chuck E. Cheese and Family Dollar.

I was tired of being blackmailed into taking their moms to the market or the hair store to buy a ponytail, so that they would sign my papers without a bunch of bullshit. I was tired of being a babysitter for mothers who shouldn't have had that seventh kid that nobody paid attention to and nobody wanted.

I was tired of going into shacks and battling the roaches and mice for a seat. I was damned tired of that old, cooking-grease smell coupled with dirty dishes and ramen sauce packs.

But alas, those days would soon be over.

I had my weeks as a BSC planned, workable to ensure plenty of time for the hair and nail salon and a bi-weekly body wax. I would stop by the nasty, overcrowded schools once a week in my X5, draped in cashmere and diamonds, and get the smiles and warm greetings from teachers, the parent, and the client.

I'd bring in coloring books from the Dollar Tree and smile, pretending to listen to the TSS, who was in the school with the badass client for eight hours—and that was just school time. There might be five to twenty hours of community time on a case, in addition to the thirty-five to forty hours of school time.

I'd spend a half hour in the school with the client, smile, greet, and jet. I'd run past the shack and speak condescendingly to the mom—who never had a job or a GED—get her to sign blank forms, and bill the agency for the entire two hours I was supposed to spend with the client at the school and the shack. It would be great. I couldn't wait.

I had busied myself over the past sixteen months studying, stressing, and worrying about graduate school. Now that herpes was no longer a concern for me, since I was marrying the man who had given them to me, I didn't have to worry about confessing to another man that I was infected with an incurable, transmittable virus. I didn't have to worry about anyone contracting herpes from me and I felt better about myself. There was no longer secret shame or guilt on my conscience and I felt a combination of relief, joy, depression, and only occasionally, anxiety.

As usual, I lost track of Brand from time to time as I struggled through graduate school. We definitely didn't break up, but I took little breaks from him and our relationship throughout the sixteen months of school. I called them "station breaks," but they were really breaks from Brand so I could breathe and concentrate on something other than him. I couldn't bring myself to stray, even if I wanted to, because my diamond winked in my direction each time an attractive man or woman crossed my path, reminding me of my commitment.

I had no reason to doubt Brand's sincerity and faithfulness and worked hard to ensure that he, too, was secure in our relationship. We had a checkered past that involved Brand being unfaithful with sixteen women while we were together, and me dealing with feelings of insecurity and doubt. Long before Brand proposed to me, I found out during a visit to my gynecologist that Brand had given me herpes. I thought the word *herpes* was shock enough for the day, but the telephone call from Sheila to my home, asking for Brand, was almost more than I could take that day.

Apparently, Sheila had been dating Brand for five months during our relationship. I found out during our telephone call that he had promised to introduce her to his family and take her on a trip to Jamaica. She went looking through his cell one night while he was sleeping at her apartment, looking for information.

Well, she found my number in the phone. Honestly, I was so relieved that they hadn't slept together, that I wasn't fazed by their short-term liaison. The denial of sex was confirmed by both Brand and Sheila.

I'd been contemplating how to confront Brand with the knowledge of the disease he had given me. I dreamed of sensationalizing the confrontation. I was disgusted, hurt, and ashamed of the news I heard from the doctor. I'd been attempting to deal with the horrific news—and the possibility of not having an eventual vaginal birth due to possible complications of herpes— when the phone rang. Sheila's news just rocked my world further.

Don't get things misconstrued. I was no angel. I had done my share of dirt, lying, and being less than forthcoming with certain information. But, damn. All of that? A few lies versus a nasty transmittable disease that would live within my body forever? Life was not fair!

Sexually transmitted diseases were a new concept to me, even though I had gotten the crabs from either Brand or Daren, my ex from Villanova. But they were just crabs! You know: comb the special shampoo through, let it sit, rinse, and presto/bingo, it was over.

Again, I had hardly been an angel, but Brand's shit had been extra, and I eventually left him because of it. Yet we always found our way back to one another. And the makeup was orgasmic, as was most of our sex and lovemaking.

Beyond the sharing of the nasty, incurable virus that Brand had gotten from a jump-off named Jeanine years before he met me, we were soul mates. In many ways, we considered ourselves two halves of the same whole. Brand understood and encouraged my goals and dreams. He also understood my attraction to women, helping to orchestrate my first lesbian experience with a woman named Kristal.

I'd had enough bullshit during the first three years that I'd been with Brand, and my main focus now was my upcoming nuptials. Brand

and I had fought long and hard over the location of the ceremony and reception, from how many from each side were invited, to who was absolutely excluded. My list of exclusions was long and was comprised mostly of Brand's friends, who were thuggish and fine and too much of a distraction. Just look at Evan!

I couldn't wait to marry Brand, and I wasn't letting anything or anyone get in the way this time.

# CHAPTER 7

I thought of the night I first met Shawna often. When we met at Scooters Pub in West Philly almost two years ago, I'd been checking her out all night, not willing to make the first move. Who knew that I even liked chicks? But that face was gorgeous, with a body to match. Shit, it made even a straight chick like me look twice.

*I saw her checking me out a few times and then we were looking at each other for the next hour. Yeah, I had checked out a few chicks in the past, but damn! I thought I felt my dick getting hard, and I didn't even have a dick!*

*She had short, strawberry blond hair, not quite blending in with her caramel-colored skin and small lips. Her red, fitted tee said SCREW YOU across her tits, worn to display the D-cups she carried so well. Some red-pocket, Apple Bottom jeans finished her look, and I was hooked. She was a cutie without makeup. The bitch knew she was fine and knew that her natural beauty would catch the eye of everybody within eyesight.*

*Well, I was staring at her ass. After my second Long Island Iced Tea, I got real bold and kept staring at her, daring that ass to look away. I gawked at her tits and then moved my eyes to her face, and then back down again. I wanted her to know that she was being watched by me, and I was undressing her. Shit. I wanted to see what was under those clothes.*

*After my third Long Island, I was caught off guard when she popped* up next to me. Then this sexy woman whispered in my ear with her shiny-ass lips. I know that she knew those lips were touching me.

"I been checking you out checking me out, you know?" Her breath was warm on my face. I felt goose bumps on my arms. What the shit?

Yeah, I wasn't going to deny it. I turned around and looked right at her pretty face. I could smell Issey Miyake. "Okay. You got me. What? You got a problem wit' that?"

"No, I don't have a problem with that, but women don't usually stare me down at the bar all night and now you got me curious. And that's different for me, because I'm usually not curious this way." I felt her right arm on the back of the barstool, and then on my waist. I tried to suck in my stomach slowly so she wouldn't notice, and cursed myself for not doing those hundred crunches this morning.

I turned some more until I was between her legs. Every time I turned, I moved closer to her to see how far she would let me get to her. I put my hand on her waist and pulled her forward till she was between my legs. I had to see this chick up close. Her body was giving me rhythm and I felt like I might like this shit too much. My hand was real close to grabbing the apples on the pockets of her jeans.

"What's your name, Apple?" I asked, giving her a nickname based on her choice of attire. Now that she was close again, her tits were in my face and I started breathing hard. I watched her nipples get hard and my clit jumped. This was getting real interesting, and I tried to remember how all this started but the iced teas were blocking my neurotransmitters..

Shit. I just came in for a drink. Now I was feeling all on this chick and basically putting my mack down. This drinking had to stop. But not tonight.

"What you drinkin'?" I asked.

She stared at me for a minute, I guess trying to figure out where I got the name Apple. But, first things first. She got all sexy on me.

"I'm drinking Absolut and grapefruit." I felt her hard nipples on my arm. "I'm not sure how I feel about you calling me an apple, but I figure I'll let it pass, especially since you're buying drinks."

I turned away to order Apple's drink and let her go. Shit. This was some new shit for me, and I was trying to get a grip on myself before I did something stupid at this bar. I'd been coming to this bar for years and had bought plenty of drinks at the bar before—for dudes and chicks. Shit, I'd been the life of the party, flirting with anybody that was around. But that was harmless flirting and completely different, and I was feeling something in this bar for this Apple chick. This was something else altogether.

I needed another Long Island. I gave Apple her drink and asked again, "So, what did you say your name was?"

"I didn't, but thanks for the drink. Drink up, even though you look like you been more than enjoying yourself. The next one's on me." She took a sip and stared at me. She was standing over me, next to my barstool, and I could see her looking me up and down. Then she whispered in my ear.

"So what's your name, and do you usually stare at women's breasts in the bar, or should I be flattered?" I must've blushed or something, because she said, "Don't be shy now, 'cause you were staring through me over there." She pointed across the bar at her prior seat.

She made a face at some chicks across the bar. I figured the chicks staring in our direction were her friends, and they were probably wondering what she was doing with me.

I saw her wave and raise a finger to somebody, indicating that she needed a minute. I looked across the bar ice-grillin' three sets of eyes staring back at me. I wasn't sure what was going on and wondered if I was flirting with somebody else's chick. Fuck it. I decided I didn't care and looked back at Apple again.

"So, what did you say your name was?" I started playing with the straw paper of my drink that I wasn't drinking. I may have been treading on some dangerous ground, and I was trying to figure out if Apple was worth fighting over tonight. What if one of those chicks was her "man" or "woman?"

"For the second time, I didn't say, but I kind of like the apple part, so let's stick with that." Apple watched me play with the cherry in my mouth. I didn't even like the imitation cherries that came with Long Islands and usually threw them away; but Apple was staring at my mouth and I was thinking that I might want to kiss this chick.

I ordered my fourth Long Island, and Apple was driving me crazy. She was all in my face, and I was feeling the attention she paid me. She whispered in my ear again, but the music was too loud to hear what she said. This chick must've been feeling me, and I wasn't about to tell her to stop.

Since Apple was taking liberties, I asked for her name again.

"Okay, so what did you say your name was again? I don't think you told me the last time I asked you."

Her hand was on my hair and she acted like I didn't ask her a question at all.

"Before I go back across the bar, do you want another drink?" she replied instead. Her hand was inside the back of my jeans and I was wondering if I'd had too much to drink.

I was kind of scared of what another Long Island would do to me.

"Not right now, but ask me again in a few and I'll let you know. And my name is Taylor, but my friends call me Tee." I decided that maybe she had told me her name and my drunk ass must've missed it when she said it.

Maybe I did want another Long Island, and fuck the consequences.

"Okay, Taylor, you do just that. Excuse me a moment while I curse out my friends for being assholes across the bar." Her friends were loudly calling to her, laughing, and gesturing to her, calling her something that sounded like Dawn. "Oh, and Taylor, please order us another drink. I'll be right back," Apple said.

She sauntered that fine ass away, her Apple Bottoms swinging viciously while Lil' Wayne and Robin Thicke's duet "Shooter" blasted from about eight speakers. I watched til she walked to the other side of the bar and then checked myself.

I looked around the bar, feeling a little conspicuous, wonderin' if anyone had seen me staring at her onion like it was the last supper. I was trying to shake my head clear of the alcohol and buzzing in my brain, to see if anyone was looking at me.

With Apple, a.k.a. Dawn, out of my space for a minute, I wondered what the fuck was happening to me tonight. I came to the bar by myself, planning to stay by myself and get a couple of quick drinks. I hardly ever drank alone, and I was planning to make this an in-and-out trip without a bunch of bullshit. Depending on who was in the crowd, I could count on a round of free drinks from the bartender or a couple of the regulars.

Scooters was the hangout for cops from the nineteenth district in West Philly. Since it was usually filled with the law, it got loud and crowded, but nobody was willing to start some shit and catch some hot shit in the ass. There was a takeout menu that sold cheesesteaks, hoagies, burgers, chicken wings, and fingers. Customers from the bar and the street bought food until two AM.

I looked over and saw Dawn talking to her friends while putting on a denim half-jacket. Her friends were giving her grief and holding on to her arms, like they were trying to keep her on their side of the bar. I saw her pointing in my direction and throwing fake jabs at them so they would let her go.

I caught her eye as she pretended like she was struggling. I mouthed to her, "You want some help?" I was holding up my arms like a bodybuilder, showing off my biceps. She slapped at their hands, and they finally let her go.

Blowing kisses and waving good-bye, she walked away backward, like she was coming back to my barstool. Shit. I forgot to order her drink. I called Sissy, the bartender, and ordered another round. Sissy was good at her job and never needed to be reminded of your drink.

The next thing I knew, Dawn popped up next to me like she did the first time. Silent and sexy, she was in between my legs and those lips were driving me crazy again.

"I sent them away," she whispered. I must've been looking at her like she had too much to drink, because she pointed across the bar. "My friends. I told them that I was staying with you. I told them that we knew each other from school and that you'd make sure I got home safely."

I wasn't paying attention. I was feeling this chick and the way she was up on me, and saying cute shit in my ear. Those Long Islands had me thinking that Dawn was some fine-ass dude up on me, and she was making me feel some shit that I couldn't believe I was feeling. I was trying to play it off, watching Sissy make our drinks and bring them over to us, looking at this chick in my face. She looked at us like something was off, and I knew eyes was watching.

Sissy had been serving my drinks for two years, and she'd met most of the dudes I dealt with. She knew she never saw me with another woman. But, shit, tips were tips and my money spent the same, whether a chick or a dude was in my face.

Dawn was talking to me again.

"So, what are you going to do with me, now that you have me all to yourself?" she asked. She hopped onto the stool next to me as soon as it was empty. She moved closer to me, dragging her stool across the floor, til her stool was touching mine. My fifth Long Island sat in front of me, turning watery while she rubbed my leg under the bar.

"I don't know what I want to do wit' you, but I'm not goin' to be able to do nothin' at all if I drink this iced tea." The music was loud as shit and my head was pounding. I needed to get some air and I had to pee like a goddamned racehorse. But I must've been tripping, because I didn't want to leave her. I wanted to make sure she would be waiting for me when I got back.

Dawn took sexy little sips of Absolut while staring at me. She was damn near sitting on my lap, and I could smell something peachy in her hair. I knew *we were causing a scene, but I guess those four Long Islands were making me not care.*

*"Okay, Taylor, what would you like to do to me?"*

*When I looked at Dawn across the bar before, I didn't think she was into chicks. Not that there had to be a look or a type. I just wondered if this was something she was into all the time. She didn't seem to have any problems with being next to me, and being in my face in front of so many people.*

*Yeah. Dawn looked like she was enjoying herself, like this was something she did every day. For some reason, I didn't like thinking of her being gay. I wanted to pretend that she was a straight chick who just happened to be attracted to me. But watching those lips when she talked to me, feeling that body right next to me—, I didn't give a shit what people thought.*

*Lucky for me, Sissy gave me a glass of water, because she knew I needed it even if I didn't ask. She had been a barmaid forever and knew that I had drunk too much and needed to get home.*

*I was thinking,* Fuck the consequences. I'll worry about my actions later.

*"Let me see, Dawn. I think it's time to see if you know what to do wit' them lips you had on me all night. And I need to know what's in them Apple Bottoms."*

*She laughed at me. I didn't think I said shit that was funny.*

*"Well, let me see if I can help you figure that out, Taylor, okay?" She signaled to Sissy and asked for the bar tab. She placed two twenties on the bar. "Here. Put this toward the tab, drink your water, and be ready to go when I get back from the bathroom."*

*Wow. I wondered if she had a set of balls. That didn't seem to bother me because I drank my glass of water and paid Sissy what we owed. I left Sissy a tendollar tip and told her I would be back soon.*

*"You can tell me what you think about what was happenin' here tonight," I told her. I knew Sissy saw everything. She had been around too long to miss much at her bar.*

I pushed myself from the barstool, weaving and trying my damnedest not to embarrass myself before I got to the front door. I made it, thanks to the barstools around the bar, and darted outside to get some fresh air. I'd pee later.

Dawn met me outside, looking worried. She'd gone back to the bar, looking for me and to leave Sissy a tip. When she found me gone and Sissy already tipped, she hoped that I would be outside getting fresh air. Such a smart girl.

"Taylor, give me your keys so I can get us to your place in one piece. You do have a place of your own, don't you? I guess it's kind of late to ask if you live with someone, right?"

She snatched the car keys out of my hand and started walking away. I could hear her talking to herself about being dumb, and not asking the right questions first. Then she stopped and turned back.

"Taylor, let's go. Wait. Where's your car, and where are we going?"

# CHAPTER 8
*Taylor*

I told her how to get to my 1991 Nissan Stanza. I know, I know—they didn't even make those anymore. But it was cool. It got me where I needed to go most of the time.

Somehow, Dawn found her way to 52nd Street and to the 5800 block of Ogden.

The water at the bar and the night air had worked wonders on my head, and I felt all right when we got to my security door. We walked inside the house where I grew up and now lived in by myself. My mother had moved to Charleston, South Carolina to be with her sisters and left me the house. I had three bedrooms and one-and-a-half bathrooms. Somehow, I scraped up the money to pay the utilities and the property taxes each year.

"Naw, Dawn, I live by myself. I heard you talkin' shit all the way to my house. And thanks for lookin' out, getting me home in one piece. Ain't nobody here but us. Give me a minute to pee, so I can take you on a tour around this mansion. Sit right here on the couch and watch some cable before they turn it off." I damn near ran to the closest bathroom, which was behind the kitchen.

I barely made it in time. I did brush my teeth real quick, though. Then I did the sniff test—you know, when you checked the hot spots for hidden funk: underarms, pussy, and between the butt cheeks. I passed with flying colors.

I thought I needed some more water.

"Dawn, do you want somethin' to drink? I got some Dasani and a flat

two-liter of Dr. Pepper." I had to admit—since I was no longer so drunk—
that I didn't know what I was going to do with this chick; but I didn't want
to be too drunk to remember it. No more drinking.

When I got back to the living room, Dawn had removed her jacket and
was watching HGTV. She was all stretched out on the couch. I sat down on
the love seat because one, I didn't trust myself to be that close to those tits lying on my couch, and two, I was trying to see everything she did so I could
know what to do.

I gave her the Dasani and called myself playing it cool.

"So, Dawn, what's up? What's a nice chick like you doin' here with me?
Is this your thing?"

She frowned for a second and then laughed.

"Is what my thing, Taylor?" she asked and laughed again, but I must've
missed the joke. "Why don't you ask me what's really on your mind?" She
sat up and crossed her legs. "And do me a favor, will you? Stop calling me
Dawn."

It was my turn to frown.

"Well, what do you want me to call you? And is goin' home with strange
chicks your thing?" I watched her like a hawk, looking for somethin' that
would help me know what was goin' on wit her.

"You could call me my name to start."

"Look, Dawn, no, I'm not into this type of thing. I don't hit on chicks at
the bar." I thought about it for a second. "Put it this way, I've never been attracted to a woman like this, and if I was, I definitely didn't try to bring her
to my house." I could not read this chick and it was really starting to bug me.
"So, what's really good, Dawn, and what's so damned funny?"

"First of all, my name is Shawn. It's actually Shawna, but my friends
call me Shawn. I've been laughing at you, calling me Dawn all night. What
made you think my name was Dawn?"

She laughed again and didn't let me answer her question.

"Never mind, don't tell me. C'mere and sit next to me, so we can talk for real." She patted the cushion next to her and crooked her index finger, motioning me over.

Part of me wanted to jump over the table to get close to her again, and the other part was embarrassed as shit. I needed to work on my pickup lines. I thought I was doing something while flirting with her all night, but instead I was just calling her the wrong name.

"Well, ain't that fuckin' great, Shawna! You coulda said somethin' before now. I feel like the world's biggest dickhead. Shit." I was feeling like going to bed and kicking her the fuck out, but I moved over to the couch.

I sat one cushion over to give her space, but she pulled me closer to her. Her thigh was touching mine and now I was feeling shy, like a sacrificial virgin over an open flame.

"That's better," Shawn said. "First you're acting like you want to fuck me, and now you're acting like a virgin."

Bingo! I tried to play it off, though.

"Don't even bother to say anything, Taylor. I know when somebody is tryin' to get in my panties. Now, about this 'thing' you've been asking about. No this is not my 'thing.' I'm trying not to blame it on the alcohol, but I saw you looking at me in the bar and after a while, I started looking back. You are a very pretty girl, and I was feelin' the look in your eyes when I looked back at you."

Shawn stopped to take a sip of her water, then continued.

"I kept trying to convince myself that it was the alcohol that had me checking you out, and after a while I had enough nerve to say something to you."

"So what made you want to approach me?" I asked. "I mean, you were in my face like you knew me, or at least wanted to know me. Why was you so bold tonight?" I thought for a second. "Should I be the one flattered?"

"Yeah, you should be, Taylor." She looked at my face and I could see her eyes dip lower. "So now what? You want that kiss you was talking about earlier?"

*Aw, shit. Now I was really feeling like a virgin. It was all fun and games before. This shit was getting very real all of a sudden.* Now what? Shit. Maybe I shouldn't have brought this chick here with me.

*"Shawna, look, I'm not sure—" I started to say, but then she took the decision away from me.*

*She leaned over and kissed me on the lips. It was a soft, quick kiss, but I swore I felt that shit in my stomach and I thought my dick might've gotten hard—if I had a dick. She stayed in my face for a few, then pulled away a little bit.*

*"So how was that?" she asked me. We were nose to nose. She cocked her head to the side. "Not so bad, huh? I thought it was rather nice, but it could be better if you participated."*

*It must've been all of those Long Islands, because all I could think of—other than why I was getting turned on by this chick—was that her breath didn't smell like Absolut or grapefruit. She must have snuck in a mint or something.*

*Fuck it. I was here now. I moved closer, turned my head, and kissed her this time. Then, like it knew it was supposed to be there, my tongue was on hers and she started sucking it.*

*She touched my hair, which was a little longer than hers, and her hands massaged my scalp. It was awkward at first until she sat on my lap and turned her head the other way. Then it turned into a real kiss, like one of us was a dude.*

*I swear I didn't know how my hands got to her tits, but she was rubbing them all on me, so I squeezed them and rubbed her nipples. Aw, shit. I liked this kissing and shit a little too much.*

*We stayed like that, Shawn on my lap, kissing me like one of us was going to Iraq the next day. We kissed for like a half hour, and then I took her ass home with wet panties.*

*Shit.*

# CHAPTER 9

*Eva*

Everything between Brand and I had been perfect lately; too perfect, probably. Because I had been lulled into a false sense of security by the quiet before the storm, I was completely unprepared and blindsided by the reemergence of Tomboy (TB), a.k.a. Lisa. Tomboy and her association with Brand had always been somewhat of a mystery to me. I met her in Atlantic City about three years ago with Brand's best friend Evan. Brand and I were at the Showboat Hotel and Casino for the weekend. We had reserved a suite of rooms, just in case his friends stopped by during our stay.

Evan and TB had walked into the suite and my interest was piqued as I watched Brand emerge from the bathroom, greet Evan with a handshake, and hug TB. I had never seen or heard of her, so I was immediately curious about the association between them. A hug with my man was and will always be something that deserved a second glance, and definitely a bit of investigation. So that weekend ended up being a wild, orgy-filled time.

Unfortunately, TB unexpectedly came back to ruin my perfect little relationship with Brand. Taylor called me one Saturday afternoon with the bad news. The conversation started out as it usually did, with us catching up on what happened over the last twelve to twenty-four hours. Since we spoke daily, sometimes multiple times a day, there wasn't much new information to trade. Taylor was my moral compass in life. She kept me honest with myself and in line with reality.

"What's up, girl?" Taylor's first question was the standard opening. "I know you are not still sleeping at this time of the day."

I snorted in response. "You sure got some nerve, questioning my daily activities when you normally keep bat hours. What's up, girl?"

"Oh, you know, sitting here on the bed, strokin' this beautiful breast that's resting in my palm. I just knocked Shawn out. You know my oral game is tight and she's snoring prettily, as only a fine-ass woman can."

"Girl, please. I have had more than enough of you and Shawn and your sexual mess." I grinned at the thought of their overactive sex life, so deliciously described by Taylor. "Honestly, Tee, do you do anything but squeeze her D-sized tits all day? God, you are sick. Leave that girl alone sometimes."

I wasn't jealous, really. I had been, though, at one time. For a while, it seemed like all Taylor could talk about was "Shawn this" and "Shawn that." I thought, for a minute, that she was trying to replace me, but I was cool with it now. Honestly, though, I had met Shawn at Savannah Soul Food Bar one night, and I could see why Taylor couldn't keep her mouth or hands off her.

"So anyway, Evie, what are you doing for the rest of the weekend?" Tee was hedging, as she normally would have lapsed into some type of gossip or complaint about someone or something. Plus, we'd already discussed our weekend plans.

"Spit it out, Taylor. What's up?" I never called her by her full first name, so she should have known that I was on to her. It had better not have something to do with Brand. Somehow, Taylor knew everyone who knew someone. Therefore, Taylor knew a little bit of everything and a little bit of everyone.

"What? I didn't say anything. Damn it, Eva. I don't know. Now I'm not sure I want to say anything at all. I was trying to work my way into this thing. Can we pretend that I didn't call you at all?" She sighed long and loud into the receiver. "I really hate to have to even get into this. I hate having to ask you about any of this. Fuck it. Maybe we should just forget it. I don't even want to have to get into this with you."

I had heard enough and figured that this was about Brand. I really wasn't trying to hear anything about him, and from her tone, it wasn't good information that she wished to share. I felt like my bubble was about to burst, and I was going to fight whatever it was with all that I had.

"Jesus, Taylor, just say it. Stop dragging this bullshit out and get it over with."

"Eva, look, I've been thinking about this long and hard. I've been debating this back and forth. I am, and have been, really reluctant to say anything to you at all. Fuck it. Do you know where Brand is?" I could hear something that sounded like anger and impatience in her voice. "Do really know what he's doing and who he's with?"

I let out a sigh of relief. "Is that all? Of course I know where he is. Girl, you almost scared the absolute crap out of me." I glanced at my winking diamond. With a lighter heart, I asked, "Why, Tee? What do you think you know, and who told you?"

"Look, don't ask me. Don't take this the wrong way. I'm just passing on information that came to me. I don't know for sure if it's valid. I'm just looking out for you. Let me ask you this question: Is Brand with Evan in Atlantic City this weekend?"

Okay. I was suddenly silent and not smiling anymore. The conversation had taken a sudden, nasty turn and changed my thought process. Yes, Brand was in AC with Evan this weekend, and no, no one else should have known that. My heart was suddenly hard and heavy and I wanted to know what was going on.

"Okay, give, Taylor. What's going on? What do you know?"

"Look, girl, I'm telling you what I overheard from some chicks in the cafeteria. These bitches was trying to be smart, because they suddenly started talking loud when I sat down. At first I ignored their silly, giggling asses, but when I heard the name Brand, I started listening. They weren't giving up much information, but then I heard something about Atlantic City and Evan." Taylor's voice was rising and I could tell she was angry at the possibility that Brand was being deceptive at this point in our engagement. "One of the girls at the table's name was Jessica. Her voice was the loudest, and she kept mentioning Brand and someone named Lisa."

"Taylor, are you sure? I'm supposed to be getting married in four months."

Taylor was quiet for a brief moment.

"So now what? Seriously, in your heart, what do you want to do? Are you really ready to find out something? Do you think you could get over this, or get past it?" She sighed again. "I'm with you, Eva, for whatever. Whatever you want to do, we'll do it. Say the word and we are on Route 42. We can be in AC in an hour."

I couldn't think and didn't want to reply. I was devastated, hurt, and unwilling to believe that I could possibly go through this again with Brand. We had put this shit behind us long ago. Or, at least I thought we had. Now, I wasn't so sure. I didn't know if I wanted to know the truth. I wasn't sure I wanted to go to Atlantic City, and I was afraid of what I might find.

It was all too much—the herpes, the other women, Brand breaking my heart, leaving me hanging, not communicating with me. The list went on and on. I could go on for days about the things that were wrong with our relationship, now and in the past. But I was in love. Plus, I needed Brand and the comfort and acceptance he represented in my life.

"Taylor, I need to call you back in a little while. I can't do this right now. I'm not sure I even want to know what's going on, if there is anything to know. Maybe I need to pretend that we didn't have this conversation. I need to call you back, okay? Thanks, Tee, really. Bye."

Of course, after we hung up, I couldn't concentrate, or eat, or sleep. I didn't want to believe the things Taylor told me but in my heart, I knew that some part of it was true. I felt tricked and stupid, again.

Maybe Taylor's information was flawed and she'd heard incorrectly. Maybe the information wasn't about Brand. Maybe. Maybe. Maybe. I was almost scared to find out. I thought that maybe I really didn't want to know anything about anything at all. I didn't want this right now. I didn't need this right now. I wanted to be secure and happy in my relationship. I needed to be secure in my relationship.

I couldn't go through that herpes shit again with anyone else. Honest to God, that shit with Brand the first time, almost broke me. I couldn't go through the lies and deception anymore for my own sake. I was tired of meeting new people and wondering how and if I was going to break the news to them of an STD that was impossible to cure. This was a disease that might kill a newborn baby if it got infected coming through the birth canal. I mean, really. What kind of shit was that?

How did you explain that to an eagerly expectant father? *Oops. Sorry. You see, I should have told you that I might kill our baby by accident. Yes, I know that I should have told you long ago that I could possibly pass this disease to you and ruin your life, along with mine. We can take pills every day for the rest of our lives to keep the virus at bay, though. What's for dinner?*

And in the end, I chose not to go to Atlantic City. I chose not to know for a time.

I called Taylor.

"Tee, it's me." As if I would be someone else. "I'm not going to AC. I can't go. Don't ask me why. I just can't do it right now. I appreciate you telling me, though. I appreciate your loyalty, and for you just plain looking out for me." I sighed and bit back tears. "I know you want me to go, Tee. I want to go. I'm just not ready for what this may do to me. I'm sorry for disappointing you and me, because I know I deserve better than this."

Taylor was silent for the most part, and let me get it out.

"I understand, Eva, and I can respect your decision to withhold judgment until further notice. I just wanted you to know what I knew. I want you to be happy and I want you to be happy with Brand, just not like this. Not at a sacrifice of you or your happiness. So keep that in mind, and let me know if you change your mind. Okay?"

I let Taylor go and let the tears flow. I cried for my sanity that was at stake again. I cried for the Eva I used to be. I cried for the happiness that I thought I'd never see again. I cried for the Brand and me that might never.

# CHAPTER 10

## *Eva*

Of course, I never went to Atlantic City. I wasn't strong enough then. I watched instead. And waited. I watched and waited for signs that Brand was not as faithful as I'd imagined. I wondered and hurt. I prayed and tried to believe. I put the doubts behind me and prepared for Brand's return home from his weekend away with Evan, and God knows who else.

"Brand, baby, when did you get back?" I had been blowing up his phone on Sunday morning, as I was expecting him home any minute. He walked into the house to find me waiting for him in our bedroom, lying across the bed, wearing only a white lace thong. I'd been thinking about him all weekend. I pushed Taylor's words far from my mind and decided to concentrate on what I did know was true: I knew that I loved this man, and would marry him in a few months.

"I just got back. Evan drove down in the Escalade. That was him dropping me off." He walked toward me and stopped short, looking down on the bed. "Damn, Eva, you look good as shit. I can't wait to marry your sexy ass. You know I'm ready to do this." He knelt on the floor at the foot of the bed and kissed my stomach, up and down my rib cage. In between kisses, he asked, "What was with you blowin' up my phone like that?"

I lay on the bed, lost in his kisses that were creeping back and forth, toward and away from my favorite places. My body vibrated slightly as I was overcome by Brand's physical closeness and the emotional wringer

I had been through during the weekend. Taylor's words threatened to enter my thoughts again, and I pushed them aside and pulled Brand to me. We lay on the bed, side by side, me caressing his head and face, and he rubbing my arms and shoulders.

"Nothing. Just missing you and wanting you here with me. You know I usually go to AC with you, and I was lonely." I pushed him onto his back and straddled his body, sitting on his flaccid penis. My mind paused. Anger flashed and I wondered why he wasn't aroused. I mean, here I was, almost naked, and he was caressing my body, but he wasn't horny yet? "Why, didn't you miss me?" I asked.

I kissed his neck and nibbled my way over to his ear. My kisses continued down to his chest and over toward his arms. I circled back over and latched onto his left nipple, licking and biting, hard and soft, alternately. "Didn't you miss me, Brandon?" I heard him mumble something and my mind pictured that Jessica chick or Lisa kissing him the same way in AC.

I moved slowly up his body and kissed his lips, feeling the proof of his arousal during my ascent. He kissed me in return, pulling me tightly against him and wrapping one of his legs around mine. It was a possessive move and it was a welcome feeling as I kissed him in return, and wondered if another woman had been kissing him within the last thirty-six hours.

Brand sat up, supporting my weight on his chest, and unbuttoned his shirt as he continued to kiss me, his tongue moving around in circles, sucking my tongue farther into his mouth and then retreating. His mouth dipped below and licked my nipples, his hands now free to tug and pull at my warm globes. I moaned as his teeth scraped my hardened tips.

My arms hung loosely around his neck while I strained and arched my back to allow total access to my neck, chest, and breasts. Brand was holding me, almost crushing my body into his, and he told me he loved me over and over, kissing my mouth, my face, my hair. I was aroused and in love, and almost desperate to prove to myself that he was mine, alone.

I pushed myself up and reached under me to unleash his throbbing penis and we touched sexes, blending ourselves at the same place and the same time. The tumultuous feeling of his love inside me—soothing, touching, loving—was almost more than my emotions could stand. I lost myself inside and around the softness of his hard, masculine body against mine.

This was the Brand I loved and knew. This was the Brand who loved me and wanted to marry me. This was my Brand, his love evident as he stroked himself into my wet, welcoming warmth. We loved slowly, working our hips, gently stroking, pulling and claiming as he came inside me with a grunt and a harsh whisper of my name, sweating, gripping my neck as he touched down back to earth. The warm, welcome feelings slowly softened my body and thoughts as I lost myself in the comfort of my fiancé's love.

But I didn't cum.

After he passed out—he obviously didn't get much sleep in Atlantic City—I went through his pockets and through his cell phone. I loved him, but I hadn't really trusted him since he cheated on me years ago. I loved him and would marry him, but I didn't put anything past him when it came to other women.

Of course, I didn't find anything. Brand was too smart for that. I knew that just because there were no obvious signs of another woman, didn't mean that there wasn't one, somewhere. I just hadn't found them yet. But I would.

From that day forward, I watched Brand like a starving hawk. I double-checked his whereabouts and stories of hanging out all night, gambling. If he said he was with Evan, I checked with Evan's latest jump-off. If he said he was with Sharif, I followed in my car. I didn't care. I loved Brand and would do what I needed to do to hold on to him and keep him with me.

I fucked him like a mad rabbit, too. Every time I saw him, I clung to him, kissed him, and hugged him. I stalked around the house naked or nearly naked, daily. I pranced my ass in front of the television as he played Xbox 360 on Saturday nights and Sunday mornings. I licked his ass when I joined him in the shower uninvited. I gave him blowjobs as he shaved in the mornings and sucked his toes at night.

I made my body open and available to him at all times—oral sex in the Range, anal sex in the garage, and good, old-fashioned pussy all over the house.

Then I found out the truth about Lisa, Jessica, and Atlantic City. Of course, Taylor had been correct. As usual, she had the scoop about any and all goings on in the city.

One Saturday night, soon after Brand returned from AC, we were out at Walts Devils Island on Hunting Park Avenue. I was drinking Thug Passions and eating mussels and snow crab legs. Betting on who would get drunk first, Brand and I were throwing back shots of tequila in between eating our food, when some chick and her gang walked up on us at the bar.

I didn't know who the main ho was, initially. I saw a light brown, short (barely five feet tall), thick chick walk up in jeans and a fitted, long-sleeved tee that said LIMITED TOO. She was tiny, almost childlike in size. Her black weave was long, hanging over her breasts and below her bra strap. Her little feet were in black, knee-high, fur lined Timberland Boots.

"What's up, Brand?" this chick asked my man. She totally ignored me, looking only in Brand's direction. "You were supposed to call me, correct? Don't tell me you forgot what you told me at the hotel. Do you really want me to remind you right now, in front of your company?" It was her only reference to me. She turned to her gang of friends and laughed at herself. The gang was looking at me.

At first I didn't pay attention to her, thinking she was another of Brand's adoring fans, as they flocked wherever we were. But her mention of AC—and Brand's lack of response—caught my attention, forcing me to pay attention to her. I caught on quickly, realized she must be the infamous Jessica, and tossed back the rest of my Thug Passion.

"Why *don't you* ask her to remind you, Brand?" I pushed myself forward in my seat, positioning myself near enough to him so there'd be no misunderstanding that we were together, but far enough in case I needed to spring on Jessica or her friends.

Brand had no response. Jessica turned to me.

"Oh, you must be Eva. Brand did mention you, briefly, that weekend. He told me about you right before I was riding his dick in the Range Rover, third level, section F in the Showboat Casino parking garage. Yeah, it was good too, wasn't it?" She was speaking to me, but never looked at me as she stared into Brand's face.

I sprang forward and smacked Brand in his face. He didn't see it coming, but Jessica screamed and jumped out of the way. I knew it!

I was going in for a second attack when Brand recovered and grabbed my hands. I screamed in his face.

"You fuckin' bastard! This is the shit she was talking about. She said your ass was out of town with some bitches, and I didn't believe her. You dirty, nasty, cheating bastard. I can't believe you would even look at this tack-head bitch."

I could see Jessica responding to my choice words, and none too happily. She swung around to her gaggle of friends with attitude and they glared at me in unison. But I wasn't done.

"While I'm home, waiting on your dumb, fuckin' ass and sending out wedding invitations, starving myself to fit into a dress for you, you're out fuckin' with cheap-ass McDonald's whores. You ignorant asshole." I was too stunned to cry and I couldn't breathe. "Fuck you, Brand! Marry this tacky bitch if you want to. Fuck you. I'm done with this. You won't get the chance to marry me."

Now it must be love, 'cause I really considered cold-cocking that bitch where she stood. And I don't fight. Never had to. My favorite moniker was, "I'm a lover, not a fighter." I told myself I would see that bitch again and when I did, I would do my best to beat her ass like she stole something. I looked at Brand in disgust. His sappy, sorry ass was sitting there, looking caught. Men were such assholes! He never said a word. Not in defense of himself, or of our relationship.

And that was it. That was the end of the wedding, and the end of us.

I left the bar alone, leaving Brand to deal with Jessica and her friends. I caught a cab and made it home before he did and cleaned out as many of my things that would fit into Brand's weekend Louis Vuitton bag. It was huge, and I'd always had my eye on it. He wouldn't give it to me, and rarely let me use it. Well, he'd have to catch me with it red-handed before he got it back. I also took a red Polo shirt and a leather lambskin jacket that I loved, and didn't want him to have anymore. I couldn't believe that I was leaving my car behind. But pride goeth before . . .

I cried as I left my three-carat marquise diamond on the nightstand.

The thought of going back to my Aunt Mirabelle's house was too depressing and had been the center of too many bad memories from my crazy twenties. I'd run there to recover from the heartbreak by Cory, and the subsequent abortion of our baby. It seemed like I ran home to her house after every setback in my life. Plus, Mirabelle was getting older, and I didn't want to drag her into the new single-life mess I was about to start.

I went to Taylor's instead. *Please,* I prayed silently, *don't let Shawn be there, naked and writhing in her bed.* I needed my best friend. I needed a place to sleep. Then again, did I really want to sleep in the mess they'd left in Taylor's bed? I'd take the couch.

# CHAPTER 11
### *Taylor*

Why was I not even surprised when Eva came knocking at my door? How had I known, somehow, that she'd be at my door or her aunt's, fleeing from that asshole, Brand? I must have had some kind of Eva-tuition, because I knew. I just knew that something was going on with them. I could feel their trouble brewing a mile away. Or maybe I simply knew Brand too well.

Lucky for Eva, Shawna wasn't with me. She was damn lucky. Shawn damn near lived at my house and had only been gone for that one night that Eva popped up of course without calling first. I loved Eva, but I felt sorry for her.

I swear, I felt like my heart broke every time Eva's broke over some dumb shit. I listened while she stomped around my living room, ranting and cursing Brand's existence. I made fruit smoothies with brandy because I knew we would need an alcoholic haze to get us through to the next day. And because I knew just how much of an asshole Brand could be.

"Of course you were right, Taylor. That sneaky, nasty, asshole bastard was in Atlantic City with some bitch. This whore Jessica walked right up on us at the bar. Can you believe that shit? She walked right up to him, like I wasn't even there, and asked him why he hadn't called her. Can you believe that?" Eva looked like she wanted to punch the mirror on my wall. I hoped she didn't.

"Then she had the nerve to tell me that he 'mentioned' me when she was riding his dick in the Range. She knew the hotel name, the parking space, everything. That bitch fucked him; I know she did. I should have gone there. We should have gone to AC that weekend. We should have caught him red-handed. We should have kicked his ass and hers. I can't even believe I'm going through this shit again!" She kicked my stuffed panda. "I'm done with men, I swear."

I watched Eva go through the motions and felt even more sorry for her. I watched her and wondered. I wondered if Shawn and I would ever be going through this type of shit. I was waiting for the tears. I figured they'd follow the ravings about deceitful men and their unfaithful penises.

"Sit down, Eva." I followed her into the living room, handing her a mixed drink as I passed. "Drink. Take a deep breath. Let it out and let it go, at least for right now. Brand is an asshole. He's always been an asshole so while this is fucked up, this shouldn't be much of a surprise."

Because I was an asshole and I didn't always think about what I was saying, I had to watch tears start falling down that pretty face. I thought about it for a few, and then spoke again.

"Evie, I don't mean to be a bitch about this, and I'm not being um . . . inconsiderate, but I'm tired of that asshole hurtin' your feelings, like you ain't shit. I'm so tired of his shit, so I can't even imagine how you must feel."

My phone rang. I looked at the Caller ID, saw that it was Shawna, and considered letting it ring. I looked at Eva, trying to think about her feelings, while the phone kept ringing. But, shit, I wanted to talk to Shawn. I finally answered on the fifth ring.

"Shawna. What's up, baby?" I listened to her giggling on the other end. I never called her Shawna.

"Shawna? Oh, shit, what did I do?" She was suddenly sounding sexy and almost whispered, "You miss me? Is that it? What are you doing, Taylor, other than thinking about me, obviously?"

"I'm sittin' here with Eve, havin' a drink. She's going through some shit with Brand and we're getting drunk. But I'm more interested in you. When you comin' back to me?" I did miss Shawn, more than I was willing to admit. Maybe I missed her more now because Eva was going through this bullshit with Brand, a man. I was feeling Shawn's and my shit more than before. "Tell me the truth: you out with another chick or what?"

"Yeah, right. And, what, wait weeks to find out if she can eat pussy like you? Or worse, she might have some funky diseases and I find out too late? No, thank you, Tee Tee. I think I'll stick with you."

I looked over at Eva as she finished her drink and went to the kitchen for another one. We was definitely getting fucked up tonight.

"Oh, it's Tee Tee now? Yeah, well, Tee Tee got somethin' for that ass when you get it back here. Seriously, though, Shawn, I do miss you like crazy. You just get that sexy li'l ass back here."

Eva returned from the kitchen and I blew Shawn a kiss through the phone.

"You get that fine ass back here and give the girls a kiss for me. Call me tonight, so I can make you cum on yourself in that twin-sized bed." I laughed, just thinking about that shit. Then I started getting all horny, thinking 'bout Shawn holding my favorite D-cups, kissing her hard-ass nipples goodnight.

"Bye, cutie," she said, and we hung up.

Eva sat down when I hung up. She looked miserable as shit and I could have fucked Brand up, right then. She was drinking her second smoothie and I saw her looking at me. I felt sorry for her all over again. She just kept catching a bad break. Eva was really pretty and I couldn't figure out why she had so much bad luck in relationships.

And while I watched her, my left nipple started twitching.

"Evie, you okay? Bring me my drink and come sit next to me." I plopped down on the sofa bed couch. "You goin' to be okay. I promise. That asshole will not get away wit' this shit. Let's sit here and drink and think of ways to fuck his life around while we get fucked up."

Eva dropped next to me on the sofa. She let her head fall back onto my outstretched arm. Her head leaned into the space between my arm and rib cage. I looked at the phone and wondered what Shawna really thought about my friendship with Eva. Eva nuzzled the side of my right breast, and I figured that she must be drunk.

"Tee, you're gonna take care of me, right?" She looked up at me.

"Of course, Evie. You know that I always take care of you." I tried to move away from her, because something different was happening.

"I know you will. I'm not worried about you." She stared at me for a long minute, then picked up my hand and kissed my palm. "Taylor, I want you to take care of me and make me feel better."

I thought I had lost my mind when I let her move closer and kiss me. It was slow and soft, so unlike Eva herself. She was normally a whirlwind of doing and going. I allowed myself to kiss her back. She took my drink from my hand; I only know that it disappeared. To this day, I still don't know what happened to it.

My first and last thought was, *Eva, why now?*

And then I gave into her softness. I thought I felt her hesitate but since she started this shit, I was going to finish it.

I wanted to see her naked, and I realized that I had always wondered about her slim physique. I had only seen one woman naked in my life. I only knew one way to fuck a woman and Shawn had taught me well. I was the man in our relationship, and I acted like one in bed.

"Take off your clothes, Eva." I stood up, dragging her shirt up with me as I went.

I didn't play into that soft, subtle petting and foreplay. Or if I did, I saved it for Shawn. I wasn't sure what Eva was used to, but I'm sure I wasn't it. I would have never made the first move on Eva but now that she had, I was with it.

I stood over her on the couch, watching her stare up at me as she did what I asked her to do. She pulled her fitted tee over her head and pulled me down on the couch to kiss me again. Eva's kiss was different than Shawn's. Shawn was soft and smooth. She kissed me like a girl, and I kissed her like a man.

But Eva was used to being in charge.

She stood up as she reached around her back to take off her bra. I turned her around to unhook her bra and ran my hands down her back and waist. She slowly pulled the straps down her arms.

Eva's every move was strategic, and she moved like she was on stage, stripping for a crowd. Her performance turned me on in a different way than Shawn's quiet sexiness.

Eva stepped away from the couch and stood still, watching me watch her. She put her hands on her hips and smirked, as if she dared me to touch her.

Without knowing her heritage, Eva looked like a light-skinned sista. But up close, her face and body were something else. Her skin, the part you never saw, was pale and almost white. It was obvious that she took after her Italian father more than she did Mavis.

Because I'd always wanted to, I pulled her wild-ass hair, which was tangled and curly and ran down her back. Then I was on my knees in front of her, pulling her in front of me by her belt buckle.

"Eva, take this shit off."

She removed the last of her clothes, staring at me the whole time. When she was done, I kissed her stomach. I pushed her legs open and dove into her pussy, noticing the difference between Eva's taste and

Shawn's. She grabbed the back of my head, forcing my tongue deep into her wetness. I didn't even think about herpes.

Eva was beautiful, her body slender and less shapely than Shawn's. I rubbed her nipples between two fingers, watching them get hard and feeling her body shake. I ate the shit out of her pussy, doing all the things that made Shawn go crazy. I listened to her take deep breaths and then she moaned.

She kept moaning and pulled my head close, pushing her tits on my lips.

I felt my panties getting wet.

I had tired that ass out and then she decided to be the dude. She got bold and started moving my head back and forth across her tits.

"I want to cum again, Tee." She came down to kiss me and lick herself off my lips. My eyes were open and I watched her watch me as she kissed me harder and longer, licking inside my mouth and over my teeth. She had bragged to me before about her legendary kissing skills, and now I was a believer. I knew she wasn't bullshitting.

Eva wanted to be in control, so I let her. She unbuttoned my shirt, licking my stomach and tits as she went. She stood up, pulling me with her. Somehow she got me unzipped real quick.

I shook off my Capris and stood there for a few seconds, letting her take it all in. Yeah, her body was tight, but so was mine. Plus, she probably wondered what my body looked like, just like I wondered about hers.

I didn't know how I felt about her laughing at my attempt at the Venus de Milo. She pushed me back down on the sofa, leaned over me while still kneeling on the floor, and kissed my eyelids. She licked down until she got to my lips. When she had her lips right over mine, she stopped.

She grabbed my head and started kissing the shit out of me. *Damn, this bitch is bad!* I was all caught up in her sexual shit, getting turned the fuck on while she licked my lips, teeth, all on my chin, and in my nose.

She moved my head from her mouth, back to her tits, moving her body across my mouth, holding my head still. I was wet and horny and couldn't wait to feel those soft-ass lips on my pussy.

Eva held me close to her, chest to chest, her nipples rubbing all over mine, and I felt all of it down to my clit. I was turned on, but in a different way from sex with Shawn. With Shawn, I felt all in love and shit. With Eva, I wasn't sure what I felt yet.

Sometimes I felt like I was gonna leave Shawn hanging if I didn't make love to her. It felt like passion and the need to get all inside her to make her cum. With Eva, it was like I knew her and knew that we shouldn't be here, like some forbidden shit, some sinful shit.

And that turned me the fuck on.

Eva pushed me to rest on the back of the couch and moved between my legs.

*It's about damned time,* I thought to myself. Shit. I was ready to bust, or explode, or something. Her lips touched my clit and I still couldn't believe this shit, but I came all over us.

My clit was on fire and I felt one hell of an orgasm moving through my body. Then Eva shifted and started to French kiss my clit. I jumped up on the back of the couch. I was mad as shit! I was about to get that fuckin' mouth—those sexy–ass, full lips that were made to win sex awards—all over my dripping pussy, and I played myself and came faster than a virgin trying to get his first piece of ass.

I lay my head on the back of the couch and figured I was dreaming or I had lost my mind, because I couldn't believe I had just had sex with Eva.

The phone rang and I almost ran to it, hoping to death it was Shawna. I really needed something to save me from having to talk to Eva, now that we had just fucked. I was at a loss for words and didn't feel like trying to find none.

"Shawn! Baby, I'm glad you called me." I glanced over at Eva, who was looking at me like she couldn't believe what we'd just done, either.

I motioned upstairs with my thumb, in the direction of the spare bedroom. She grabbed her clothes and walked up the stairs and out of sight.

I was already lost in thought about Shawn, my mind on something else all together.

"Shawn, baby, I miss you. You gonna cum for me tonight?"

# CHAPTER 12

*Eva*

"Oh, my God, I fucked Taylor." I was speaking aloud to myself as I drove Taylor's car from my interview at Mountain View Center for Mental Health and Mental Retardation. My ten AM interview ended at approximately eleven twenty-five, and I was now officially employed as a Behavior Specialist Consultant with eight, six-hour cases.

It had been at least two weeks since the INCIDENT with Taylor, but I didn't know exactly how long because I had conveniently eviscerated the mishap from my memory. Only at times like these, when I was excited and anxious after my interview that went surprisingly well, did memories of the INCIDENT creep into my mind.

I knew that it had been two weeks and four days since my breakup with Brand. Hence, two weeks and four days since the INCIDENT, but I chose not to remember that.

I was on my way to Don Rosen BMW. I was going to reward myself with a brand new X5 for a great interview, a new position at Mountain View, and to combat the depression I had fallen into since my breakup with Brandon. Plus, I needed to flex as I cruised around town in my linen and diamonds.

Trust me, black people were the only people to work in the hood and drive around in luxury cars, wearing diamonds, furs, and stilettos. For the CREAM, black folks would do almost anything, including wearing a full-length fur into the hood to see lazy baby-moms and badass clients.

Anyway, I was meeting Bryce at Don Rosen so he could help me negotiate the purchase of my new SUV, and because I was feeling the need for some male attention after staying at Taylor's with her and Shawn and their sexual mess. The guilt from that night that never happened was overwhelming at times. I loved Taylor and was genuinely fond of Shawn. THAT SEXUAL INCIDENT WITH Taylor SIMPLY DID NOT HAPPEN!

The past two weeks had been a whirlwind of activity, planning, plotting, and being plain miserable. I had been staying with Taylor, Bryce, and Desiree, my old neighbor. Feeling like shit and trying to forget the INCIDENT, I sought out Bryce, contacting him through his mother in Mount Airy. I knew where he lived, since I helped christen his new house with loud, orgasmic sex the night before Brand proposed to me. But popping up on a guy I hadn't spoken with in almost two years was not my style.

Of course, he was ecstatic to see me. Yes, he'd been wondering where I'd been. And, yeah, he felt used and played because I'd fucked him, gave him back his engagement ring, and then never called him for almost two years. Oh well. His house was big and lonely, and the other women he'd brought home were no match, sexually, for the vibrant memories of my sexual prowess. I swear those were his exact words. I gave Bryce some bullshit excuses about needing some *me* time and getting my mental together over the last two years. I could tell he didn't really buy my explanation and probably wanted to call me on it but he didn't at the time. I think he missed me too much to start something he might not really want to finish.

Desiree used to live in the apartment building where I stayed after I left Mirabelle's at age twenty-four. She was an exceptional cutie who had been dying to give me the pussy. Or was that wishful thinking? Running into Desiree was a bit of circumstance, luck, and carefully chosen placement. Okay, I went to her job. Luckily, she was still a bartender at the Eagles Bar/Max's Steaks at Erie and Germantown Avenues. I floated into her life and job almost two years after disappearing, ordered a Blue Kamikaze, and pretended that I didn't know that she was working there. Surprise, surprise. I was back in the saddle. I'd been staying with her as well as with Taylor and Shawn, but, ironically, no sex so far with Desiree.

My cell phone rang and I saw that it was Bryce, with his impatient self. He was at the dealership already, waiting for me.

"Bryce, baby, I'm already in Bryn Mawr. I just crossed City Avenue and I'm three minutes away. How about you congratulate me on an interview well done, and my new job as a BSC?"

"Yeah, yeah. Just get here. I've already congratulated you all that I'm going to, Eva. First, you pop back up in my life without apology after years, after you were supposed to be my fiancée. And do I complain and curse you the fuck out? No. Now you order me to help you buy this truck and I'm trotting along behind you, as usual. You're luck is gonna run out soon, Eva. Just get here." And then he banged on me.

Well, now. I just needed to fuck him again, real good. Then he'd get rid of that attitude.

*Oh my God, I fucked Taylor!* The thought slipped in before I could banish it as I drove into the lot at the dealership. I immediately looked for Bryce's sexy, fine ass, but I didn't see him. Instead, the sea of new vehicles stopped me short.

Don Rosen BMW and Subaru was a cacophony of sensual, luxurious eye candy for the road. Forget the Subaru's. My senses led me to the BMWs like flies to shit. Ooh, goddamn they were beautiful, if a car could be beautiful—325s, 525s, 535s, 745s. I jumped into each one. Smooth leather, cup holders galore, TVs, navigation systems, Sirius satellite radio, backup cameras, and DVD players. But, of course, I was there for the X5, and that was it.

I was drawn to and wanted the 2009 X5 Sport Package, hunter green, with ivory, heated leather seats.

"That's my truck right there," I told Richard, the car salesman. I got in, adjusted the driver's seat, and test drove speedily around Bryn Mawr, terrorizing the senior citizens out for a stroll.

However, after reality set in and the sticker shock wore off, I settled for the 2007 X3 basic model. It was still priced at an ungodly $37,367, but much more manageable for my budget. Credit. What credit? I barely had any, except student loan payments. After I wandered back into Bryce's life, he agreed to cosign for me. Lucky me. Otherwise, I'd been in a nice, new Subaru wagon.

Hours passed and we were still at the dealership, closer—but not close enough—to driving off with my dream truck. Bryce almost had to get physical with Richard over the final price and warranty, but we left—me several thousand dollars poorer, but happy as hell. My certified pre-owned X3 would be detailed and delivered to me at Taylor's house by seven PM.

I broke Bryce off a nice piece of oral aerobics in broad daylight inside his Suburban, for all eyes to see. I felt slightly whorish, but damn, Bryce had just helped me get my dream car. And it wasn't like I hadn't been getting my knees dirty at the house in Chalfont—and God only knew where else—for much less.

I was beyond words, really. I mean, how did you say, "*Thanks for co-signing for my dream car. I know that I'm not your girl, and that I stopped calling you for almost two years and all. Oh, and I'm still lying by omission 'cause I haven't mentioned that I was engaged to Brand when*

*I wasn't calling. Yeah, he's the guy that gave me the herpes. Yeah, I know you really like me, but I think I may still be in love with Brand. But thanks for the BMW."*

I let my amazing oral Olympics speak for me and left Bryce panting, sweating, and smiling. But his smile was not bigger than mine. I would have done this—and more—to get my new truck. Fuck it. Welcome to whoredom. The truck was the most expensive thing I'd ever fucked for. I could definitely do this.

I was happy and satisfied. I promised to call Bryce as soon as the truck's keys were in my possession, and I almost floated back to Taylor's car, glad to say good-bye to her wreck. I couldn't wait to return it to Taylor. Not that I hadn't been grateful for the lemon over the last two weeks, but damn. Shawn had to be in love, and/or the sex was phenomenal, because it definitely wasn't Taylor's lifestyle.

I couldn't wait to get back to Taylor's to share my exquisite news. I barely got inside before I heard squealing from the bedroom.

*Damn, doesn't anybody work around here?* I didn't want to know how Taylor sustained her and Shawn's lifestyles, when I couldn't think of the last time either of them worked for a paycheck. I knew that Taylor had been living off grant and loan refunds, but damn. Somebody needed a job—more working and less fucking.

"Forget trying to get their attention. Knowing them, they'll be at this shit all goddamn day. Nasty asses! I'll just celebrate by myself." I was talking to myself—mumbling, really—as I was a little perturbed that no one was available to listen to me rave about my new truck and all the attention I'd get by driving it. I wanted Taylor to be the first to know, but if she'd rather be knee-deep in Shawn's pussy, so be it.

I went to the kitchen to search for something to drink, in celebration of my accomplishments for the day. *Champagne would be nice,* I thought. *Yum. Okay, or maybe some Belvedere vodka, aged perfectly, odor-*

*less and tasteless as it had to be by law. Yummy. Or some Bacardi dark rum, which sneaks up on you just when you're trying to drive home. Yummier.*

Well, none of the alcohol I'd been dreaming of was in the house. Instead, I saw apple cider, which looked tantalizing in a champagne-looking bottle with a pop cork. Well, I could pretend.

The cider didn't do the trick, but I made do. Soon I heard Shawna's giggling and Taylor's slightly deeper voice.

"Shawnee, baby, go wash that pretty body and come back to me. I'm getting something to drink. Do you want something?" I heard water running, the shower curtain moving around, and then I guessed that Taylor smacked Shawn on the ass. More giggling. I was about to gag.

Sipping my cider Champagne, I listened as Taylor approached the stairs. It occurred to me that femme-ass Taylor was the butch in their relationship, which was really surprising as Taylor was the prettiest, most feminine woman I knew. She was a five-two shorty, slim with big boobs. Her closet was filled with pastel sweaters, tiny fitted tees, and more shoes than Macy's shoe department.

I guessed that Shawna—who was taller than Taylor and slightly heavier, with bigger boobs—was even more femme, forcing Taylor into the masculine role. Amazingly, Shawn, with her cute, round face and dimples, was the one who wore loose-fitting fatigues, Timberland boots, and was always in green, black, or gray clothing. I guessed they liked it that way and it must have worked, because Taylor fucked that girl every day, sometimes while I was on the phone. They really had no shame.

Taylor walked into the kitchen, looking only slightly surprised to find me there.

"Goddamn it, Tee. Will you leave that girl alone for just a few minutes, please? Does her mother know that you fuck her like this, day and night without rest? It's a good thing y'all can't make a baby 'cause that poor girl would be perpetually knocked up." I waved my cider at her to emphasize my point. I sometimes wondered if they even talked at all.

"I've been here for more than half an hour listening to you torture that poor girl," I said. "I was excited when I got here 'cause I had some good news. Now it's old, boring, and I can barely remember what I wanted to tell you." She just stared at me, used to my ramblings and guilt trips. "I'm surprised you came up for some air."

Taylor still wasn't responding to my rantings, so I gave up and just spilled my news.

"Tee, I bought a truck today! It's being delivered at seven, and you'll never guess what it is and who helped me get it. Oh, and I got the BSC position at Mountain View and I start my six cases in two weeks! I can't believe this. This is my lucky day, and I'm celebrating with cider wanna be-champagne. By myself. 'Cause my best friend likes pussy too much." I looked at her with attitude. "Did you even go to class today?"

"Well—" she started. I didn't let her finish.

"Damn it, Taylor, you can't give up on school now, not because of a relationship! I know you're feelin' Shawn right now, but don't let this interfere with the rest of your life. Plus, isn't your job at the NDC about to start?" I looked at her. "Never mind, I won't preach, and you're as grown as I am. But did you at least feed the girl and brush your teeth? Nasty asses. I can't believe either one of you."

I smiled when I was done because I loved Taylor. Her relationship with Shawna was special for both of them. They were still crazy about each other, which was why I couldn't believe I had fucked Taylor! And even worse, I had fucked Shawn, too! I tried to convince myself that since we did little more than petting, not full out-sex, it didn't really count, and I didn't have to feel guilty around Shawn each time I saw her.

Then thinking about their relationship made me think about my breakup with Brand. I wondered what he would think about my new truck. I knew he was wondering how I was getting around without the car he gave me, since I left it behind when I dumped his cheating ass.

Why the hell was I thinking about him? I hated his cheating, nasty, herpetic ass. I had been stressing and worrying over the weeks since the breakup. As far as the world knew, we were still together and the wedding was still on. I hadn't had the heart to tell anyone other than Taylor and Desiree. I still wasn't admitting anything to Bryce.

But I didn't want to think about him right now.

"Tee, go get Shawnee out of the tub, let her get dressed, and keep your hands off her so ya'll can join me. I want some company to help me celebrate my job, the new truck, and the fact that Don Rosen is classy enough to deliver my truck to your door. Damn, I didn't mean to tell you where I got it from. Do you think your mom will let me use her address to register it in South Carolina? Girl, you know my insurance will be high as shit in Philly."

What I didn't admit to Taylor was that I couldn't wait for Brand to see me in my new truck. I couldn't wait for him to see my accomplishment.

# CHAPTER 13

*Taylor*

I let Shawn get dressed without getting all in her personal space, and we went downstairs to help Eva celebrate her accomplishments. That cider was the worst, though. But Eva was happy, so I was happy for her. She was acting like she was getting her life back on track, and I was glad that I could help.

Surprise, surprise. The truck came at six-thirty and I was shocked to see that it was an '07 Burgundy BMW X3. After jumping up and down like a preschooler, Eva made Shawn and I get in the back while she took us for a ride around the way. We made Eva play chauffeur for us. Shit. She wanted to show off.

Now that she was happy as shit, she told us all the details about buying the truck, including Bryce co-signing for her and her oral Olympics in his front seat. Now that information actually surprised me. I didn't even know Bryce was back in the picture. But I was not surprised that she had sucked his dick in his truck right after he signed for the BMW. I should have known she was fucking somebody. Would she be Eva if she wasn't?

She dropped us back off at home without saying where she was going, but I knew she was probably to Desiree's or to go lookin' for Brand. We were supposed to be going out but it turned out to be more like Eva driving us around a few blocks and that was that. She did tell me that Desiree was back, but she said that they weren't messing around. My money was on Brand. She hadn't really been talking about him that much lately, but I knew she missed his ass.

I knew she would want him to see her in her new BMW. She was so broke when she met him that she would want him to see her come up, and rub it in his face that she got her truck without him.

After Eva kicked us out of her new truck, I walked back in the house with Shawn, thinking that we had some time to get busy. Shit. Now I was wondering if Eva was right. Did I fuck the girl too much? I hoped not, but I couldn't help it.

Once inside, Shawn and I sat on the couch and love seat, in the same places we sat the first night that we met. We just looked at each other while Shawn threw me little smiles, but she didn't say anything. I had been feeling kinda fucked up and guilty since fucking Eva, and I wasn't really proud of what we had done.

Aw, shit. Why did I feel like doing something stupid, like telling Shawn what I did with Eva? I must be on that shit.

"What's up, Shawnee? What's up wit' you? You know somethin' I don't? Come clean, girl. Get that ass over here and sit next to me."

"No, you come to me. Just because you wanna act like the dude in this thing and fuck me with that plastic dick, don't mean that I gotta do what you say," she said with a smile. Shawn still loved dick; she just wanted it from me. "You get your ass over here and sit next to me."

I did as she said because she didn't ask for that much, except when I was fucking her in my bed. I shook off my sudden need to tell Shawn the truth about Eva and me. I sat down next to her and put my head on her shoulder.

My cell phone buzzed in my pocket and I knew that I had a text message. I felt guilty when I sneaked a look at the name of the sender. Brand. Why was he texting me right now? It felt like too much of a coincidence, and especially since Eva had just dropped us off in her new BMW truck. Was this nigga stalking her? Did he know about her truck already? Why was he bothering me? I tried to play it off and turned my attention back to my baby.

"What you want to eat tonight?" I asked Shawn. "Let's go out, somewhere close that don't cost too much. Thanks to you, I'm a little light on cash right now. I feel like a burger and nachos, or fried fish and mozzarella sticks. What you got a taste for?"

"I don't know. Whatever you want, Taylor. What time do you want to go? 'Cause I would like to change my clothes and do something with my hair." Shawn kissed me and walked up the steps without saying anything else.

Was I missing something? Was Shawn really acting strange, or was I being paranoid?

Goddamn it. Why was I still feeling like doing something stupid and telling Shawn about what I did with Eva?

I didn't get the chance to do something stupid. We wound up at T.G.I. Friday's on City Avenue. Plenty of action going on there. Allen Iverson was at a table near the bar, and there was some bitch getting her knees dirty under the table. Damn, what a shame; but maybe not. Maybe she'd get a kid or a Porsche Cayenne, out of it.

Shawn and I sat close to the bar because we wanted to be close to the action and refills. We weren't really groupies, but who didn't want to be close to a star, especially one like A.I. with all of his tattoos and all that extraordinary skill on the basketball court? That was some sexy-ass shit, watching that li'l sports phenom playing against and scoring on niggas twice his size. He only had to look at me once and my mind went blank. Shawn who?

I ordered us two vodkas and grapefruit juices. We were on a budget.

"So, what's up, sexy?" I asked. "What's on your mind? You ready for this beatin' I'mma put on that ass when we get home?" For once, Shawn didn't feed into my sex bullshit.

"No. The question is, Taylor, are you ready?"

"I was born ready, miss. But I'mma let you talk your shit, if it makes you feel better."

"So when do you start working at the prison?"

"The Norristown Detention Center ain't hardly no prison. They're kids who got caught doin' dumb shit out in Montgomery County. It's probably like a country club for young white kids, and you know how white people take care of their own." I stopped and looked at her. "Why, you worried about me 'cause this is my first real job, and I'm gon' be workin' with some baby criminals? Aww, that's so damned cute! Is that why your ass is lookin' like you lost your best friend?"

"I'm cool, Tee. I'm just gonna miss you when you go to work now. I guess I got a lot on my mind lately and you working with criminals— even juvenile ones—is part of it." She changed the subject. "What are we going to eat? I'm starving."

"Yeah, well, don't worry about it, Shawna. When I went on the interview that day when Eva took you to your doctor's appointment, we did a walk-through of the facility, and the staff seemed to have the kids in check. There weren't even any real bars or gates. It looked more like a boarding school, if you ask me. It looks like a piece of cake, and I can't wait to start working all that overtime."

While we looked at the menu, Shawna dropped the motha-effing bomb on me.

"Taylor, did you have sex with Eva?"

Just like that, she dropped it, and I stumbled and couldn't get my lie together quick enough. I think I said something stupid, and then I just shut up and sat there, looking dumb.

Why the fuck was I still feeling like I should just admit what happened with me and Eva? Was I fucking stupid? I already knew that if it wasn't on DVD or recorded on a camera phone, deny, deny, deny!

I didn't know what to do, so I told Shawn the truth and hoped she could get over it. I still didn't know what I was thinking, and why the urge to save my relationship didn't kick in.

"Shawn, it's not what you think."

The alcohol gods smiled down on me. The waiter delivered the drinks and I had a few seconds to think of something to say.

Then I had to look at her, and all the bullshit stopped.

Shawn cried quietly. Her hands covered most of her face, but I could tell. I felt like shit because she didn't deserve this shit, and I knew it.

I wasn't ready for being here, and for Shawn to ask me that question, —even though I kinda knew I would have to tell her. I had felt it in my heart. Eventually, I would have to be honest with her. I felt like I owed it to her.

I was prepared for hateful and nasty words that she would apologize for later, when I had her begging for forgiveness. I was ready for Shawn to want to fight me. I was prepared for her slaps and punches. I was ready for that.

I wasn't ready for tears of anguish and hurt. I didn't know how to respond. I didn't know what to do.

"Why, Taylor?" Her question was simple. "How could you do that?"

I didn't know the answer, and for once, I didn't have a response. I had hurt Shawn, and I didn't know if it could be fixed.

"Shawna, I'm sorry. I didn't mean to hurt you. I don't want to say that it was an accident, but it was. It was something that just happened. Shawn, she needed me that night. I felt like shit 'cause I wanted you that night, but she needed me."

I started getting pissed because I could see that Shawn didn't understand. I tried to explain to her that I didn't want to lose her because I took care of my best friend on the day she needed me the most. I started thinking that I really didn't want to break up with Shawn.

"Taylor, I trusted you. I knew that you and Eva were close, and even though I didn't like it at times, I dealt with it because you are the first person in a long time—male or female—that I have loved. I don't even understand my attraction to you. I don't understand half of why we do what we do."

The waiter came back and she waved him away.

"When you kiss me, I respond to you, to your love. I can feel it. I can feel love in your kiss." She laughed through her tears. "I can feel your love even when you don't know how you feel about me."

I opened my mouth, probably to say something else stupid. She waved me quiet and continued.

"You never talk about it, but I know that you're not gay. I know that you struggle with your attraction to me, and for me. So often I want to say to you, 'I'm not gay either!' when you're kissing me the way you do or just touching me, telling me how pretty I am. I want to say it, but deep down inside, I know that what I feel for you is special and different. I don't even try to understand it anymore."

She was crying, and it was killing me.

"I don't know what to say or do, Taylor. I'm hurt and confused, and I don't know what to do anymore. I thought you would be different. I love you, and I don't know how to handle this. I wasn't prepared for you and us, or your effect on me." We were attracting attention, but I didn't care. "What am I supposed to do now?"

I felt like shit. I had fucked up, and I didn't know how to make it right. I didn't have an answer for her.

Shawna told me that she wasn't hungry anymore and wanted me to take her home. What the fuck was I supposed to say?

She walked out on me.

I let her go, watching as she walked out in gray fatigues, that apple ass swaying from side to side as I paid the tab. She left me in Friday's by myself—a first. Shawn was, if anything, loyal to me. She did not leave me hanging, ever. Even when she was mad as shit at me, her loyalty to me was irrefutable.

I took her to my house and helped her pack her bags. I wouldn't let her see me cry. I held the tears inside. I didn't ask her to stay.

When Shawn said she wanted to go home, I assumed she wanted to go to my house on Ogden Street, but she meant her parents' house. So that's where I took her.

After she slammed my car door closed and pulled off, I checked my text message from Brand: *i need 2 talk 2 u tee.*

Now what?

# CHAPTER 14

*Eva*

My first drive, after dropping Taylor and Shawn off, was past Brand's house: a drive-by without the guns. I was not going to stop, of course. I thought I missed him. I wasn't sure if it was him that I missed, or if it was the sex and comfort factor. I thought that maybe I needed to talk to him, because I never did get his version of what had happened in Atlantic City. I was so enraged after we were confronted by that girl and her posse of friends at the bar, that I took only her word and fled my relationship.

Then I was worried about my friendship with Taylor. I could not believe that we had sex. I wasn't even attracted to her that way. Yeah, she was cute, but we didn't get down like that. I wondered if our relationship would ever be the same again. I wondered if Shawna knew or suspected anything. I wondered if Taylor suspected anything about me and Shawna. I didn't think any of us had been acting differently, but then again, what the hell did I know? I didn't even have a man anymore.

I had been thinking about herpes way too much since Brand and I broke up. My peace of mind was gone. All the thoughts that had been at bay were rearing up, making me sick to my stomach. My attempts to keep busy—running from house to house and buying a new truck— were not working. I had to admit that being with Brand was easier on my mind.

The outbreaks weren't back yet, but I was sure they were on their way. I was stressed and unsure of my future again. I was having unprotected sex with Bryce, even though he knew that I had herpes, but my mind was not at rest. Bryce had once dated an older woman with herpes, so he knew the risks and the probabilities almost better than I did. From previous conversations, he knew that I would let him know if I felt any symptoms of an outbreak. No, it was not a flawless set of circumstances, but it was more than I could ever have hoped for. Bryce understood and accepted me, yet I kept thinking about giving him the virus. Yes, he knew the risks and continued to see me with full knowledge of the possibilities. It really should have given me a clear conscience and enabled me to sleep at night. But it didn't.

With Brand, I didn't have those worries. Yeah, so I had other worries—namely Jessica—and whether or not his dick was greeting another woman when he was away from me. With Brand, my future was intact. I knew who I was and where I was going. I could get pregnant, schedule a Cesarean section before the onset of labor, and not have to worry about passing on an STD to my baby. My life would be worry free, for once. I wanted my life back.

In attempting to get my life back and forget about Brand, I had been fucking Bryce like a fiend; but he was not Brand, and he did not offer the same sense of past,—good or bad. I could admit that having sex with Bryce in his new home was much more exciting than our first kiss in his mother's basement. Sure, Bryce knew that I had this nasty disease, and accepted me as I was. But for how long?

Of course, I stopped at Brand's house. I couldn't help it. I admitted to myself as I drove toward his home, three weeks into our breakup, that I was miserable, tired of running to and fro, and wanted my life back. I really didn't want to fuck Bryce, as fine as he was and as good as the sex was. I didn't want to sleep on Taylor's couch. I didn't want to stop in on Desiree and lust over her body for hours. I didn't want to ponder what a relationship with Desiree might bring me. Then again, maybe I'd get a chance to know what Taylor and Shawn shared.

Before I knew it, I was at Brand's door. I knocked and waited. I questioned myself as I stood there, almost hoping that he didn't answer. Then, I heard multiple feet approach the door. The door handle turned and after some unsuccessful pulls, the door finally swung open. Small, pink Adidas appeared in the doorway.

It was Brand and his younger sister, Angelique. That explained the delay in opening the door. I looked behind them for his other sister, Tasha, who was never too far from Angelique.

"Eva."

"Miss Eva." The two greetings were spoken almost simultaneously.

"Brandon." I used his first name because I needed to show him that I meant business. Now what that business was, I didn't know. But I wanted to look serious.

Then softer, I said, "Hey, Angie. What you been up to?" I reached down to hug her tiny body. She had nothing to do with our relationship woes, and the fact that her brother was a cheating asshole.

"Watching *Chowder*," she said.

"Where's Tasha?"

"She had to pee." Angelique was not impressed that I was at the door, so she returned to watching *Chowder* without saying good-bye.

We were suddenly alone. Brand had yet to say anything beyond the initial greeting. Maybe he had nothing to say. Maybe Jessica and I said it all. I could see Brand looking around me, beyond me, to see what I had driven to his door. Suddenly, I was not interested in bragging about my new truck. I just wanted to know what was going on with us.

"Brandon," I said again. I never called him Brandon. It was his given name, but one I rarely used. I was introduced to him as Brand, and it was the name that fit the best. But I was angry about Jessica and the disruption of my otherwise perfect engagement. I wanted to hurt something or someone, and he was high up on my list. I was still standing in the doorway.

"Eva." He sounded stupid, saying my name and not much else. Maybe we both sounded stupid. "Can we talk for a minute?"

"I guess. Brand, honestly, I'm not even sure why I'm here. Something was steering me to your house today, despite the fact that I had no intention of coming by. We have a wedding planned, people are coming here to see us get married within months, and you have bitches walking up on us while we're together, out in public."

"Come in the house, Eva, and don't stand out there and give the neighbors more shit to talk about. They're mad enough that black people could afford to move onto this block. At least have a seat and let me talk to you for a minute." He pulled me into the foyer and closed the door. I was awestruck, as always, when I walked into a DeLoache home. Their money, taste, and home décor always made me feel like a semi-worthy houseguest, like I shouldn't sit on their furniture and eat off their china. I wondered, for the thousandth time, how Brand remained so unaffected by the wealth. Or maybe he wasn't, and I failed to notice.

I followed Brand to the family room, which was so much more appealing than the stiff, formal living room. I mean, really, how did you enjoy yourself in a home where the furniture was so beautiful and hard that you couldn't kick back and get comfortable? We sat on the same part of the oversized sectional. I declined his offer for refreshment.

"Brand, again, I don't know what led me here to see you. But I'm here now, and I'd like to talk about what got us to this point." I ran my hands over my hair. "Wow, I don't know what's wrong with me. Apparently I sound and appear much calmer than I feel inside." My hands were moving, driving home each point as I expressed my feelings. "Maybe I'm still in shock, or maybe I'm in love. I just know that I want to smack the shit out of you right now. I'm so tired of going through this shit with you! I want to know why we can't have a relationship with just the two of us. Why must there always be another woman—fuck it—other *women* involved, when it comes to you?"

Brand looked guilty and ready for flight. Maybe he was worried that I might really jump up and smack the shit out of him. I most certainly felt like it! I wanted to fight somebody. I would've fought Jessica if she was around, but she wasn't. So Brand might have to get it.

"Eva, let me start by saying that I'm glad you're here. I'm glad you stopped by and I don't care why you did, or why you chose tonight to come. I owe you an explanation of what Jessica said at the bar. I wasn't completely honest with you before we ran into her, and I can understand your reaction to how things went down."

I interrupted him. I was furious and had lost all hope that there was no truth to what she said. I jumped to my feet. "What the fuck do you mean, you weren't 'completely honest?' You mean to tell me that you allowed some tack-head bitch to have intimate knowledge of you, and then allowed her to get to me and tell me before you did? What the fuck were you thinking, Brand?"

"Eva, calm down."

"Fuck that. Was she in AC with you?" I asked. My mind was racing. I wondered just how much more I didn't know.

"No, she wasn't in AC with me. Yes, she was there, but not all weekend, and I did not invite her." He stood up and grabbed my arms. "Eva, sit down. Let's get all this bullshit out and over with."

"What else didn't you tell me about that weekend, Brand?"

"Look, Eva, you know most of it. Evan and I went to AC for the weekend. We've been working on a few deals and needed to put our heads together and relax for a few. I had been working like a slave at the office, so we decided to take a break, go gamble, shoot some dice, and kick back for the weekend. He wasn't taking any females, and I said I wouldn't bring you."

I snatched my arms away and sat down. I was stunned into silence.

"We got to the Showboat, and I blew like a grand at the tables, so I decided to crash. I went to my room and he went to his. I didn't see him til the next morning. I didn't even know that he had Lisa with him until the next day, and by then she was there with that whore, Jessica."

"How long have you known her?" I asked, referring to Jessica. I was thinking back to when I met Lisa in Atlantic City,—ironically,—years ago.

"A few years, I guess. I don't remember, Eva. I met her back when Lisa and Evan were fuckin' around for a while."

"Did you ever fuck Jessica? Ever? At all?" I was steaming mad, thinking of that bitch with the tacky weave fucking Brand.

"Look, Eva, the point is that nothing happened with me and Jessica that weekend. She was there for a while. I made it perfectly clear that I wasn't feelin' either one of them bein' there. Yeah, Jessica wanted to fuck, but I left. Evan fucked Lisa for a while, and Jessica needed someplace to chill while they got busy. I gave her my room and left." He stopped and looked right at me. "I left the hotel and went to another casino."

I just stared at him. I didn't believe one fucking word that came out of his mouth.

"So, yeah, she'd be able to say that she knew what hotel I stayed in. If you gave the bitch one more minute at the bar, she would have told you what room I stayed in, too. But nothing happened that weekend. I did not fuck her."

I found my voice.

"Okay, so you didn't have sex with her that weekend—, so you say. But you didn't answer my question. Did you ever fuck Jessica?"

"Look, Eva. I'm not going to lie to you. Yeah, I've fucked her before, a couple of times in the past when we broke up. The bitch don't mean shit to me. She and Lisa are a couple of thirsty bitches, always hanging around Evan. He was fuckin' Lisa, and Jessica heard that I had a couple of dollars and wanted to get with me, so I let her suck my dick in the men's bathroom once." Brand almost smiled as he told me about it. "If you have to know, the first few times I get with her, I only let the bitch suck my dick. She don't know nothing about me. She don't know where I live. The bitch don't matter."

But it did matter. She did matter. I knew that Brand was an attractive man. I knew that he was hardly a virgin when we met. I also knew that I had broken up with him, allowing other bitches to get close to him in the time that I was gone. I just hadn't imagined that he'd fuck with little tacky bitches like that. I also was mad that she knew something that I hadn't known.

"Brand, I'm not going to comment on who you stuck your dick in while we were broken up. But what I don't like is this bitch having information over me. There's no fuckin' way that she should have known about your trip to AC before I knew, and she did know before I did. You should have called me and told me that Jessica and Lisa were there, so that she wouldn't be able to spring it on me like that."

How did you explain some shit to a man that he should already know? Couldn't he understand that he put me at a disadvantage by allowing her to have knowledge and information about him that I should have been privy to? He looked guilty, plain and simple. If nothing went on, then why didn't he mention that they showed up? Why did I have to find out from Taylor first, and then be shocked and embarrassed later at the bar, in front of Jessica's friends?

"You're looking guilty as shit, Brand. The bitch was in my face, telling me that she was riding your dick in the Range. How am I supposed to feel about that? I was looking like an asshole and she knew that I didn't know she was in AC with you. That shit was not cool, and you could have prevented that whole scene. If I had the information beforehand, I could have played that bitch before she got the chance to play me. If the roles were reversed, you'd feel the same way." I got up and walked toward the door.

"You make me sick, Brand. You do dumb shit, catch me all up in it, and then expect to walk away unscathed. It's just like you giving me herpes. You let some bitch catch you up in some nasty shit, and now I'm paying for your stupidity. What else aren't you telling me? What other bitch is going to walk up on me and tell me some shit that I should have known months ago?"

Brand followed me, trying to interject, but I wouldn't let him. I was too pissed. I yanked open the door.

"You need to get your loyalties together. You can't serve two masters, and I am not taking a backseat to anyone, male or female. You let me know what you want to do when you figure it out." I was outside on the steps. "Unfortunately, this hasn't increased my faith in you or our relationship. As far as I'm concerned, I'm still not marrying you, so tell your people that the wedding's off."

It felt good stalking to my truck, knowing that he was watching and wondering what had just happened, and what he could have done differently.

# CHAPTER 15
## *Taylor*

Okay. I had to shake this shit off. Yeah, I knew I had been fucking that girl for, like, two years, but that shit was over now and it was time to move on. If I tried real hard, I could pretend like it was just a sex thang, and that I didn't dig her.

Goddamn! That girl could eat some pussy.

Let me stop fronting. It was more than that. I knew Eva thought that we didn't talk. I knew I fucked that girl like there was no tomorrow, but really it was way more than that. I honestly thought that she might take Eva's place. I could never admit that to Eva, but Shawn had been working hard for the best friend position.

Plus, I couldn't keep my hands off her.

Damn, I had met her parents and everything. No, she hadn't introduced me as her damn near live-in lover-girlfriend, but I got to know them and kind of liked them. Shawn had an eight-year-old brother who had a crush on me, and tried to hug me and get free feels on my butt whenever he saw me. We thought that shit was cute.

I must've been kidding myself about my real feelings for that chick because I hadn't dealt with anyone else for a long while. I hadn't thrown my li'l black book away, for real, but I damn sure didn't know where it was. I couldn't even remember when I saw it last.

I mean, yeah, in the beginning, I was still fucking dudes. I had a few male sponsors, but they all just disappeared over time. I couldn't even remember when or how they stopped coming by or calling. One day they were there, and the next they weren't.

Yeah, I fucked Andrew for a few. Then Chris popped up, and I had to pretend like I wasn't home so Shawna wouldn't pop up on us doing the wild thang or something. Oh, yeah, Carlton made his way back to this pussy long enough for me and Eva to spend like $4,500 of his money at Pier 1 to decorate her first apartment.

Shit. Now that I thought about it, I had sucked much dick and ate pussy for a minute. Damn. And then there was just Shawna. Shit. I don't really remember missing dick after a while. I must've lost my fucking mind.

All that shit. Over a bitch.

I called Eva because I needed to shake this shit off.

"Evie, what's up?"

"Nothing, girl. Why do you sound like somebody just stole your bike? Did you start that job yet, Tee and how many times have you put off the start date? They're not going to hold your position for long, you know. You need to stop playing games, get the damned job so you can stop fucking Shawn for free. I know the bitch needs new clothes, or her hair done, or something. Keep playing and she's gonna go get some real dick from a nigga that's willing to break her off a few dollars, and keep her fine ass laced."

"Bitch, please. I started that fucked-up job last week while you was probably doin' . . . what? Suckin' Bryce's dick or something? No, boo, that's you who fucks for money. I don't need money to make Shawn cum. Keep your perverted shit in your own backyard, please."

I didn't even know why I was faking the funk. I didn't bother to tell Eva that Shawn figured out that we'd fucked, and had dumped my ass at Friday's in front of A.I.

After Shawn dumped me, the NDC finally reached my name on test score list and I started working the four AM to twelve PM shift. I had been on a hiring waiting list for almost two years when they finally called. Due to the amount of overtime and the outrageous amounts of money you could make, everybody was dying to work there.

"So how is it? I can't even believe you didn't call and tell me all about your first day. Are there some cute dudes? Are the chicks fat and ugly? I know they was hating on you, Tee. Did some of those juveniles ask you to marry them yet?"

"I don't know, Evie. I guess it's okay. I just started the five weeks of training, and I met this wild and crazy chick named Nadia who got all the dudes drooling over her already. Some nigga named The Prince takes her out to lunch damn near every day, and we're not even supposed to be talking to the regular staff right now. She is cute as shit, though. Not cute as us, of course, but the niggas seem to love her."

"So, what, you thinking about hitting that? What about Shawn? What's up with you two, anyway? You haven't been talking about her lately, and I miss listening to y'all having loud sex over the phone."

I didn't know how to tell Eva that Shawn dumped me, so I played it off. "She's cool, but I'm not sure this gay thing is for me no more. You know Chris has been texting me, and I actually been thinkin' about gettin' some dick lately."

"Bullshit!"

"Um, excuse me, Miss Thang, but before Shawna, you was the only one switch-hittin' all over the city. You was eatin' pussy long before me."

"Whatever, Tee. Tell that nonsense to somebody who don't know you. You love that girl and until I see some dick at your house, you won't make a believer out of me."

"Yeah well, too bad I ain't in the mood to convince you. I'll talk to you later, Eva."

I didn't even bother to tell her that Evan had been texting me like a fiend, too.

First Brand, and now Evan. What the hell did they want?

# CHAPTER 16

*Eva*

After Taylor basically hung up on me, I looked at the phone like it was about to sprout wings. Something was definitely up with them, and she was holding out on me. Shawn kept calling me, and I had been ignoring her calls. Whenever I talked to Taylor, I always felt about two seconds away from telling her that I had sex with Shawn.

I called Taylor's ass back.

"Tee, um, you do know you just basically hung up on me, right? Anyway, girl, please tell me why I'm still thinking about Brand? I hate him. In fact, I hate all men. Let's go out tonight. I think it's SEPTA night at Lou & Choos. Hell, even if there aren't bus drivers there, we still need to get out and go have some fun. I'm tired of staying at home, worrying about some nigga who done me wrong and ain't thinking twice about me." I stated those words as if they were fact, when I really felt like I'd never find love in this lifetime.

"I don't know, Evie. I'm sittin' here, waitin' for Shawna to call me back." Taylor paused for a few seconds. "She hasn't been actin' like her usual self lately . . . and I'm not sure what's goin' on with us right now."

Taylor started to speak again and I thought I heard a bit of uncertainty and evasiveness in her voice, so I cut her off mid-sentence.

"No, I'm not taking no for an answer, Taylor." I used her first name, so she knew that I was serious. "I'll come by at nine-thirty to get you, so be ready. I mean it. We are bright, intelligent, beautiful girls and we will NOT sit at home, waiting for the phone to ring. We don't wait for men or women to call. Toodles." I slammed the phone down in her ear. She was getting worse than me, worrying about Shawn, and going this one night wouldn't make a difference.

# CHAPTER 17

*Taylor*

"I'm not sure I want to do this, Eve. I don't think I'm ready—" I started to say when Eva rudely cut me off.

"No, I'm not taking no for an answer, Taylor." Oh, shit. She was for real. Eva never called me Taylor. I was stuck now and she'd never leave me alone. Shit. She had a spare key to my house, so she would stress me the fuck out, then come into the house and drag me out. She was like that when she swore she knew what was best for me.

Maybe going out with Eva was what I needed. Maybe it was time for me to get over Shawna. Okay, so maybe it was time for me to get to living again.

Maybe I needed to thank my lucky fucking stars that she was out of my life, and now I didn't have to worry about being in a 'same sex' relationship, explaining that to my mother or wonder how I was going to have a baby. I'd just go out and get me some random, regular old dick, get on with my life, and forget this gay shit.

If I left it to Eva, she'd find me plenty of available dick and then some nigga would get my mind off Shawn for a few. Shit, if Eva just gave me a portion of the dick she got on a regular, I'd be cool.

Damn, that girl could fuck. I guess I should know.

Damn, I gotta shake this shit off.

# CHAPTER 18

*Eva*

F orget what ya heard, Lou & Choos was poppin'! SEPTA night, Amtrak night, school bus drivers' night, stay-at-home moms' night. Who cared? The niggas were out and buying drinks. This was what I had been missing, sitting at home, blubbering over Brand.

"Let's go upstairs to the back bar and see who's serving," I yelled at Taylor over the music, which was pumping from the speakers courtesy of Kenny, DJ extraordinaire. I'd always had a soft spot for Kenny, and tonight was no different.

We walked past the DJ booth and fine-ass, chocolaty rich Kenny was spinning records on two tables, old-school style. The music and beat were undeniably catching, old and new played back to back, relentlessly daring anyone dancing to think about sitting down.

"What's up with you, Kenny?" I purred in my sexiest voice 'cause, damn, the man was looking mighty fine. How was it that the ones you wouldn't look at in high school became gorgeous fucking studs a mere few years later?

"Eva! Damn, girl, what you doin' here? I'm surprised to see you." Kenny was up and out of his seat after making sure he played a song that would give him a few minutes of uninterrupted time with me. I was engulfed in his strong arms and back, feeling safe. I briefly wondered if Kenny would be worth a quick roll in the hay. Really, who would have to know?

But, alas, after a few quick feels, I reluctantly let go of the rock-hard body and stepped back. He was looking absolutely fuckable.

"You know Taylor, right?" They said hello and Taylor moved on to the back bar.

I stayed behind to flirt with Kenny a little longer.

"Damn, Kenny, you're looking awfully good these days. What's up with that?" I didn't bother to disguise my appreciation of his physical appeal. I looked him up and down like he was a piece of meat. I secretly hoped he felt cheap, as if I was undressing him with my eyes, which was what I was doing. It was okay to turn the tables on men once in a while.

Chocolate-covered Kenny managed a blush and a smile.

"The question is, what's up with you, Eva? You know where I am Thursdays, Fridays, and Saturdays—right here. You should come by more often, and we can talk about us."

Okay. For real. Kenny had been a fan since high school at King, but he was just a regular dude then. Nothing about him particularly stood out. We were cool, don't get me wrong, but cool as in, I knew Kenny was one of my fans but he had not a snowball's chance in hell of getting with me then.

The new Kenny, though—he definitely had a strong back and was a small leap away from getting the panties. Funny how a few years changed things so drastically. I flirted a little longer, got another hug and a kiss on my neck. Beautiful lips. I could only imagine them all over my body.

"Why don't you play something for me? Dedicate something to Eva, so the niggas know that I'm ballin' out of control and that there's a female don in their presence." I made what I hoped was a sexy exit, blowing kisses in my wake. Damn, I would really have to consider a roll in the hay with the new Kenny. What was one more dick up in me?

"What you get me, Tee?" I asked as I made my way to the bar and dropped down into the empty seat next to her. I rudely interrupted whatever conversation she was having with a skinny little ashy dude in a South Pole sweat suit. South Pole: played out since—well, were they ever in fashion? Little did she know, I was saving her from herself and this loser.

"A watermelon martini, and they are delish. Three of these, max, for me, or some lucky dude or chick will get me to their home or car and have their way with me." I could see that she was already on her second martini and Mr. South Pole had his paycheck—in twenties—on the bar. Okay, so maybe he'd be good for something.

"Eva, this is Trevor. He was kind enough to buy us a round of drinks." We exchanged the usual pleasantries and I wondered if he thought he looked like a baller, with his mini-knot on display for all to see. I sipped my martini. Strong. Taylor was right—they were delish.

"How you doin', ma? I'm just here keepin' ya friend company till you was done. You shouldn't leave such a beautiful woman alone by herself." South Pole was laying it on thick. "You hungry? Go ahead and get yaself somethin' to eat. Tracey already ordered us two pounds of Alaskan snow crab legs. She said you probably would want a fried shrimp platter."

I was trying not to burst out laughing in South Pole's face when he called Taylor "Tracey." This was the name she gave nut-ass dudes like South Pole so she could bleed them all night. But who was I to complain? I just hoped that I didn't wreck her cover by blurting out the wrong name, especially considering how strong the martinis were tonight.

"Eva? I wasn't sure if it was you. Damn, you look good." The voice was deep and I tried to place it before turning around, so that my face would show the appropriate surprise and excitement.

I turned around and was pleasantly surprised to see this dude I matriculated with at Villanova University. Wow. Roman (*or was it Roland*) was six-seven, medium brown-skinned, and wiry as hell. An All-City basketball player from the Baltimore projects, he made it to Villanova on a basketball scholarship, and he was too sexy. He was also two years younger than me and four semesters behind me in school, so that had been a major problem cause I didn't do the younger generation.

Roman was definitely a fan when we were at 'Nova. Okay, I was a fan as well and seriously considered a bone-fest a time or two, while I was on a station break from Brand. Once, I went to Roman's on-campus apartment as a kind of date. He definitely put the moves on me and we shared a few kisses and some grinding that almost morphed into dry sex, but my wits resurfaced and I dashed from the devil's lair just in time to keep my campus reputation intact.

Afterward, it was like, *"Yeah, Roman, you're sexy as hell and I'd love nothing better than to ride the wild pony for a few, but I'm kind of in the middle of a relationship right now and why don't we revisit this conversation at a later time, ya know?"*

Some major ducking went on henceforth, mostly because I didn't trust myself to be alone with him anymore. I also didn't want my first forage into the younger male species to be with a well-known jock.

Now, it was a completely different set of circumstances. We were both college graduates and that made us all even at this point, didn't it? Or was I now making allowances for wading into muddy, unknown waters? Was my break with Brand the reason for this un-Eva-like behavior? Who knew? Who cared?

Seriously caught by surprise, I squealed and rushed into Roman's open arms. Oh shit, he felt as good as he had two or three years ago. And that same smell—something close to Bvlgari BLV. Damn, he looked and smelled awfully good. What the hell was I going to do?

"Tracey, get ya ass over here and meet somebody." I motioned Taylor over. She came over to us and shook his hand.

"Taylor," she whispered. "How are you?"

"Roman," he whispered back. "How are you, Taylor? Is there a specific reason that we're whispering? I'm cool with it, but if you're in hiding or on the run from state parole, let me know now." He paused to sip his Heineken and introduce us to his friend. "This is Shajid."

I said hello and jumped to her rescue, explaining that she was Tracey to South Pole.

"What are you doing here, Roman?" The name issue had been resolved, thank God. I knew it wasn't a common name, and I was glad I didn't embarrass myself by calling him *Roland.* "Are you still playing basketball? What have you been doing with yourself since 'Nova?"

"I've been playing in Barcelona for the last year and a half. I'm on break for the summer and I bought a condo in Pennsauken last month. I'm here with my boy Shajid. We usually come here once or twice a month. What are you doing here? I've never seen you here on a Thursday night."

"And you probably won't ever again, trust me. I dragged Taylor out here tonight. She's having problems with her girlfriend." I watched one of his eyebrows rise. "I'm having a bit of man trouble myself, and I thought we could use some bangin'-ass music, strong-ass drinks, and whatever company we could conjure up."

My mind raced. Damn, what treasures one finds in the hood! Was I seeing a trip abroad in my near future? Suddenly, my looming single life was blooming with possibilities! Mere issues such as Roman's age—and the fact that I only came up to his rib cage—seemed to be minor inconveniences.

"Well, Roman, I'm certainly glad I stopped by Lou's tonight. I couldn't have imagined what happened to you since 'Nova, and I definitely didn't think I'd see you slumming in North Philly." I pasted on my best smile and added, "It's been great seeing you again. I hope we don't let time and space separate us this way again."

"Shit, Eva, I ain't lettin' you get away this time."

Bingo. The words I wanted to hear. Now I only had to get on-line and check the starting salary of a second-year player in one of the Spanish basketball leagues. There really wasn't much more to do.

Brand who?

# CHAPTER 19
## *Taylor*

I really had to shake this shit off.

When I got home, I had two messages waiting for me. One was from Shawn: "Taylor, I'd like to talk to you. Call me back." The other was from Brand, wanting to know where Eva was, no doubt; I erased his message before he could mention her name. The nerve of that bastard! If she only knew.

I had to admit, Eva was right and we had a fucking ball at Lou's the other night. I danced a little bit and shook my ass because I saw the niggas hawking. I wasn't feelin' anybody, though, for real. I let South Pole, um, Trevor—Eva had me calling that man all out of his name—buy us drinks all night, and I knew he expected to at least get the digits before he left. Too bad. He didn't get shit.

The bad part was that I knew I wasn't giving him shit the minute I told him my name was Tracey. They never stood a chance when my night started out with the alias. Too bad for him.

There were some fine-ass niggas out that night, looking at me—and truly, I hawked right back. I didn't even give the bitches a once-over. I was done with chicks.

But I hadn't had no dick in a minute, and I didn't see nobody worthy of getting my Virginity of the Second Coming. There were plenty of niggas to choose from, though, because all three bars had been packed.

Of course, Eva got her flirt on and seriously put her mack down all over all over the bars. She was truly shameless, and a master bullshitter.

The niggas loved her and all the drama that surrounded her, wherever she was. She had that Roman eating right out of her claws all night. I didn't even remember him from her college days. She claimed he was making major dough overseas, and I was sure it was only a matter of time before she was flying over there on his dime.

She had that fine-ass DJ Kenny dedicating songs to her all night and she thought I missed them little kisses she threw at him. I had to admit, Kenny looked like a chocolate éclair, ready to be slurped through a straw, if you were into dudes.

He'd probably be Eva's newest boy-toy. Domestically, that was. Roman was sure to be her new international sponsor.

I caught myself checking out the crowd, but for real, I was just chilling. I tried to get my mind right and figure out if I really missed Shawna, or if I was just tired of being by myself.

Plus, I hadn't had no lips on this vibrating pussy in weeks.

Shit. Somebody better watch out.

I was about to catch a rape charge.

# CHAPTER 20

*Eva*

After meeting back up with Roman at Lou's, I was *so* over Brand. I wasn't about to play myself out by blowing up Roman's celly, so instead, I called Bryce. No, I didn't want to fuck him, and I didn't particularly want to see him right then either, but I was mad, angry, and disgusted with Brand. Plus, Bryce generally got Brand's sloppy seconds and castoffs. He just didn't know it.

He opened the third garage door when I got to Chalfont and I parked the truck inside. *Nice automatic garage door opener.* I wondered if I could get a remote for my car. Wouldn't that be a nice coup? I followed him through the door into the kitchen, and sat at the island counter before he waved me over.

"What's up, Eva? Did you get here by accident? figured you'd be in New Jersey or Delaware, riding around, showing off your X3. I'm feeling almost honored that you'd come by here when, I'm sure, there are other places you'd rather be."

"Damn, Bryce, it's like that? I can't come see you and thank you for what you did for me?" I plucked a handful of cashews from a container on the island. The kitchen was nice as shit. Every appliance was Bosche, stainless steel, and obviously designed to complement one another. "You don't think very highly of me, do you?"

"You're wrong, darling Eva. I think you are a wonderful person, when you care to be. I must admit that I'm a little tired of you popping in whenever you feel like it. You don't give a lot of consideration to me and how I feel when you're in my life, and then back out so quick." He walked over and stood in front of me. "What's up with that?"

I made the first move and draped my arms around his neck and pecked him on the lips. Bryce was about six-two, and nicely chiseled— gifts from nature, and the gym four days a week.

"What can I say, Bryce? I don't mean for it to feel like that. I try to spend time with you when I can. I try to be up front with you and let you know what's going on." *Lies, lies, lies. Is my nose growing?* "I truly appreciate what you did for me with the X3." I kissed him again. "My first stop was to Taylor's place to brag, and rightly so. Don't get me wrong, I went cruisin' for a few, made sure I was seen on the scene. Oh, they'll be talkin' 'bout Eva all around Germantown by tomorrow."

"Oh really?"

"But seriously, Bryce"—I snuggled closer—"I don't want you to think or feel that I come and go as I please, and without thought for your feelings." Although that was exactly what I did each time Brand got on my nerves. Why shouldn't I, when Bryce let me get away with it? You know what they said about teaching people how to treat you.

"You know I care about you," I continued. "At least, I hope you know. If I haven't said it before, I'm saying it now. I don't want it to be a problem between us."

"It's not necessarily a problem, Eva. It's just that I can't seem to read you at all. You're here, and then you're gone. We fuck all weekend, and then you disappear for months or a year."

I tried to suppress a giggle. Oh, God. It was so true. Bryce was smarter than I previously thought, and appeared to be on to my games. I should have felt guilty because he was right about me, and I had been bullshitting him from the beginning. Yeah, I had learned to like him, and his résumé was packed. I didn't know what I was waiting for. Bryce was a successful businessman, a handsome, sexy, eligible bachelor, and an all-around nice guy.

But maybe that was the problem. Maybe he was too nice. Maybe if he called me a few "bitches," didn't put up with my shit, and was unavailable when I popped up in his life after being gone for almost two years, things would be different. Don't get me wrong. I was not looking for a man who would physically, mentally, or verbally abuse me, but a li'l spice never hurt.

"Well, why don't we work on that, then, Bryce? Why don't we figure out what's going on with us, and I'll figure out how not to disappear for long periods of time?" I moved away from him and sat back down at the island bar. "If you don't mind, I'm here for the night. So what would you like to do while I'm here? And what you got to eat, 'cause I'm starving and I gave Don Rosen all of my money." I didn't mention being at Lou's the previous night, nor did I feel guilty about giving Roman my cell number and planning a trip overseas.

Bryce stepped forward until he was standing between my legs.

"We can eat whatever you want. We can check the freezer or check the menus; you choose. I'm just glad you're here now." *Sound familiar? Didn't someone just say those same words to me?* He put his arms around me, looking directly in my face. "I'd like for you to stay, Eva. But you know that, don't you? I've told you before."

He pointed me in the direction of the floor-model freezer in the pantry.

"No, I didn't forget that you just started your new job and I'll give you some money to hold you over until you get your get back on your feet. Why won't you let me take care of you, Eva? I care about you and I hope you give me the chance to show you how much."

I checked the freezer, found nothing I wanted, then perused the menus. Great, Pizzeria Uno delivered til midnight. What more could a chick ask for? Great pizza, and then scrumptious sex afterward. I didn't know what to say in response to his confession, so I opted for silence.

Bryce poured champagne while we waited. I guess we were celebrating me being back on the scene. I didn't know, and didn't question it. I just knew that I was enjoying myself, and why shouldn't I? Men did this shit all the time, and no one questioned them—least of all, themselves. Plus, I didn't know what would happen between Brand and I, and I wasn't going to sweat it. Bryce was virtually drama-free, at least for the moment. He was single and, best of all, he wanted to be with me.

We changed out of our clothes and wound up on the carpet in front of the fireplace. We lay on the area rug and talked while we knocked off two bottles of Moët & Chandon champagne and one extra large, extra cheese pizza. We occasionally spooned and kissed as the champagne worked its way into my senses.

Bryce rolled onto his back and pulled me on top of him. My head nestled onto his shoulder and I fell asleep to the rhythm of his breathing. In my sleep, I wondered if my dreams were erotic because I was feeling good and wondering what could be making me feel like this.

I awoke to his hands rubbing up and down my back, shoulders, and ass. His mouth was on my neck and I could feel him leaving trails of kisses from my jaw to my ear. I didn't know if it was the champagne, sleepiness, or the fact that I had broken up with Brand. Whatever the reason, I felt good, slightly tipsy, and Bryce was wreaking sexual havoc on my senses.

I lifted my head and kissed Bryce, opening his mouth with my tongue, lightly stroking his tongue with my own while rubbing my hips into his hardening penis. I let my lips leave a wet trail across his cheek to his ear where I hummed softly, darting my tongue in and out. I whispered his name and told him how much I wanted to make love to him—here, now, any way he chose.

I returned my kiss to his lips and breathed into his mouth, "Tell me, Bryce, what you want." I straddled his body as he lay on the floor. "What do you want, Bryce, and how do you want it?" I asked between kisses. I wouldn't have guessed that he was shy, but he wasn't saying much other than groaning and sighing as I worked my lower body on his.

I ground my body into his when I heard him gasp, "Oh, God, Eva, whatever you want to do." He writhed beneath me, pulling and pushing on me as if he was unsure of how to proceed.

I was back in his ear, the left this time, urging him to tell me. "What, Bryce? I want you to tell me, so that I'll know."

"Eva, whatever you want."

"I don't know what that is, Bryce." I rubbed his head and face. I was breathing hard, almost panting in his face. He still wouldn't tell me. "Is it down there?" I rubbed his ass, kneading and massaging. "Is it down here?"

His eyes were closed. His body jerked as I rubbed his hard dick, moving slowly down until I was rubbing his asshole with two fingers.

"Is this it, Bryce?" He muttered in agreement, but it was not enough. I felt his hips rise and fall, pressing into my hand, which I roamed over his lower torso and between his legs.

"Talk to me, baby. Tell me what you want from me." I applied pressure in response to his physical and verbal reactions.

"Eva, please, just touch me."

I'd had enough. I moved down his body, my mouth following my hands on his neck, shoulders, and nipples, right then left, across his abs, and lower. I pulled his Lacoste pajama pants down to his knees and his dick sprang from his boxers and stood at attention.

I knelt between his legs and rubbed the head of his dick, then up and down the shaft with one hand, and then two. His dick bobbed back and forth with each brush of my hand. I stared at him, and it. His eyes were glazed over and semen slowly rose from his dick and spilled down the sides, running over the bulging veins and down to his sack.

"Just tell me, Bryce, and I'll make it happen for you. I want to know what you want, and I want to do what you want." I rubbed the perineum between his anus and the base of his penis. I got the greatest response when his hips moved so that my fingers were accidentally, *or purposefully*, rubbing his anus.

"Like this? Is this where you want me?"

I watched Bryce nod in agreement. It was not enough.

I brushed my lips over his abs and moved lower, rubbing my face in his pubic hair and licking the shaft of his dick, running my tongue over and around his bulging dick, while my fingers probed his ass. I opened my mouth wide and engulfed the head of his penis as I slowly inserted my finger into his anus.

I was expecting a surge of anger and immediate displacement of my finger; what I got was whimpering and soft shrieking. As I sucked on the head of his dick, swirling my tongue around the head and into the hole in the tip, Bryce's hips moved forward as I sucked and fucked in a fast rhythm, withdrawing and plunging forward. My finger was slick in his asshole and I was suddenly excited when he pulled my head toward him and worked his dick into my mouth.

His hands pulled me forward and his hips pushed onto my finger as I moaned, saliva pouring from my mouth, wetness everywhere. I felt his dick swell, his veins pulsating.

I finger-fucked his asshole with reckless abandon as Bryce strained forward and backward, pressing down on my finger to increase the penetration. When I heard his usual pre- orgasm moans and groans, I pulled back and watched the semen shook up like a detonated missile, even as his hips continued to ride my finger. After he came, I slowly removed my finger and watched him come out of his trancelike state.

I might just have to keep good ol' Bryce around. Crazy sex and a BMW truck—who knew what else he might have in store for me? Plus, he kept my mind off Brand for a little while.

# CHAPTER 21
*Taylor*

I needed to shake this shit off.

I was sitting on the bed that I'd slept in with Shawn for most of the two years we'd been fucking around. Okay, I admitted it. We were in a relationship.

We did the gay thing for a minute—and it was good, too. Carpet muncher, lesbian, dyke, lesbo—whatever you wanted to call us, it was damned good while it lasted.

I didn't have time to ask Shawna how she knew that Eva and I had fucked around. Fuck it, we'd had sex. I was still fucked up that she broke up with me at Friday's while we were looking almost directly at A.I. Damn, didn't that mean anything to her? Then his ass got traded to Denver and now we'd never get another chance to sit across from him at dinner. Damn!

I still couldn't believe she broke up with me, forcing me to listen to her politely tell me that I broke her heart, and then rolled out on me. I knew she would be mad. I thought we would argue, maybe she would even swing on me a few times.

I was cool with that. She had to right to be mad enough to try to whip my ass, and I would've given her the first few hits. I would've taken it like a man. I would've taken that shit and then fucked the shit out of her when we got home. I would've accepted her apologies and let her kiss away the hurt, and then make it up to me.

Okay, that was what I was hoping would have happened. It never crossed my mind that Shawna was going to break up with me and leave me sitting there, looking like a nut. Shit, I was hungry and we didn't get a chance to order food, *and* she wasted her Absolut and grapefruit. She knew I was leaking and damn sure didn't have no money to be wasting.

I felt like I needed to be angrier. I wanted to call her all types of trick-ass hoes.

I mean, yeah, I fucked up. Eva didn't rape me. I knew what I was doing, and I went along willingly. Okay, now what?

Didn't two years mean anything to her?

Fuck it. Where had I last seen that damned black book?

That night after Eva, I had phone sex with Shawna and had her cumming on herself in the bed she slept in until she was seventeen and left home to go to college. That was a fucking thrill and a riot. I forgot that Eva was even upstairs, until I heard her flush the toilet.

Damn. Now I was thinking about how happy I was with Shawna. She had graduated from Widener University with a bachelor's degree in math. I had myself a smart, fine chick, too. Then I started thinking about how I fucked up my relationship by fucking with Eva.

What the fuck was that about? Why had I fucked Eva that night?

Then I started getting suspicious about what happened between us that night. Was I subconsciously trying to fuck up what I had with Shawna? What was Eva's motive in kissing me that night? Was she trying to fuck up what I had with my girlfriend? Did she want me to be miserable, like her?

Had I unconsciously used Eva so as not to accept Shawna in my life as someone other than a fling, or simply something to do? Why did I really allow myself to have sex with Eva that night? Why didn't I stop myself, or stop her?

Goddamn it. Why was I thinking like Eva now? It was a damn

shame. That girl was rubbing off on me. I was sounding like her in my thoughts now. I really needed to get Shawna back in my life.

I wanted to call Eva. No, I wanted to call Shawna.

I really had to shake off this shit.

Maybe it was time for a change. Maybe I should sign up for some overtime at the NDC. Yeah, the job was fucked up, but I wasn't making no money sitting here at home, thinking about Shawna, when I could've been at work. I obviously needed to meet some new people and broaden my horizons.

Damn it, I was tired of missing Shawna.

We did talk a lot, despite what Eva thought. We didn't fuck all of the time. Well, we fucked a lot, but that was what we wanted. In between sex, we talked about our goals and future plans. We talked about gay couples, how we were going to have babies, and wondered about the stigma that still existed, and if we really wanted to be bothered with all of that.

Shawna was a good friend. At times, she was almost closer to me than Eva. I'd never admit that to Eva, but Shawna and I talked about how much closer we were getting. Sometimes I couldn't tell that we weren't a male and female in a heterosexual relationship.

Shit, when I strapped on that dick, Shawna couldn't tell either.

I wondered if she missed me. I wondered if she was cool, and wondered about her overall well-being. Shit, I wondered if she was eating somebody else's pussy. I wondered if another bitch was sucking on her gorgeous titties right now. Or had she crossed all the way over, and was fucking dudes now? I wondered if it was possible to have a soul mate of the same sex. I wondered if we could have been happy together.

I was tripping. I sounded like Eva. This sad and dreary shit might call for a good stiff shot of Stoli. I turned on my old Sony five-CD changer. Mary J. Blige came on full blast. "*I wanna be with you . . .*"

Right on point. After about five shots of vodka, I decided to admit to Eva that Shawna broke up with me.

I dialed the first three numbers and passed out.

# CHAPTER 22

*Eva*

I t was Monday morning and I was at Bryce's after he left for work. I dressed swiftly and grabbed breakfast. I resisted the temptation to snoop through his closet and pockets. My first and only attempt at snooping revealed that my ex-boyfriend, Cory, was sleeping with this ugly chick Therese, a.k.a. Zimbabwe. I found cards from her, thanking him for wonderful sex; pictures of them kissing; and pictures of him jerking his penis in bed. Needless to say, I didn't snoop anymore.

After a breakfast of burnt toast and orange juice, I rushed from Bryce's place before my curiosity got the best of me and I started looking in the medicine cabinet to see if he had Viagra or an HIV cocktail hidden away. There had to be something wrong with him, other than his dry lips and dry personality. I would find out, but not today.

I called Taylor on my way to work.

"Tee, where the hell have you been? Girl, let me tell you how Bryce is a fucking freak," I whispered conspiratorially into my Bluetooth. "I had my finger all up in his ass the last time we fucked. It was a mess! He must have some bitch all up in him to like that shit."

Tee giggled. "Mmm. That's a little scary. You think that nigga on the down low? Eww, I hope you two are still wearing condoms! What else do he like in his butt? I know Shawn loves it, especially when I'm licking her tight little asshole, but it even took her some time to feel comfortable with me touching her that way. And then I had to almost bribe her." Taylor clucked her tongue like an old woman. "I'd watch that shit if I was you."

"Wait, I can't front, though. I was getting all into that shit while we were doing it. I felt like I could cum just from finger-fucking him like my bitch." I paused to relive the sensations I felt while I was finger-fucking Bryce up his ass. "It was weird. I always wondered if Brand would let me do that to him. Now, why am I thinking of him right now? But anyway, I'm almost glad he didn't let me. I'd hate to have to wonder about Brand, too."

Taylor agreed with me. "Yeah, girl, you probably sleep much better at night, not having to worry about it."

"Girl, you ain't never lied. Listen, I have to get to this client's house before his mom disappears and I haven't gotten all of my signatures yet. I'll call you later."

My first case of the day started at approximately eleven AM at Anderson Elementary School at Sixty-first Street and Cobbs Creek in Southwest, Philly. The client was eight-year-old Patrick Barclay. Before I went to the school, I had to stop by Patrick's home on Sixtieth Street. The twenty-two-year-old mom, Sandra Watson, was appropriately dressed in laying-around-the-house, no-job, about-to-go-get-some-crabs-and-shrimp-with-my-Access-card gear: a velour Baby Phat sweat suit and leather DKNY slides.

There were at least four small children of various ages—from about three months to four years old—milling about the house in search of food. Patrick was the oldest of five children by four different men. The smaller children were in various sizes of diapers, and looked and smelled like day-old Similac.

Something like, "Jamilla! Git the fuck back in this fuckin' door before I slap the shit outta your dumb ass," spewed forth from the mom's lips as she lit up a Newport. These particular words were for the two-year-old who was watching videos on MTV right before the front door opened and I entered, revealing the portal for Jamilla's attempted escape.

The words were coupled with the mom dragging the child by one arm and back into the living/dining room, to be discarded once again in front of the television. A one-year-old, runny-nosed boy had changed the channel to BET and watched reruns of Lil' Kim's reality show as she bid her fans a final farewell, as she prepared to enter a federal prison for 366 days. The child sang along with Kim as her latest video played.

As this was our very first meeting, I attempted to get vital information from Ms. Watson about Patrick. I was constantly cut off by her verbal outbursts.

"Who da fuck is in my refrigerator? Rafeek, git your dumb ass off your sister and go watch TV!" These outbursts were usually accompanied by the lighting of another Newport.

I didn't get far with Ms. Watson, but I was not surprised. Patrick had been diagnosed with ADHD, ODD (oppositional defiance disorder), and dyslexia, and it was apparent that he had acquired those genes from his mother. I grabbed the required signatures, checked myself for roaches, and jumped into my X3, happy that I didn't have to come back for another week.

I drove to the nasty, overcrowded elementary school and met with the guidance counselor, where I identified myself as the BSC for Patrick. The guidance counselor walked me to the classroom and I met the TSS. The TSS was young, a recent graduate of Temple University with a BS in criminal justice. She looked stricken and was grateful to speak to me outside of the classroom.

I spent ten minutes with the TSS, listening to her account of their typical day at the school and Patrick's home. She had forty hours each week in the school and fifteen hours in the home and community. She described the client as having an attention span that lasted approximately four-and-a-half minutes, unless he was playing PlayStation 3 or Xbox 360. He could count to twelve, but could not read. He did not know the days of the week or his birthday. Alrighty then.

At the time, Patrick was sleeping off his mega dose of Strattera or Concerta in class, so our introduction would have to wait. The Special Education classroom was filled to capacity with five other students, four of whom had a TSS in attendance. There was also a teacher's aide to round out the crowd of adults in class. I had never seen such an amount of supervision: six students and six adults in one classroom. There had better be some major learning going on in room 203.

I spent eight additional minutes going over the old treatment plan and jotting down notes from the TSS to create a new, updated plan. I spoke briefly to the Special Ed teacher and her aide, and was told basically the same information the TSS had provided. I promised to see the TSS in one week with a new treatment plan, left the Dollar Tree coloring books and flash cards, and jetted back to the comfort and safety of my X3.

I only had to do this five more times this week, with other families in other parts of the city, and then I could sit back and watch my dollars stack.

That old, broke Eva was gone, never to be seen again. I didn't need Brand and his father's money anymore. Suddenly the DeLoache clan's money didn't seem so impressive.

Later, at Bryce's, my cell phone rang and Alicia Key's "Karma" startled me out of my get-rich-quick-daydream. "Karma" was Shawn's personal ring tone because she wouldn't stop calling and because I couldn't forget fucking her on Taylor's couch. I needed to stay away from her. I debated on whether or not to answer the call. I quickly thought about Brand and his bullshit, Bryce and his boring routine, and decided that talking to Shawn might be interesting. What did I have to lose?

I pressed "talk" and put on my sexy voice. "Hello?"

"Eva, it's about time you stopped playing around…" Shawn sounded just like I remembered: bossy and sexy.

My other line clicked. "Shawn, hold on."

It was Taylor, and she sounded drunk. I could almost smell the vodka seeping out of her pores over the phone.

"Evie, she dumped me. She dumped me at Friday's, in front of A.I., right before he got traded to the Nuggets. I can't stop thinkin' 'bout her crazy ass. What the hell am I gonna do now?"

*Oh, shit.* "Hold on, Tee." I clicked back to the other line. Shawn was gone.

Why was I not surprised? I clicked back over to Taylor.

"Tee, what the hell happened?"

"I don't know, Evie. Somehow she figured out that we fucked and when she asked me about it, I couldn't even lie to her. I call myself being strong and not admitting that I been thinkin' 'bout her a lot lately. I don't think I'm over her and the fact that she left me hangin' at Friday's. She ain't even call me or nothin'! I'm 'bout to say 'fuck her,' but I can't. I'm a sucker, and I would probably get back wit' the bitch if she called."

"Tee, trust me, I know all about broken hearts and whatnot. I'm feeling you, Tee, really I am. I know you're feeling some type of way about Shawn and I'm sorry that I'm part of the reason why you two broke up. But if y'all ain't getting back together, then you need to find someone else to help you get over her. You know what they say: 'Don't nothin' help you get over a broken heart like some new sex,' or something like that."

"Yeah right, Evie, like you got over Brand so fast." She sounded like she was drinking her way into the bottle, face first.

"I'm not saying it's easy, Tee, so give yourself some time. Trust me, it will get easier."

"Yeah, if you say so. I gotta go. I'm 'bout to finish off this bottle of Kettle One and go to sleep. Call me tomorrow."

What could I say? I was busy trying to forget that Taylor and I had done the wild thang. I didn't want to think that I had been an integral part of their relationship while they were together and had partly caused they're break up.

I didn't even put up a fight and try to talk sense into Taylor. I simply hung up and tried to put it out of my mind.

# CHAPTER 23

*Eva*

I figured out how to work three days a week and still manage to bill for all 48 hours. During my two days off, I got weekly massages and slept like a pregnant woman in her first trimester. On my three working days—Monday, Tuesday and Thursday—unless a crisis or meeting arose, I ran ragged around West and Southwest Philly in my X3. I worked, literally, from eight AM to eight PM, making sure I hit each home and nasty school for signatures.

I spent a few hours on Wednesdays shopping for items to distribute throughout the weeks ahead. National Wholesale Liquidators, Dollar Tree, and Big Lots became my favorite shopping haunts.

I basically lived with Bryce, as was his initial wish. I loved staying in the house, with or without him. I was throwing myself into my work as my wedding date passed, trying not to think about Brand and the future we had planned together.

Bryce tried hard to please me and had been hinting around about another engagement. I couldn't even pretend to think of that right now. I played it off with my fake self, explaining that staying with him at his house should be enough of a commitment.

I found myself thinking about my defunct relationship with Brand and what went wrong, even though I was trying not to think about him. I felt myself falling back into the feelings that plagued me back when I felt I couldn't keep a man, any man, and had considered a relationship with a woman.

Bryce smothered me, asking questions about my past disappearances. I kept giving him the same old excuses about needing time to find myself but he was buying my story less and less as time went on. I was starting feeling overwhelmed out and knew that stress would bring back the herpes outbreaks.

I missed wearing my engagement ring from Brand. I wondered if I should give us another chance. When I talked to Taylor, she said Brand had been inquiring about me, wondering where I was and how I was doing. I told her to ignore him and instructed her to give him no information about what was going on with me. I wondered when they had gotten so cool and how that came about.

Taylor had been acting strange and a little distant. She was not answering the telephone and we hadn't been having our daily chats. I hadn't heard anything about Shawn in a few weeks, and even though they had broken up, that was definitely strange. I almost missed hearing them having some sort of sex at least once a week.

The INCIDENT continued to flash through my memory, despite all of my attempts to forget it and put it behind me. I had not talked to Taylor about the INCIDENT, and I was wondering if she, too, was having difficulty dealing with it.

I thought Taylor and I would have to discuss the INCIDENT and get it out and over with. I was not looking forward to it. I'd rather pretend that nothing ever happened.

I briefly wondered if all was well with either of them, but quickly forgot my concerns as I was consumed with my own drama. I was tired of being homeless. Bryce was and had been a wonderful host, but it felt like it was time to stop house hopping.

My paychecks from Mountain View were averaging $2,900 every two weeks, and I was saving about $2000 of that. I was seriously considering purchasing my first piece of property. Hell, I was on the fast track to independent wealth.

But first, I had get over my feelings for Brand. Or should I? My choices were pretty limited. Maybe I needed to get out and make some new acquaintances. Bryce was paid and had turned out to be a giving, thoughtful lover, but I wondered what was really going on in his head. I wondered if he was thinking about herpes when he was with me, when he was running up in this gushy raw dog. I wondered if he still considered me wifey material. I knew that Bryce talked a good game, and I truly believed that he believed what he was telling me. But when it came down to it, would he really be willing to wife me?

Maybe I should just start over with an all-new lineup.

# CHAPTER 24

*Eva*

At the moment, I was at Bryce's house, alone. I wasn't shit, for hopping from Bryce's bed while thinking of Brand and Roman and karma was gonna kick my back in one of these days.

"You know how to get here?" Roman sounded so damned sexy over the phone.

Yes, I was at Bryce's house, talking to Roman while Bryce wasn't there. Karma was coming.

"Yeah," I replied. "I go over the Tacony-Palmyra Bridge and make the first left into your complex. I got it. It should take me about forty-five minutes to get there." Fuck it. Roman and I had exchanged phone numbers at Lou's that night. We'd been on the phone every night since then, having phone sex and talking shit about the things we'd do at our next meeting.

"All right then. Call me when you're making the left into the complex. The guard is going to stop you and ask for ID and my condo code. I'll call them and let them know that you're on the way, and to let you in. I'll get you a passkey so you won't have to go through this anymore."

I don't know. Maybe it was me, but this was sounding more and more like the brotha was planning on keeping me around for the long haul. Passkeys to the entrance one day, master keys to the front door the next. It all seemed like I'd be moving to Barcelona soon. Or maybe I was rushing things a bit. Maybe the nigga just wanted some older woman pussy, and I was the flavor of the week.

Whatever. I was gonna ride this puppy out, and see what I could see.

I jumped into the X3 and tore down Route 309 like a bat out of hell. I let my mind wander and tried to keep count of how many times Brand ran through my thoughts. By the time I hit the bridge, I'd counted seven. Brand-7, Bryce-0. Way too damned many thoughts of Brand, when I was literally driving to my future.

I grabbed my phone and hit "talk" twice to redial Roman's number.

"Roman, it's me. I'm waiting for the left turn signal to turn green, so hop on it or whatever you have to do to get me past security." Now that I was here, I was ready to do the damned thing. I was ready to get to it and be done with it. I'd been curious about Roman's flow and tonight, I'd find out.

After a too-long delay with security, I was finally on my way. I looked around as I walked up to Roman's open door. No key yet, so he made it easy for me. The grounds were filled with lush greenery, strategically placed foliage, and colorful flowers. It looked like money. Just what I needed.

Suddenly Roman was at the door. Barefoot, bare-chested, and wearing a pair of basketball shorts. Damn. He was long and lean and sporting a grin. All six feet, seven inches of him leaned down to hug and kiss me with thick, warm, inviting lips. I was pulled into the front door and we stood chest to chest—or maybe chest to stomach—smiling at each other.

"Shit, it took you long enough to get here. Where were you coming from? I didn't think it would take that long from Mt. Airy." He leaned down to kiss me again. Roman thought I was coming from home. He thought I lived in Mt. Airy, in my old apartment. He had no idea that I'd been hauling ass down Route 309 to get to him. As the saying went, what he didn't know . . . I just played it off.

"I'm sorry. I was driving as fast as the law would allow. I coulda swore I got here pretty quickly. You know it wasn't so easy to get here. Maybe you should have come to me." As if he could. As if I had a door to allow him entry. I was basically homeless, driving around in a BMW X3. But he didn't know that. As the saying went . . .

Roman's complex was comprised of two–story, duplex-style condominiums ranging from $291,000 to $1.4 million. The Internet was the best place to research anything under the sun, and it held no secrets. No one was safe.

Roman had a one-bedroom condo, completely furnished. He had paid roughly $314,000 based on the going rates listed on the Internet. Fucking A. Truly impressive. Of course, I played dumb. No way was I letting on that I knew how much dough he was rolling in. Not quite DeLoache money, but damned close, and it was all his. Not passed down from Daddy.

I rolled into the condo like my shit was on fire, which it was. I looked sexy as hell in an Adrianna Papell fitted dress and some Barbara Bui boots. My hair and makeup were fierce.

We ordered dinner from Italiano Bistro a few miles down the road. He uncorked a bottle of Gypsy Canyon Ancient Angelica wine, and we ate and drank while we watched *Nip/Tuck* from his DVD collection. I also watched him play *Madden 2008* on his Xbox 360. We kissed, cuddled, and spooned, all almost in total silence. His period must have been on because all he wanted to do was eat my pussy. Okay, that was cool with me. Funny, though, he didn't want to talk much about himself or me. He seemed to be on some kind of weird silence kick. Okay. Cool with me. Less lying I'd have to tell and remember later.

We spent the night together—I was naked and he was as dressed as he was when I got there. We slept like babies.

I jumped up in the morning at 7:31 AM. I quickly calculated the hour, distance, travel time, and commuter traffic, and figured that I'd miss seeing Bryce by a half hour. If I played my cards right, I'd get back to his house and forgo the story of spending the night at Taylor's, at least until later that evening. I took a bird bath, searched the cabinets till I found a spare toothbrush, kissed Roman good-bye, and headed for Bryce's.

I took a moment to reflect on what hadn't happened that night. What the hell happened to the phone-sex fiend who had me cumming over the phone? Yeah, the nigga could kiss his ass off, and his oral game made me cum quite a few times, but it was a little short of the sex fest I'd imagined from our daily conversations.

However, Roman was way too paid for me to count him out and merely dismiss him without further proof that his sex was bad enough to make me forget about moving to Barcelona, Spain.

# CHAPTER 25
*Taylor*

After my and Eva's night out at Lou & Choos, I was at work at the NDC more than I was at home. Overtime kicked my ass, but I was happy on payday. There was something almost erotic about being in a jail for up to fifteen hours at a time, the thought of death and dismemberment hanging over your head the whole time. That place must have been getting to me because my coworker Nadia's boytoy—the wanna-be pimp named The Prince—approached me one night in the male infirmary unit, and I actually played into his bullshit.

"What's up, Ms. Houston? What's good wit' you?" he asked.

"Um, Prince, you ain't hardly workin' the female infirmary tonight, so what you doin' over here? Where's your partner? Is he gettin' his ass beat over on your unit 'cause you over here, sniffin' around?"

The Prince was a real male whore, and shameless in his womanizing and shit. I couldn't front, though: he was tall, dark, and almost pretty with his dark velvet skin and white teeth, if you were into dudes. Picture Adewale Ogunleye from the Chicago Bears, mixed with Kelenna Azubuike from the Golden State Warriors, in all their fineness and glory.

"Damn, Houston, it's like that? I was just coming by to compliment you on your nice, fitted uniform pants. They let a little tiny girl like you work in here with these criminals?"

"Mr. Prince, or whatever your name is, I'm busy and obviously they let women—big and small—work here. Don't bring your shit over here, and I happen to know for a fact that you're currently fuckin' wit' my girl, Nadia, so fall back. I don't get down like that."

"True, true, about everything you just said. Yeah, your girl Nadia is fuckin' wit' me and fuckin' me quite nicely, I might add. But, come on, you heard 'bout me. You know what it is, just like Nadia knows what it is. I don't belong to nobody, and we all like it like that. That way, everybody can get their share of me and I don't have to leave a trail of broken hearts all over this place."

Of all the ignorant, conceited assholes! I couldn't even believe he was over here with that you-know-you-wanna-fuck-me bullshit! Even worse, I couldn't even believe I was entertaining this bullshit.

The supervisor was probably sleeping off his break at the sports bar around the corner. It was well known throughout the facility that he drank every day and if management didn't care, neither did I. I heard one of the crippled inmates bang on the door, and left the conceited asshole standing at the desk.

While I walked down the hallway with the key, I wondered what the real deal was with The Prince. His reputation was disgusting around the NDC, yet that didn't stop chicks from standing in line to fuck him on a regular. The nigga did look good as shit, but knowing that he'd been passed around—and was currently dicking down Nadia—didn't put him high up on my wish list.

Then again, Nadia wasn't really my friend.

After I locked the inmate's door and walked back to the desk, I had to admit I was a little curious about Prince, and if he actually lived up to all the hype surrounding him. I wondered if his ass was as freaky as they said, and if he really made bitches lose their minds up in his house.

"So, what you got in mind, Prince? What you got that would make me forget that Nadia is my girl 'round here, and that you might be worth a roll in the sack?"

"Why don't you come past The Den, and I'll show you? You know you're dying to know if chicks be tellin' the truth about what goes on in there. Why don't you judge for yourself? You can come through and if you see something you like, then stay. If you don't, you're free to leave." He grinned, showing off his pearly whites. "I'll bet fifty that you stay. Y'all always do."

So, I ended up at the Prince's Den, his den of sin, home of all things sexual and nasty. I went to his house in the Wynnefield Heights section of Philadelphia after my shift ended at midnight. I got there close to one AM, and when I got in the door, Prince had on a Mardi Gras mask and some tighty-whitey Fruit of the Looms. I almost wasn't sure if it was him, and I was almost hoping it wasn't.

Then his ass yanked me inside and started ripping off my uniform, right at the front door. He was rough, but that kind of turned me on. This nigga pulled on my clothes with this crazy look in his eyes and got rougher by the second. I went along with it for a few, then the scene started to remind me of an episode of *The First 48*.

"Whoa, big boy! You might want to slow down a little bit. It's been a minute since I been wit' a nigga, so calm down." He had one of my tits out of my bra and was trying hard to remove my nipple.

"What?"

I pushed his ass—hard.

"I said, calm your ass down! I ain't been wit' a nigga in almost two years, so slow ya roll!"

"What? So what, you into chicks or something?"

"Yeah, I guess you would call it something like that. I mean, I like dick, but I ain't been strictly dickly."

"Damn, shorty, I ain't know all that. Shit, you don't even look the type." Prince paused and backed up. "Yeah, all right. I got something for all that. I'll be right back."

This nigga left me standing in the living room with my tits hanging out of my bra. I looked around the crib and noticed that Prince had damned good taste, because everything was leather and oak. It looked like there was a white bear rug in front of the lit fireplace; it wasn't even that cold outside.

I was standing there, looking stupid, when he walked back in wit the baddest chick I had seen in a minute.

"Ms. Houston, this is Aisha, my gorgeous girlfriend. Aisha, this is Taylor." I just stared at her for a quick second before I tried to cover my boobs.

"Oh, please don't cover up, Taylor. Percy tells me that you prefer the more civilized species in your bed—females. Don't worry; most times, so do I. This man here, however, is like a chameleon inside the bed and out. He is whatever I need at the moment." Aisha moved closer to me and dropped to her knees. "So, what are you doing here tonight, Taylor? What's on your mind? Tell me how I can please you tonight."

✻

After Aisha finished fucking me with about a thousand dildos, and eating the shit out of my pussy, plus feeding me and speaking in several different languages, I fell asleep. When I woke up, I watched Nadia and Prince on the big screen, fucking like the end of the world was one hump away. They must have been in another part of the house and the room resembled a strip club. It looked like Nadia didn't know she was starring in her own porno, and I wondered where they had the camera stashed.

Aisha was on the bed grinding on some big, purple, ten-inch dildo, watching her man bang the shit out of another chick, straight getting her shit off. After a while, I just joined in. I had to admit, Aisha was damned good.

Not as good as Shawn, though.

Damn, the shit that went down in the Den.

# CHAPTER 26
*Eva*

M y cell phone was flashing a red light in the passenger seat of my truck. I almost didn't want to check and see who'd either left a voicemail or text.

Just like that, Brand left a message on my cell phone. A complete and utter no-no. Sneaky as hell, and just enough for the bastard to find a way back into my thoughts. It was Monday morning and Brand knew that I'd be out and about town, running to and fro to see my clients. He knew I'd check my voicemail and that I wouldn't ignore the possibility of missing an important message. If Brand knew nothing else, he knew that I wouldn't do anything to mess up my money.

I listened to his message on speaker.

"Eva, baby, I been thinking about you all night. I miss you, baby, and I gotta make things right between us. I told you, I didn't fuck that girl that night. She just tryna throw salt up in our shit, and you lettin' her. I love you, Eva. Call me. I just want to talk to you. You owe us at least that."

*Please bastard, don't even.* But I could feel myself weakening. He knew me too well.

Oh, but he wasn't done.

"Please, Eva, don't do this to us. We were supposed to get married a few months ago. We'll just talk, I promise. We need to figure this out."

Yeah, well, he should have been thinking about that when he was fucking that tack head, instead of coming home to this sweet-tasting pussy.

Brand sighed. I could tell he was stressed and I found perverse pleasure in that. He really didn't need to know that I had come from Roman's condo earlier that morning and had shit, showered, and shaved
at Bryce's.

"I love you, Eva," he continued. "You know I do. I know I'm not
perfect, but I need you. I know you love me, so stop being stubborn.
Call me on Bright's phone, and Bethany said to call her; you know my
brother and sister still love you, even if you act like don't know me. Oh,
and the girls said hello."

He was such a sneaky bastard! Why did he have to bring his family
into it? Especially his cute-ass little sisters? Those memories, I didn't
need. Because I was a wimp, I saved the message, but I would not return
his call. I would not. I could not.

Instead, I called Roman who was at basketball practice apparently—three-days-per-week practices for returning players. No problemo.
One needed to stay fit for the migration back to Europe. Let's not do
anything to compromise my future. I mean, our future. I left him a
voicemail.

"Roman, sweetie, it's your darling, Eva. Sexy, where are you? I just
wanted to say hi, and let you know I'm thinking about you this morning. Call me back when you get a moment. Toodles." I layed it on thick.
I truly needed to be on my best behavior. I could not fuck this up. If I
did, I would never forgive myself.

True, Roman hadn't even hinted at inviting me to Spain. But why
wouldn't he? Why would he be able to resist this sweet-smelling pussy
when no one else—male or female—had been able to?

I was gonna lock this pussy on that fine-ass giant and not let go. He
wouldn't be able to resist my sexual wares once he got his paws on them,
in them, around, and all over them.

But I digress. I was on my way to West Philly to see another client.

This time the client was Coco-Samyka Lexus Wriggs. I truly believed the mom was high, coked up, or drunk when the badass client came forth into this world. Then, if that wasn't bad enough, she straight made up her child's names. There were no such words in the English language.

Anyway, Coco-Samyka was eleven years old and in the third grade. She was as tall as her teacher and wore a misses' size ten. I hoped she never got buck, because I was not looking forward to gripping up a grown-acting, woman-sized child in a school uniform.

I stopped past their house because Coco-Samyka's mother said she would be home for a few hours. Yeah, right, as if she really had somewhere else to be. She had probably never paid a dime into Social Security or Medicare.

Because it was my job, I pasted a fake smile on my lips and held my breath as I entered the house. As usual, the familiar smells and sounds beckoned, and I offered up a quick prayer to exit the home in a similar state of mind and being as when I entered.

Not to be.

Some little being that shall remain nameless to protect the innocent met me at the threshold and challenged me to a duel. Seriously; she appeared to be about four years old and told me that she'd kick my ass because she was from Fifty-eighth and Chestnut. Then she proceeded to stick her filthy hands on my silver cashmere BCBG dress.

"Samyra! Stop it and leave that lady alone." The mother actually reprimanded her daughter. Imagine that. "Git yo' dumb ass upstairs and git the baby. You know you hear yo brother ass cryin'!" Oh well. I knew it was too good to be true. She turned her attention to me. "Hi, how you doin'? I'm Shuleesa. Can you take me to Aldi food market? I need to git some food before the li'l baby wakes up."

Samyra was sliding down the steps with a toddler almost her size.

"Samyra, I got to leave, so git the baby his bottle. I'll be right back."

Shuleesa apparently needed a quicker response from Samyra.

"I said move, girl! Git that bottle for the baby, sit down, and shut up! Ms. Ledochy is gonna take me to the store, so I can feed yo' greedy ass later on."

I hadn't heard Samyra utter a word since our initial meeting, and I let the massacre of my surname go unchecked. Why bother? Would she understand anything that I said?

I didn't remember actually agreeing to take Shuleesa to the store, but she knew I would do her bidding. She knew how the game was played, and so did I.

"Ms. Wriggs, could you place your signature on these forms for me?" I whipped out the forms; this bitch wasn't going to play me out like that. We weren't moving one inch closer to that store until I had her John Hancock in place.

Shuleesa grabbed a Fendi Mix Small Metallic bag bucket that was more than likely real, because she was pulling in approximately $2,700 a month in cash and benefits from welfare and other programs. I knew this because Cynthia, the TSS, spent fifty-five hours per week at school and in this dismal home with a family that could probably win awards for being dysfunctional.

Though I knew I should be more professional, Cynthia and I talked about this family and their drama at least a few times a week. This Shuleesa was scamming welfare, the Philadelphia Housing Authority, Section 8, and every other program available to those of her ilk. She was trifling beyond belief and dressed better than most working-class folks I knew.

While honest, tax-paying citizens were tending to her brood of unruly varmints, this woman was shopping and flossing all around town.

Welfare gave her $200 a week for daycare for each of her four children under five years of age, because she was supposed to be attending GED classes, which would enable her type to get a job that afforded her a salary to care for her ever-growing family. Yeah, right.

She got $800 a month in food stamps and $600 in cash. They gave this money to her on an Access card. Picture a debit Visa with someone else's money on it. Priceless. It didn't get any better than that.

Two weeks ago, Shuleesa threw out all of her living room furniture, half of the kids' beds, and her refrigerator. SCOH (Services to Children in their Home) replaced everything within four days. The Department of Human Services—and its affiliated organizations—was the watchful eye of the local government that ensured that children weren't neglected. Or starved to death. Or beaten to death or burned with matches by a deranged parent. However, they seemed to be dropping the ball on Shuleesa and her brood.

I was seriously ready to bare my womb for all to partake, so that I could push out five quick kids and get $4,000 a month, tax-free. If this lumbering idiot could get $2,700 a month in benefits, surely someone like my savvy, intelligent ass could get more.

"Can I call you Shuleesa? I appreciate you taking a moment to sign my forms and now that we've concluded our business here, we can move forward. Now, in what direction is the store? And why don't you tell me about Coco, while we're on our way?"

Mirabelle ain't raise no fool, damnit.

# CHAPTER 27

*Taylor*

Shawna called me! Then she apologized and said she had dialed the wrong number. I wanted to talk to her. I fucking missed her like crazy. I wanted to find out where she had been and what was going on, but I refused to play myself. I thought my heart jumped when I answered the phone, but it may have been my clit. I couldn't tell.

Besides, Carlton was knee-deep in my pussy at the time. So I let Shawna go, unmolested.

Yeah, Carlton had resurfaced and kept my mind and pussy occupied.

One day Carlton's cell phone number appeared on my CallerID. He said he was outside my front door. He whined and pleaded his case. He missed me and wanted us to try again. He moved out of the house he bought for his kids' mother, Tanya. He had only been staying with them for a couple of months after she lost her job. He figured he'd have to pay her bills anyway, so he might as well get all he could out of the deal. Yeah, three hots and a cot. Free pussy at night and home-cooked meals. Tanya, the mother of his son and daughter, didn't play that shit and had probably whipped that ass while she was kicking his ass out.

Yeah, right he moved out. It probably was more like, "Nigga, get your cheating ass out of my house and go get a HIV test before you try getting this coochie again. And don't come back without an engagement ring!" I knew that was what I would have said.

Carlton fancied himself to be a rap producer. A small-time Diddy and Jermaine Dupri in training. Seriously, he had a few acts and some wannabe gangsta rappers on his roster. You know the story. Former drug dealer turned rap star, washing all that dirty money clean in the studio. Whatever.

Whenever Carlton appeared, the nigga knew not to come empty-handed. He had gotten all the free pussy he was getting from me in this lifetime. He had those two babies with Tanya on me and if he expected me to take that shit lying down, he was the fuck stupid.

I had to admit that the first baby broke my goddamned heart. I cried and flipped out and busted that nigga in the head with a twenty-two-ounce Heineken bottle. He got four stitches and I got a shopping trip to New York. Thank you very much, Louis Vuitton. And Gucci. We hit all the major stores over that long weekend.

When he had the second baby, Carlton was smarter and disappeared for a whole year. When he resurfaced, he came back with a Sony laptop and paid my mother's back property taxes for the previous year. For real, I'd been fucking that nigga for too many years to have nothing to show for it. He was not getting out with his wallet intact.

This time, he popped up with a 2006 Honda Pilot. Okay, I'd take it, thank you very much. That was how his ass got in the door. I was almost waiting for his ass to disappear again. Ain't no telling what I just might get the next go round.

Now, if I could just stop thinking about Shawna.

Shawna must've been clocking me. Hard. I never thought her to be the stalking type, but she must have been. No lie, at least three times last night somebody called from an anonymous number and then banged on me. It wasn't a weirdo pervert, because there was no heavy breathing. Then she popped up at the door last night.

Carlton was out at the studio, laying down tracks with his latest rap group, Rappin' Paper or something like that. They had this single out and it was getting a little play on the radio, mostly locally. It didn't matter; Carlton was all excited and thought he could get some of the big boys in the industry to take notice. Whatever; it was his money.

I let him move in for a few. He was basically homeless and I *was* feeling him at the moment. He whined about sleeping at the studio, but I knew that was just game to get back into my door. I did get rid of the Stanza, finally. I was kind of getting used to driving the Pilot, and I was feeling having a man in my life again. I forgot how cool it was to have some muscle and strength around. And the dick was definitely hitting on something nice.

Anyway, Shawna was at my door about fifteen minutes after Carlton left to go to the studio. She had to have been watching and waiting and, for real, I was kind of flattered that she was stalking me like that. I knew my eat game was fierce.

The funny thing was, I hadn't been sweating her lately. Yeah, I knew I was wrong when I got with Eva on the sex tip. It was fucked up and I should've done Shawna better than that. I knew all this already.

But Shawna? Maybe knowing that I was moving on without her, had her feeling some kind of way about it.

"Hello, Taylor. How are you? Do you mind if I come in for a minute? If you're not busy, that is." She had on the same type of clothes she had on when I met her—tight-ass Chip & Pepper skinny jeans, a tight, fitted tee, and some Timbs.

Knowing that I shouldn't, I let her sexy ass in.

All of a sudden, I didn't feel like the chick I was when I was with Carlton. I felt like the horny-ass dude I was when Shawna and I were together. I watched her walk into the house, swaying her hips like she did when she got my attention at the bar. This was frustrating as hell. I thought I was getting over this gay shit. I was trying to work things out with Carlton and get back to my regular self.

"So, what's up, Shawna? Ain't you slummin', down here in the city?"

Shawna's parents lived in Bryn Mawr. The cheapest house in that rich part of Montgomery County probably cost $750,000. Her parents were lawyers who were always hangin' all over each other and kissing in front of us when we were there. I was not surprised that she had an eight-year-old brother. I wouldn't have been surprised if her forty-five-year-old mom was pregnant again.

"Oh, Taylor, why don't you quit? You know you're the reason why we broke up, not me. I wasn't giving out free pussy all over town. Do you really think that I believe that Eva was the only one?"

"Shawna, I know you didn't come this far into the city to get on my nerves about Eva. You chose to bounce. I had to deal wit' it. I'm cool now." She stressed me so bad that I had to light up a Newport, and I didn't even smoke! Well, maybe a few puffs now and then, since Carlton always had them.

"Oh, so you're smoking now, Taylor? What have you been into? I feel like I don't even know you anymore. Maybe I never knew you, but that was my fault. I don't know what I should have expected, getting picked up in a bar by another woman."

Shawna was mad and looked like she was going to cry again.

"You probably are gay, for real," she said. "You were probably talking shit when you said that I was the first woman you were with."

Oh, now she was calling me a *gay* liar.

"How long have you and Eva been bumping clits? So when did it happen, Taylor? Were you licking her clit and then kissing me an hour later?"

Shit. She busted out crying.

"That's really shitty, Taylor! I told you I loved you, and you went and fucked Eva when I was always there for you. I never said no to you, no matter what you wanted or what you asked for. You pretended to be happy with me, had me thinking that we were going to be together and have babies."

She was sniffling loudly and her nose was running. Shit. A few months ago, I would've wiped her nose with my fingers. I checked her out. Her hair had grown out a little bit. She looked like she had put on a little weight—in all the right places, I might add. Shit.

Think Carlton. Think dick. Nightly.

"Taylor, I told my mother that I was gay. I admitted that we lied to her when you met them. The last thing I remember, before you fucked Eva, was that we were talking about how I was going to carry the baby. We had everything planned. We talked about how we were going to tell people that we were a couple, not just roommates. Who was I talking to then? Who are you?"

I hated it when she cried like this, and she was definitely a crying ass because she knew she could get anything out of me when she did. I put my arms around her and felt her hands on my hips. She was a short little cutie and I felt like her strong man again.

"Shawnee, don't cry. Please, don't do this to me."

I moved in to kiss her tears, like I always did. I'd kissed more of her tears than I had ever tasted of my own.

"Shawna."

She leaned into me like she did when we was about to get busy and I was about to wax that ass.

I moved when I heard the security door open.

"Taylor." The front door opened and Carlton walked into the living room. "Oh, hey, I didn't know you had company," he said.

I moved farther away from Shawna and walked over to Carlton. She was still crying, and I felt stuck.

"Carlton, this is my old roommate, Shawna. I know you heard me talkin' about her before." I gave him a hug because, shit, I was with him now.

"Hey, Shawna, how're you doing?" Carlton leaned in to kiss me, like he always did when he came in.

I kissed him back, feeling like a traitor, like I was cheating on Shawna.

"Taylor, listen, I just came back to grab something from the basement," Carlton said. "I'll be right out of your way in a few minutes, ladies."

I walked him to the basement door. He ran down the steps and I could hear him cursing to himself while he moved boxes.

When I got back to the living room, she was gone.

# CHAPTER 28

*Eva*

U nfortunately, I had to go too far out of my way to the closest Aldi. I impatiently waited while Shuleesa leisurely sashayed her welfare-scamming ass into the store. If she thought I was going in with her in my knee-high Tory Burch boots, she was sadly mistaken.

Oh, well. I hoped she didn't think I was going to help her carry boxes filled with food to the truck. Luckily for her, I drove curbside so she wouldn't have to pay someone to assist and help her pack the trunk.

I swear, this family better not be more than I bargained for, and I reminded myself to have a packed schedule the next time she desired a free trip to the discount food market.

I drove faster than the law allowed back to Chestnut Street. The scent emanating from the passenger side of the truck smelled something like Similac, dirty diapers, and morning breath. I was ready to hurl all over my plush leather. I couldn't get the windows open far enough or fast enough.

In record time I was back at her house, my foot on the brake, the X3 still in drive. Shuleesa went to the front door and commanded her troops out to the truck to remove the food, while she sashayed into the house without so much as a thank you. Really, had I expected anything different?

Damn it, how the hell was I supposed to get her smell out of my truck?

While I was in the midst of creative-scents thinking, my cell phone rang.

*"I be buggin' cuz all these fake thugs is tryna press up/ I need a boss like (hey)/ who's flossin' like (hey) . . ."* Most times, I let the phone ring for a few just to hear Shareefa belt out my personal anthem.

It was Roman, returning my call. I let the ring reverberate through the soundproof cabin and then answered as if I didn't know it was him.

"Hello?" I had to throw in my business, white chick voice. Thank you, Anton (Daddy). He was apparently good for something.

"Eva, it's Roman. Sorry it took so long to get back to you. Can you talk for a minute?"

Oh, God, he sounded sweaty and out of breath. I was sure he tasted like a salty morsel of six-foot, seven-inch, chocolaty male specimen.

Shuleesa's irritating smell was suddenly erased from my memory and car.

"Oh, Roman I'm surprised to hear from you so soon. Of course, I have a few minutes for you." I flipped down the visor to check my appearance, as if he could actually see me. "How was practice?" I tried to put concern and interest into my voice.

"I think I pulled my hamstring running suicides. The coach sent me to medical for ice and then a warm soak. I think it . . ."

I didn't hear the rest of his comment—not that I really wanted to hear anything that might jeopardize my chances of making it across the oceans—because my other line clicked. It was Bryce. Damn. Did I have my lie straight?

Not that I necessarily needed to have a lie together for Bryce. I mean, he wasn't my man. Yes, he had helped me get this beautiful truck. Yes, I had been fucking him on a regular for quite some time now. Yes, I had been taking luxurious baths in his spa tub and sleeping on 850-thread count, Nobile bed linens.

What was Ro saying?

" . . . the coach said he's thinking about moving our return date for Barcelona forward by three weeks. I'm not all that happy because I have plans for Labor Day . . ."

What was he saying? Had I missed that much of the conversation?

"Roman, darling, could you hold that thought for one moment, please? I have a client's parent on the other line." I needed to talk to Bryce for a few. I did owe him that.

" . . . and if I miss this barbecue, my mother will bitch about it until Christmas. Not to even mention my great-grandmother . . ."

Had I missed something? Did he have his Miracle Ear on? Didn't he hear me butting into his monologue? I clicked over.

"Bryce, darling, how are you? I'm sorry I missed you this morning." I put it on the table first, so he couldn't accuse me of being distant and uncaring. "Did my poor baby fare well without my presence?" I made appropriate kissing noises into the phone.

He fell for it.

"Eva, I'm glad I caught you. And yes, I did miss you this morning. I tried your cell a few times. Is everything okay? How'd things go with Taylor? You were at her house, right?"

Damn, a nigga was straight clocking a ho.

"Well, you know she's going through something with Shawn, and she was a little down. I felt like I couldn't leave her in such a depressed state." My damned forked tongue. "Bryce, can I call you right back? I just left a client's house and now the mother is on my cell, talking my ear off about inter-agency meetings scheduled for next week."

"Yeah, babe, listen, I gotta go anyway. I'll call you back once I finish taking this potential client on a tour of our warehouse. Love you." *Click.*

"Roman, darling, I'm sorry to make you wait so long."

". . . so my youngest sister just had another baby. This makes her fourth daughter and they named her DeJesusa. Can you believe that? I told her to stop fucking these Hispanic dudes . . ."

"Roman, darling . . ." I tried to interrupt. He kept talking as if he hadn't heard a word I said, this time or at any other time. Did he even know I had clicked over to the other line?

". . . her other daughters are by Irish and German dudes who're about to be deported because their green cards are expired . . ."

"Roman!" I was almost beside myself in frustration. I had to scream his name to get him to stop talking. "Sweetheart, have you heard a word I've said?"

"Eva?"

Oh, God, what had I gotten myself into?

"Sweetheart, I've been calling you for quite some time. I have to go. Can I call you tonight at home? I've just arrived at another client's home, and I have a scheduled appointment. Give me a time and I'll get back to you."

Lies, lies, lies!

I swear, this trip to Barcelona better be worth all this aggravation. Maybe I could buy him a hearing aid for Christmas. Then maybe he might actually hear his mother bitching. And me calling his name.

"Oh, yeah, Eva. Call me back tonight."

"*Ciao*, sweetie."

I had to hold back the bang that so impatiently wanted to sound in his ear.

I was almost ready to call Brand.

# CHAPTER 29
*Taylor*

That Shawna shit almost got out of hand. I had to stop this shit.
I looked at Carlton's interruption as a sign. I couldn't fuck with Shawna like that. I was still caught up in her sexy-ass shit.

I forced myself to stop thinking about her. I concentrated on Carlton and what we called ourselves trying to make. I went to his family cookout for Memorial Day. Things were definitely looking up with that move. I had barely met any of his friends in the past. He claimed it was because they were roughnecks and he didn't want me caught up in their shit.

I think it was because I was one of too many chicks on his roster, and it was better to introduce either the main chick or no chicks at all. But I didn't complain. Carlton kept me busy and I didn't have too much time to think about Shawna. And what she was doing. And with who.

I met Carlton's two kids, Carltona and Carlton, Jr. Their mom must've been a basehead; why else would she name those kids that? Carlton cheesed and grinned like his kids were the greatest. I caught myself before I started on his kids too badly. They were cute, though, even though his daughter did have silver fronts. I almost caught myself asking him what that was about, then I changed my mind. I didn't know why I was worried. I was damned sure not stepmom material. Why did I care that Silver, as I named her in my mind, didn't brush her teeth?

Carlton, Jr. had a large diamond stud in each ear and a gold ring in his left brow. Gold (now his nickname) couldn't have been more than six years old. Silver was a year younger than Gold.

*Silver and gold. Silver and gold. Everyone wishes for silver and gold.*

I knew I was wrong. I was gonna try to keep my comments about Silver and Gold to myself, because I might have my own kids one day.

But I had to prove a point.

"Silver!" I waved her over to where I was sitting on a bench. "Come here, cutie. Look at your Baby Phat mini skirt and matchin' sneakers. Girl, you is wearin' that outfit!"

Silver ran over to me, twisting and turning like she was on a catwalk during *America's Next Top Model.*

"Silver, let me ask you something." She did look at me kind of strange when I called her out of her name. "Help me sing the ABCs. I can't remember the words. You ready? One, two, three."

"A-B-C-D-E-F . . . P-H-my-K-K-elmo-mello-P . . ." she blurted out. Yup, just like I thought. Bet she knew how to spell *Baby Phat*, though. Bet she knew every song by Lil' Wayne and could dance like Ciara. And what were those thousands of barrettes in her hair that was only yea long?

I was getting Yaz tomorrow. The Patch *and* Lea's Shield. Depo and Norplant. Lunelle and an IUD. Damn sure wouldn't be no spawn of the well-dressed dummies here.

At least with Shawn, we could have picked out a baby's dad locally. Somebody would have to fuck something with a dick. Or, we could have picked the best of the litter at a sperm bank. That might not be a bad idea. Who wouldn't want a kid by a rich doctor? Or a top-notch lawyer? Or a Carmello Anthony look-alike?

Shit. Why couldn't I get that chick off my mind?

# CHAPTER 30

*Eva*

Before I knew it, it was August. Then September was upon us, and Roman was returning to Barcelona. I thought I might really like Roman, even if he didn't have his six-figure salary, and I would miss him when he was gone. Even though he was deaf as a doorknob and obtuse as a rock, I had gotten used to my midnight drives back and forth to New Jersey.

Then Brand, that sneaky bastard, called and caught me on my cell phone, while I was in the middle of a heated argument with Bryce. According to Bryce, I wasn't spending as much time with him as I'd promised. Okay. I did promise to make him number one in my life, but that was before Barcelona via Roman came back into my life.

"What?" I was three seconds off Bryce's ass and had basically banged on him to answer my other line. I was so incensed that I forgot to check the CallerID and see who was beckoning.

"Eva, why have you been ignoring me?"

Damn it. Brand. I didn't need this now.

"Who is this?" I knew that hurt. But damn it, I was hurting, having herpes breakouts again, and Bryce had gotten on my last nerve with his incessant whining and complaining.

"Come on, Eva, don't do this. I miss you, Eva. I love you. Why don't you give me a chance to talk to you? I'm telling you, that bitch was lying. Please, Eva, let me make this up to you." Damn it. Now Brand was whining and blubbering.

"Brandon, I can't do this right now. Please don't do this to me. I'll call you back later."

"Eva, I know you lying to me! I know you not going to call me back. Eva, please. We were supposed to be getting married! Can't you at least give me a chance? Don't you still love me?"

I was sure Bryce had already hung up on me. Now I was mad at both of them.

"Damn it, Bry—" I threw the phone in the passenger seat and banged my head on the steering wheel. They were going to fucking kill me before it was over.

"Brandon, I'll call you later," I said after picking up my phone and pushing the speaker button. *Click.*

Oh, God. I did not need this shit.

Bryce. I had to get back to him.

I hit my call history and pulled up my last incoming calls. Bryce. *Send.*

I didn't even give him a chance to say hello.

"Bryce, I'm sorry. I know I haven't been available as much lately. I've been trying to get in a little me time, and wasn't aware that you felt I'd been ignoring you."

Lies, lies, lies! My pussy was sore from so much lip action by Roman!

"Bryce, where are you? Tell me where you are, and I'll come to you. Let me make it up to you, please." I was searching my brain to find the correct words. "I'm selfish, Bryce. Is that what you want to hear me say? I'm selfish, and too often I only think of Eva."

Damn. He must have been really turned off. Silence.

"Bryce. I'm apologizing. I'm admitting that I've been self-indulgent and have been taking you for granted." I rolled my eyes in my head. "I'll do better. Please give the chance to make it right."

"Eva, meet me at the house. We'll talk there." *Click.* Wow, now that was kind of sexy.

Let me get this Brand shit over with. Call history. Brand. *Send.*

"Brandon." He needed to know that I wasn't happy about calling him back. "What can I do for you on this glorious day?"

"Eva! I didn't think you would call me back."

"Spit it out, Brand. Make it quick."

"Eva, you act like I never meant nothin' to you. Why you got me beggin' you, like a fool? Don't you care about anything we did in the past? Doesn't that ring I gave you mean anything to you at all?"

"Brand, we've been through this before. I'm not in the mood for this. Is this what you called to talk about? How you didn't really cheat on me? How I got it all wrong? How much you really love and cherish me?"

I felt myself getting emotional just thinking about that night in the bar.

"Eva, stop it, please! That's not why I'm calling. You won't talk to me. I don't see you anymore. I just want to spend some time with you." He cursed at my loud, long sigh. "Listen, I just called to tell you this: Big Tony is havin' a ski trip to New York in January. Why don't you go with me? No sex, I promise. We can make it a long weekend and talk; that's all."

I felt myself weakening.

"Eva, think about it. We got a couple of months for you to make up your mind. I promise, I won't call you every day and irritate the shit outta you, like you say I do. I'll give you some space. Just think about it."

"Okay, Brand, I'll let you know."

# CHAPTER 31
*Taylor*

Carlton and I went to the movies at the Willow Grove Mall, and then to Friday's to eat. Over dinner, this nigga started getting all glassy eyed. I was stuffing down Jack Daniel's steak and shrimp and slurping Long Island Iced Teas. I was feeling kind of nice when he caught me off guard with the question of the night.

"Whassup, Taylor? Let's talk about what you think about us living together."

I swallowed some steak. "What's there to talk about?"

"We could talk about what we're doin'. You could act like it's a big deal that I introduced you to my kids, that I care about you and want you to be a part of our lives."

What was I supposed to say to that?

"Of course it means somethin' to me, Carlton. I know how you feel about your kids. I'm still takin' all this in." Shit. I wanted to eat, and here he was, going on and on about Silver and Gold.

"I'm just sayin', Taylor, we been chillin' together for a minute. I guess their mom got tired of you bangin' on her ass every day. After you cussed her out, she scared to call the house now. And she stopped callin' my cell phone every five minutes over some bullshit, like she used to." He stopped to take a big, nasty bite out of his bacon cheeseburger. Ketchup and mayonnaise oozed all over his lips.

I had to look away because that shit looked nasty.

Shawna always took cute, sexy bites of her food.

"Carlton, we are chillin'. We been fixin' up the downstairs and painting the rooms for Silv—um, Carltona and C.J. to come stay the night sometimes. I think we're doin' okay." Thank my lucky stars he wiped off his mouth. "Why? You think we need to be doin' more? What? I'm not doin' enough?"

Shit. Couldn't he wait until I was done my food? If this was some kind of breakup scene, he could at least let my food digest good. I swear, I knew how to pick 'em. I was going back to bitches.

"You want to go look at engagement rings?" he asked out of the blue.

Goddamn it. I knew this wasn't some steak caught in my throat! I put my hand over my mouth and coughed like a sick horse. Shit. Where was my femme, girlie cough when I needed it?

"Are you okay?" Carlton asked. He had pink shit on his lips again.

I put up one hand. *Please don't come no closer,* I thought.

I coughed again, like a sick pig this time.

My steak bite came up and I spit it out on the plate.

"What do you mean, engagement rings? Don't you think this is kinda fast?" I was back to myself now. "Shit, Carlton, I'm expectin' not to hear from you again soon. You been back and forth, in and out, as long as we been dealin', and now this?" I stopped for a second, hoping he would wipe that shit off his mouth. "What happened? You musta really fucked up wit' your kids' mom."

He must've thought he was dealing with a dummy. If this nigga thought he was going to stay with me until he made up with his baby mom, he was dumber than I ever thought.

"How about nothin' happened, Taylor? How about I never gave you a chance in the past, and I'm startin' to wonder why I stayed with her as long as I did? It was real convenient to run back to her when shit wasn't goin' my way."

"And now you want to get married? To me? I barely know you, Carlton." I was thinking about Shawna and what she would do if I got married on her like that. "I'm flattered, I think. I don't think we at that point yet, though. Let's not fuck up what's workin' right."

He was not suckering me in with the bullshit. Let me finish my food in peace. Shit.

"I'm not saying that I want to get married, Taylor, so you can bring your ass down off that high horse. And stop frontin' like you're not en-joyin' this as much as I am. I could tell you wasn't gettin no dick, 'cause your pussy was tight as shit when I got in it."

Little did he know, I was gettin' plenty of dick, just the plastic kind. Shawna used to work that shit out every now and then.

"Taylor, humor me, please? Let's go look, that's all. Can we do that? And not argue, and you not complain?"

"Carlton, do me a favor? Wipe your mouth, please, 'cause you is kil-lin' me wit all that shit all over your mouth."

"Why don't you do it for me?"

Shit. Was he expecting me to do this type of shit if he gave me some diamond ring? I woulda licked Shawna's mouth clean and then ate the shit outta her pussy, but Carlton? Hell no.

"Come here. You owe me big time after all this mushy shit," I said, reaching forward with a napkin.

# CHAPTER 32

*Eva*

I was tripping. I couldn't even begin to imagine why I was even considering the possibility of going anywhere with Brand. This was how he got me the first time. I should have left his ass alone after he gave me herpes. I should have taken out that full-page ad and announced to the greater Philadelphia area that he was a nasty bastard.

I didn't have time to ponder Brand's situation because I was too busy making up with Bryce. His feelings were really hurt this time, and he actually shed a tear or two. I wasn't really fooled, though, because I'd surely pushed out a few fakes in my time.

I gave him his due. I met him at his house and took him out to dinner—Capital Grille at Broad and Chestnut. I ordered his food and drink.

I fed him calamari and steamed mussels.

I kissed him between bites.

I fed him salmon with peach chutney glaze.

I stroked his ever-growing penis beneath the table.

I fed him fresh garden vegetables.

I kissed him again.

I poured his dry martini with olives from my mouth into his.

I begged and pleaded his forgiveness for my insufferable behavior. I cursed my selfish ways and chastised myself for failing to recognize his selfless acts on my behalf.

And then, because it had been a long time, I practiced my award-winning oral X Games in the truck on the return to his house. Two times, not once, did I have to swallow little mini-Bryce's on the ride to Chalfont.

Oh, well. Whatever. I had to play my part. I was still homeless, and I had been playing myself and Bryce with my foolishness with Roman. And now he was gone, back across the ocean, and I didn't know when I might hear from him again.

There was time enough to worry about that later. Right now, I had to maintain my rightful place by Bryce's side each night.

Mirabelle truly hadn't raised a fool.

"So, Bryce, tell me what you want me to do." I was lying on his back in a red thong, while he was stretched out on his California King. Every once in a while, he would raise his butt and I would grind on it like I was two seconds away from penetration.

When men did that, it always made me wonder.

My lips traced his shoulder blades and my hand worked its way around to stroke his penis. I humped his butt as he pushed it back on me.

What was that about? Never mind.

"Tell me, Bryce."

Instead, he rolled over, holding me upright so I didn't collapse on him.

"Why don't you give me something that you haven't given me before, Eva?"

Was this a trick question or something? What hadn't I given this man in the two years we'd been fucking? Was he playing with me? I mentally checked my sexual Rolodex, wondering what we hadn't done. Let's be real, now. When you consider what I had done sexually with just Bryce alone, the count was astronomical. If I were anyone else, I might have to be ashamed for a moment or two. But alas, this was me, the undeniable Eva, and this girl wasn't ever ashamed.

"Why don't you let me get in that tight li'l asshole you been keeping from me?" He was really planning to make me pay.

*Damn, Bryce.* I wondered if he would talk dirty to me, like he did when he called me a bunch of bitches and fucked the shit out of me.

"Tell me how you want it." As I spoke, I moved down his body so that I was face to face with the dick I had come to know and love so well.

His hands were on my head, guiding my mouth to his engorged penis, speaking through clenched teeth.

"Lick it."

Oh, please. I could do much more than that.

I swallowed his head, pulling it into my mouth, using my tongue to move it from side to side. His head was smooth and firm in my mouth and I suckled it, softly and then with more suction. Up and down. Right, then left.

My ass gyrated in the air to the motion of his hips, which pounded his dick relentlessly into my mouth and throat. He was making me pay for ignoring him, for making him miss me and wonder what this pretty, talented mouth was doing when it was away from him.

"Eat it."

Oh, please. Gladly.

I used every trick I knew: deep throating, humming, licking, slurping, noisy, and then quiet. I was caught up in the act, mesmerized in some kind of fellatio trance.

Bryce's hips were moving faster than my mouth, and I was choking as he forced me to pay him back for my actions in my absence. His dick had gone beyond deep throat and every three seconds, I was literally without breath.

Vomit rose in my throat and tears streamed from my eyes, but I wouldn't stop. I couldn't stop, and Bryce wouldn't let me.

"Eat it, bitch."

Oh my God, I was about to cum.

Bryce withdrew his penis from my mouth without warning. My jaws were still working, I was breathless, and I couldn't imagine what I must look like. My throat was raw, and strands of light brown hair lay, detached, on his stomach.

Damn, a bitch was eating that dick because the nigga ripped hair from my head and I didn't feel one strand leave my scalp.

As he pulled me up his body, my lips and tongue sucked whatever I came into contact with. His lips were on mine and I was lost in the moment of Bryce's delicious payback. If this was my makeup test, I'd truant and delinquent a little more regularly.

Juice ran from my pussy onto his stomach as I ground on his eight-pack, anything and anywhere. My clit was on fire and sought to be doused with contentment.

Kissing me senseless, Bryce situated me onto his dick that felt like it had grown exponentially since it left my mouth. My pussy gripped his dick and his rhythm burned into my mind, while his dick made music inside me.

I was not even aware that I was gliding, matching him stroke for stroke, delirious in my movement and the sensation of drag and pull on my sugary walls. Then I was riding rodeo, one hand gripping the back of his neck, the other in the air as I rode myself into an orgasm that sent me over the cliff of madness and made me lose consciousness.

"Oh no, Eva. You won't get off that easy."

I couldn't have been out long cause I was suddenly aware of Bryce, still inside my pussy, riding harder, squeezing my ribs, sweating profusely, shouting and wild eyed.

"Eva! Goddamn it!"

I burst into tears as my body reacted to a torrent of sensations emanating through my veins. My clit was distended to the point of pain. Another orgasm swam through me and I literally could not take another stroke of Bryce's dick.

I briefly wished for death and felt my limbs trembling uncontrollably. I was crying between gasps of breath, holding on to Bryce, almost wishing the pleasure would stop.

A vein pulsated on his hairline and I couldn't see anything else as his teeth ground in my ear. I tried to move my body off his so that I could bring back some sense of equilibrium.

With a death grip on my upper torso, Bryce moaned long and loud from the depths of his being and loosed his load into my tired, despondent pussy.

I was spent and short of breath as I collapsed.

Oh well, he could always get the ass another day.

Sheeit, I might just ignore him again next week.

# CHAPTER 33

## *Taylor*

We ended up at Kay Jewelers, looking at rings. I checked out bracelets that were three carats and up. I might be from West Philly, but I wasn't no slouch. Carlton was on the other side of the store with the sales clerk. Fuck what you heard: I knew this nigga was going to disappear again, and I was getting my list together. I would need at least three carats if he wanted to get close to my door again.

"Taylor, get over here. We're supposed to be looking at engagement rings, and you over there BS-ing." He had the nerve to look impatient.

One last glance and I was across the store to play the pretend, anxious girlfriend. I didn't care how nice he was being, I wasn't buying his bullshit for one minute.

"Tee, this is Tamika. Tamika, this is Taylor, my reluctant girlfriend. Tamika has been nice enough to show me rings while you was over there, doin' everything except helping me here."

He gave me a look. I acted like I didn't see it.

"Taylor," Tamika said all up in my face. I bet she was adding up her commission from the sale of the big-ass rocks that Carlton had been looking at. Damn, these diamonds were bigger than Eva's.

Tamika's voice was smooth and syrupy sweet. She probably practiced it in the mirror.

"Let me show you what your sweetheart has been picking out for you!" She was all excited. They were some bangin'-ass rocks to choose from. I noticed that she didn't have a diamond on those crusty knuckles.

"What's this one?" I asked. I couldn't even pretend like I knew what I was looking at. Shit. Now I wished I had listened to Eva when she tried to show me different shapes on a popular diamond website.

Businesslike and forceful, Tamika said, "Oh, that's our signature diamond, 2.78 carats, grade G, with a .63 carat emerald, cushion cut surrounding the diamond, and on the bridge . . ." She kept going, but I had tuned her out by then. What language was she speaking?

"Which one do you like, Carlton?" I asked. I looked at all the ones he picked out and it was hard to choose between them. I was in over my head and trying not to look stupid. It was probably too late for that, though. I picked up one of the rings and looked closely at it while Tamika continued to talk.

"Why am I not surprised that we picked out the same ring?" Carlton referred to the one I held. "That was the first one I told her I wanted to see, you know, when you was so busy over there ignoring me. But that's okay. I got you."

Whatever.

"How much does it cost?" I had the damned ring on my finger and it looked like it could send signals to the Russian Space Station, in the right light.

"Now, Ms. Taylor, a true lady never asks the price of her engagement ring. Now run along, and I'll speak with Mr. Tyson about pricing and our payment options."

What? I was about to knock this bitch out. I was about to let a "true lady" whip her ass at her job, and then walk out real *ladylike* to Carlton's Infiniti G35.

Carlton peeped my body language and pulled me out of the door and into the mall. He reached into his pocket and pulled out a stack of bills.

"Taylor, ignore her and go buy some bras, or boots, or a sweatshirt.

Do something, but do not go back into that store and say a word to Tamika. Let me handle this and her. Please, Tee, don't embarrass us in this mall, out here in the country with these white people." He kissed me on the lips real quick and shoved me toward Old Navy. "Go, and I'll catch up to you in a minute."

I walked over to tear up Old Navy. He'd better hope that he could catch up with me before I did some real damage to his knot. I was about to act a real live fool.

I'd have to thank Carlton for his quick thinking, because the last thing I needed was some bogus-ass aggravated assault charge out here in the country, where they didn't have real crime, and a struggle with a black woman would probably make their week. Add bonus points for arresting a resisting nigger.

Shit. I was lost in the women's department, snagging everything in my size. Carlton caught me coming out of the dressing room wit about $1,200 worth of clothes. Of course, he bought everything, plus a few things for Silver and Gold. Now that I might have to be their stepmom, I figured I'd have to get used to taking care of them.

Never mind. I would pretend.

# CHAPTER 34

*Eva*

It was easy to play loving, attentive girlfriend to Bryce in Roman's absence. I was home each night like a good girl. I cooked in that luscious kitchen and washed dirty boxers on weekends. I fucked missionary style each night, and it was okay. If this was what getting married was like, I could gladly give an emphatic, "No, thank you," right now.

Brand called me weekly. As promised, he didn't blow up my phone. He actually kept his word, but that was not what I needed, because I was really trying to continue to hate him immensely.

Taylor was living the straight life with Carlton. I hoped she was milking that nigga for all he was worth, because she knew he wouldn't be staying. He never did. He was in that game. Not the drug game, the rap game. But was there a difference?

Shawn called me every now and again, pleading with me to meet her somewhere, anywhere, her treat. She admitted that she missed Taylor but if she couldn't have Taylor, she wanted me. Apparently, she had been stalking the girl because she knew Taylor was living with Carlton, and knew that Taylor had met his kids.

According to Shawn, she hadn't talked to Taylor. These things Shawn knew by tailing Taylor in her mom's Audi jeep. Too much drama, and I didn't really want to remember that I had fucked Shawn and Taylor on separate occasions. I was almost glad they'd broken up. That shit I didn't need.

I was in West Philly, on my way to see yet another badass client when Jay Z's "Encore" broke my concentration. My cell phone was ringing. I had to swerve and swiftly apply the brakes as I almost slid into the Dodge Neon in front of me.

"Encore" was Roman's personal ring.

Green light.

*Eva, take a deep breath. Breathe. Don't jump. Don't play yourself. Let's not forget that he's been gone for five weeks, gone across oceans and surrounded by beautiful, docile, subservient Spanish women. Why would he be thinking about your half-breed ass, when he had pussy of another language in his face?*

I let it ring until it reached voicemail.

Red light. Fine. If he called back, I'd talk to him. If not, oh well.

Green light.

"Encore." Just as I thought.

Nonchalance.

"Hello?" Five weeks, my ass.

"Eva! I'm glad you answered this time. I just called you and left a voicemail. Where are you?" Same old Roman. I did miss him, though. Maybe I would let him make it up to me.

Indifference.

"Hello?" Five weeks up his ass.

"Eva, it's Rome. Baby, I'm so glad to hear your voice! I know you're mad at me, but don't be. Just let me explain it all to you."

"Well, Roman, I'm certainly surprised to hear your voice. I'd just assumed you'd moved on to bigger and better things." I paused for dramatic effect. "How long has it been now? Oh, two or three weeks, I guess. I've been so busy."

Lies, lies, lies!

I had been waiting, with bated breath, for the phone to ring, or email to sing, or UPS to deliver something with foreign postage. I played it off well.

"Damn, baby! I hoped you had missed me, at least. You barely knew I was gone." He sounded like he had lost his best friend. Well, let him mourn for a few.

"Roman, I'm glad to finally hear from you. How have you been?"

"Eva, it's me. Baby, I've been in the mountains at this boot camp-like training camp for return players. I've been there for five weeks, Eva. I wasn't ignoring you."

Oh, damn.

"The coaches didn't mention training camp until we landed at Barcelona Airport. We got on buses and rode for six hours into the mountains. There was no running water or electricity. It was almost like modern-day slavery, I swear. We worked out continuously from sunup to sundown, six days a week. I just got back to my townhouse. This is the first time I've had the chance to call you."

Oh, damn. Suddenly, a song of a different tune.

"Oh, Rome, I thought you had forgotten about me. I thought I was just a plaything while you were here in the States, and that there was some Spanish *chica* waiting for you at the airport. Are you okay?"

"Well, I wasn't until I got back today and checked my account. FIBA paid us a re-signing bonus of $42,000 for completing the training camp. That's really not enough for all the torture they put us through, though. Four players out of the sixteen who went didn't make it." He whistled into the phone. "One player from Boston had to be air-lifted to a remote hospital."

Oh, damn.

"But fuck that. I'm happy to be talkin' to my girl. You sure you're happy to hear from me? I know you was mad as shit that I didn't call you. Damn, it's like that, Eva?"

"Rome, of course I missed you! I couldn't wait to hear from you. I thought something must have happened to make you not call. I was going crazy, working each day and sleeping at Taylor's each night, all by myself."

Lies, lies, lies!

"I'm on my way to a client meeting and I'm stopped at the corner of Fifty-second and Girard, talking to you in the middle of traffic. That damned meeting can wait." I was suddenly all cheesing again, imagining my trip abroad.

"Eva, listen: I'm sending a $200 phone card overnight, so you can call me starting tomorrow. I can't stay on this line long, 'cause all of the guys are here waiting for me so we can go to dinner. I'm waiting for my home phone and cable to get turned on at the townhouse, and that won't happen till tomorrow."

"Rome, I'm so glad to hear from you! I'm glad you finally called. Did you include the phone number and instructions? Because I've never called an international number."

"Eva, I took care of everything. I gotta go. Call me as soon as you get the phone card, okay? Be careful." And that was it.

Oh, damn.

Well, it wasn't a plane ticket, but it was a start.

❈

The next day, at nine AM, FedEx was at Taylor's front door. I made sure I was there early, since I knew that was where Roman would send my package. I signed for the flat envelope and tore it open before the deliveryman left.

I sat on the edge of the couch where I had sucked Shawn's pussy dry almost two years ago. But I wouldn't think of that while Taylor was upstairs with Carlton.

There were two sealed envelopes inside. I did a quick eenie, meenie, miney, moe to decide which one to open first.

I palmed the one in the "moe" hand and tore it open. A $200 phone card, just as he said. So sweet of him. I had wondered how he thought we would keep in contact. I hoped he didn't think I'd be running up my Sprint bill. His oral game wasn't that damned tight.

I opened the other envelope and almost fell off the couch arm. I counted a hundred one-hundred-dollar bills and slid onto the floor. There was a note attached, but it took me about ten minutes to see it.

*Eva,*

*I wish I could have brought your fine ass with me. I liked the little time we spent together in New Jersey. I think of where we might be if we'd gotten together back at 'Nova. I worked hard for this money, but I thought you deserved some of it for being so patient over the last five weeks. Another woman may not have taken my call.*

*Get yourself something cute to wear for the next time I see you. Buy your family and friends gifts for Christmas. Stay beautiful, and keep that kitty cat nice and tight. Spend the rest on yourself, and let me know if it's not enough.*

*I can't wait til I see you again.*

*Love,*

*Rome*

Oh my God! I was about to cum on myself! I had to catch my breath because I was suddenly wheezing. Roman had sent me $10,000 because he was happy that I waited the five weeks it took for him to call? Preposterous!

"Taylor!" I screamed. I needed to share this news with my best friend.

# CHAPTER 35
### *Taylor*

S hit. Eva always gave up some serious dick sucking when she wanted to say thank you to her men. I wasn't into that type of shit. True, I sucked Carlton's dick, but that's because he ate my pussy. It was a give-and-take type of thing. But I wanted to say thank you for the clothes and ring shopping we did. And I did get a bracelet.

"Let's stop in the park before we go home." I was going to do something nice for once. Maybe that would help me stop thinking about Shawna. I needed to get into Carlton real quick if we were thinking about getting engaged.

"Can't this wait for a few? I want to take the clothes to Carla and C.J. before it gets too late. I don't want to hear their mom's mouth about shit."

He was focused on driving and probably thought that I was crazy, because I was rubbing his dick while he was at the wheel. I kept thinking, *This would be the time when Eva would bust out her oral Olympics.* But I couldn't do it. That was Eva's shit.

I had something else for dat ass, though.

"Come on, Carlton, I got something for you. I'm kinda feelin' this us-hooked-up thing, and I want to do something different. It won't take long, and we'll get to Old City soon enough." I moved over and kissed him on the cheek. "Please?"

We drove up to the Strawberry Bridge and I made my moves. I kissed him like crazy and ripped his shirt by accident, trying to bite his nipples. I think Eva said she did that to Bryce in the truck before. Shit. I was used to getting my shit off at home, in the bed.

I told him to lean his seat back and I opened his zipper. After giving Carlton a hand job and trying to get up my nerve, I finally practiced some oral Olympics that would've made Eva proud.

Carlton was quiet, like a deaf mute. I knew he thought I had been drinking while he'd been kissing Tamika's saleslady ass in the store. But wasn't this how you were supposed to keep your man? Wouldn't bitches suck his dick in the club, if his main chick wasn't?

I couldn't front and if Carlton was thinking about hanging around longer than usual, I needed to step my game way up. He was what you would consider paid, in a small-time, producer way—especially one from Philly. Not the long money like he used to get when he had niggas on the corners, but the rap game was definitely buying steaks and paying the bills.

This was a true first for me—sucking dick in a car, sucking dick this long, and about to let a nigga bust in my mouth.

I swore that Eva better not have been lying.

# CHAPTER 36

*Eva*

Like a scary broke ass, always afraid of being broke again like I was as a child, I put $9,000 in my savings account. Hush your mouth. One needed to save for a rainy day. I gave $1,000 to Aunt Mira and told her I worked overtime each weekend for a month.

"Spend it all on yourself, love," I told her.

I took Taylor and Carlton out for drinks later that night at California Café in King of Prussia. They looked cute together and I wondered if this was a record for Carlton's presence in Taylor's life. Whatever. They looked happy, and Tee told me they went to look at engagement rings.

I thought it was a great idea, if Carlton was being honest and had no intentions on disappearing like he usually did. I hated to see Taylor all caught up in his foolishness, only to have her heart broken in a few weeks or months.

She had enough to deal with since Shawn was gone. I wondered what Shawn was doing 'cause she hadn't called in a minute.

Of course, I called Rome once I figured out how to use the phone card. There were no directions for international calls, only long distance and state to state. I had to call a 1-888 number and speak with an English-as-a-second-language customer service representative. Had we closed the borders yet?

"Rome Wright! You shouldn't have." As if. "That was so sweet of you! You know you caught me completely off guard, and I haven't stopped smiling since I got your presents. You better not spoil me like this. I might get used to it."

"Eva, sweetheart, that ain't shit. Get used to it. That's nothing and I hardly felt that money leave my pocket. But I'm happy you're enjoying it. Think of me while you spend it, sexy."

"Well, excuse me, big spender. Ten thousand dollars through the mail is quite a surprise. Do it again, then. Don't let me stop you!"

I laughed at the unexpected events of the past two days.

"Seriously, Rome, I appreciate and thank you for your gifts. I had honestly thought you'd forgotten about me. I'm glad to see that I still rate high up on your list of favorites. Now tell what you've been doing since you've moved back into your townhouse."

"Eva, that shit is not important right now. What did you buy? You sure you been thinking about me? You know I'm expectin' to hear from you every night after work." Rome appeared to be a little more extroverted while he was a few oceans away.

Was this the same dull-ass dude who rambled on the phone for lapses of time, even when I wasn't listening? When it was obvious that I wasn't listening? Whatever. I would play along.

"Rome, I'll call you whenever you want. What? You trying to claim Eva? Do you know what that entails? This ain't no random-chick shit going on over here." I snorted because he was about to play himself out—and just when I was thinking that I might have grown to like him.

Despite what he thought he knew about Eva, he didn't really want it.

"Yeah, well, Eva, I'm expectin' you to be home at night in case I call you. I'm going to be busy during my day, and you know Spain is six hours ahead of the East Coast."

Oh, this nigga thought his $10,000 was going to buy monogamy?

He really didn't know Eva, then. What did they say about "a fool and his money are soon parted?"

"Rome, I'm flattered that you feel that way about me, but you know I have to attend classes to finish up my MSW. I don't want you to start thinking anything if I'm not available some evenings." I had to choke back a laugh because my most of my "MSW classes" would surely include Bryce and his talented dick. "How do you feel about having such a long-distance relationship?" I knew this nigga didn't think that because he ate my pussy and sent me some money, that I was his girl.

"Eva, I just want to know that you're there for me when I'm so far away. I want you to be waiting for me when I get back. I need someone to talk to when I've been away for road games and I'm tired as shit. I wish you could be here to rub my back, but you can do that when I come back home."

Apparently he did think I was his girl. And he wanted me to wait for him, patiently, like a good little girl. It would have been funny, if it wasn't so pathetic.

"Rome, I'm here waiting for you, right now. I, too, wish I were there with you. I would love to keep home ready for you while you were gone for a few days. I would be there waiting with open arms for your return."

Wait, please. I needed to go and vomit from this bullshit spewing forth from my own mouth. *And the Oscar goes to . . . Eva Arianna LoDolce-Wright . . . for best bullshitter in a comedy/drama!*

"Eva, I think I love you. I can't wait to see you again. Please be careful while I'm gone, and take care of yourself. If you need something, just call me at home or try the conference office. I'm in the process of finding another agent to handle my business, but until then, I'll be here or there."

"Oh, Rome! I think I love you, too. Sweetheart, be careful while you're abroad and so far away from me. I'll call you tomorrow after work."

Wait, please. I needed to vomit.

I had scarcely hung up with Roman when I returned Bryce's call.

Then I'd call Brand and see what I could see.

# CHAPTER 37

*Taylor*

It was October, and Carlton and I had Silver and Gold out at the mall, looking for Halloween costumes. I couldn't even believe I was here with them, doing this shit. I had to grab a couple shots of Belvedere vodka before we picked up his precious metals.

"Carla, girl, you look just like a princess," I told her. *Minus the white skin and flowing blond hair,* I thought. "You look just like royalty in them leopard skin, stiletto knee boots, girl. Watch your step, though." *Please. Don't even.*

"C.J., you look just like Lil' Wayne. You already got the bling, and now all you need is a 9 mm and to get yourself a corner. You got ya money, little duffel bag boy?"

What? Wasn't that what you were supposed to say to li'l ghetto kids, to boost their self-esteem? Carlton grinned from ear to ear. He didn't care what they looked like or what they bought. He just knew he paid for it all.

Shit. I was going to take two birth control pills tonight.

"Babe, I'm about to jet," Carlton told me later that night. "I've got to meet Tony D and Hakim at the studio. We're layin' down tracks here, and then we're going to Hotlanta to finish the studio work. They have state-of-the-art equipment and soundproof booths, and a four-man equalizer for . . ." Carlton was still talking while I watched an *America's Next Top Model* rerun marathon.

I wasn't being rude—at least not on purpose—but I couldn't get all into Rappin' Papers' rise to fame in the rap game. I figured that I'd probably regret it in a couple of years when they were on the MTV Awards show and not giving me shout outs, but right now, I could care less.

"Okay, just call me and let me know when you're comin' home. I'mma be right here on this couch, waitin' for you to get back. Miss me, okay?" I said. *And hurry up and get out* was what I didn't say.

Carlton leaned down and kissed me.

"Bye."

Finally, solitude. Shit. I sounded like Eva.

"It's about damned time you got rid of one of them sad and ugly, anorexic, twin bitches, Tyra." I talked to Tyra Banks like she was in my living room, and I just got the chance to kick the twins Michelle or Amanda out of the competition.

Tyra knew they were all knees and elbows and ain't have no business getting that damned far in the competition. Is it me, or should they have stayed their asses in New York, and not even made it to Barcelona?

I knew that was not my doorbell ringing when a twin was on TV, writing a bye-bye note to the other one because she just got kicked to the curb.

If Carlton would get us TiVo, I wouldn't be having these problems.

I looked through the peephole. Oh, shit. Why was he here?

"Let me in, Tee. I don't want to stay long. I just need to talk to you real quick."

"You know you playin' yourself, right? I know you just seen Carlton leave out the front door. Did you give him the chance to pull around the corner?" But I opened the door, just like he knew I would.

"Give me a kiss, Tee. I ain't seen you in a while. Where you been?" He hugged me and I felt like melting right on the floor. Damn, I had been missing those lips.

I kissed him back, giving him more than I gave Carlton every day. I gave him more than I ever even gave Shawna, and y'all know that bitch's DNA was in my blood.

His hands were on my titties, rubbing and squeezing through my T-shirt. He put his hand in my panties and fingered my pussy, making me wet.

I hated it when he did this to me.

I loved it when he did this to me.

Then he fucked it up, like he always did.

"Tee, I need to know if you talked to Eva today?"

Why did he always have to bring her up? Wasn't it bad enough that I had to see them together, and know I couldn't do a fucking thing about it?

"No, not today. Why you always gotta bring her up?" I didn't even want to say her name right now.

"Tee, don't be like that. You know you the one I love. It's always been you. You know that, right?" I started to pull away from him now that he had hurt my feelings. "Where you goin', Tee? I just need you to do a favor for me. I got to talk to you later about somethin' that's important to me."

He started walking me back toward the couch. He put my arms around his neck because he could tell I wasn't feeling him. I never did when he brought her up in the middle of us.

He turned me around and kissed the back of my neck, his hands running up and down my body, making me wet, knowing I was missing his dick, like I always did.

I could hear his belt buckle as he snapped it open. I tried to open my mouth to tell him no, just one time. But it didn't work. He didn't understand "no" with me.

"Tee, kiss it for me, just a little bit, baby. Please? You don't know how much I miss you kissing me there, on him like you used to. You know you was the one to name him, the first one to put him in your mouth and suck until he came for you."

I had tried to forget that I started sucking dick so young, and that he was the one to get me to do it. But I did what he wanted, and did it how he showed me.

"Damn, Tee, ya shit just keep gettin' better every time. Swallow it for me, baby. Put my head all in your throat, like you used to."

And his dick was in my throat and I had to think about something other than wanting to spit it out and throw up.

"Tee, pull it open for me. Uh-uh, no, leave your panties on. I like it like that."

He pulled me up from my knees to turn me around. He stepped back so he could watch me bend over and spread my ass. He wanted to watch me hold my cheeks open so he could look at my asshole and pussy, wet from his fingers and his dick in my mouth.

"Open it wider, Tee, I want to see them. You want my tongue in your pussy, Taylor? You love it when I do it, don't you? Tell me what you want me to do."

He knew I couldn't say shit when he was like this.

He was on his knees behind me, slurping my pussy and running his tongue up and down and in and out of my holes, and making me scream.

"Did you like it when Eva was eating this pussy?"

What the fuck?

He pushed me over the couch and pushed his dick in my pussy, all the way to the back of it. His hands went around my throat.

"Oh, you think I didn't know that y'all was right here, licking each other and grinding pussies together?"

Each word out of his mouth was another push and stroke in my pussy.

"Don't she taste good? I told you that bitch know what she doin', once you get her ass goin'. You believe me now, don't you?"

His hands were on my back, pushin' me into the arm of the couch. The cushion was thin and the wood dug into my titties, but I could not tell him to stop.

"Tell me how you ate her pussy. I want to feel like I'm in her pussy again."

His hands were tight around my neck. I couldn't talk. I was cumming on myself and on his dick.

"Did it feel good? I know you ate your pussy off her mouth, like you goin' to eat this nut I'm about to bust on your lips."

I sank to the floor, but his hands around my neck wouldn't let me go.

"I'm cummin', Tee! Tell me. Tell me how you ate her pussy." His dick felt like it was in my throat again, but from the opposite direction.

And then it was on my cheek and hot cum squirted on my lips and he was right, as usual. He always was right about me. About us.

"Tell that dude you got somethin' to do tomorrow night. I'mma come get you so we can talk, okay? It's about Eva and I know you're not goin' to like it, but we gotta talk. I'll call you tomorrow. Taylor, I love you. Know that."

I licked semen off my lips and swallowed it when he walked out the door.

# CHAPTER 38

*Eva*

Goddamn. November was cold as a witch's tit. However, I loved it. It must have been all that white up in me because I was the only black person I knew that loved snow and ice. I couldn't wait to get the X3 in a real snowstorm. BMW wasn't necessarily known for their off-road driving, but for that kind of money, my truck ought to cook dinner for me, too.

Brand was still calling fairly frequently. He continually mentioned the ski trip and asked if I had made up my mind about the trip, and about us.

"Eva. I'm not bothering you. I'm calling to say hello. I just wanted to let you know that the ski trip is comin' up on us real fast. I already have our tickets. Please don't start that shit, Eva." He cursed and let out a huff of breath. "No, Eva, you're not a forgone conclusion. I just wanted to have the tickets in case you decided that you'd go with me."

"Yeah? Well, Brand, I hope you can get your money back, just in case. I haven't made up my mind and can't say with certainty either way." I was beginning to feel irritated. "If my answer is not convenient or good enough for you, I can't really say I'm sorry. You bought this shit, Brand, so ride it out."

Or.

"Eva. I know you're not busy. You know I love you. How much longer you going to make me pay? If you wasn't such a typical emotional female, we wouldn't even be here. You know how bitches is, Eva. You're

one of them. You know how bitches play head games. And you're fallin'
for all her bullshit."

I banged on him.

"Eva, I'm sorry for how that sounded. I wasn't callin' you a bitch, but
I'm tired of waitin' for you to come to your senses and get over that silly
shit from the bar. Eva, we are engaged, or we used to be. We should be.
I swear, Eva, you act like you are some kind of angel or somethin'! You
did your share of bullshit since we been together. I don't even know why
I keep callin' and beggin' you to get over that shit. Fuck it. Maybe I need
to call Jessica. She knows how to make me feel like a man."

I banged on him.

"Eva. I love you. Please think about going on the ski trip with me. I
want to make you happy again. I know you love me. I know you think I
chose her over you, but I didn't. We can talk about it on the trip. Please,
Eva. Call me back."

Brand sent white roses.

He sent pink roses.

He sent red roses.

Brand picked dandelions from Taylor's yard and left them on the
porch.

He actually watched QVC and ordered this chunky-ass rose gold Rollo
bracelet. I knew it was from Brand when I saw the bill-to-ship-to label. I
knew the nigga was still in love then. A man ordering jewelry off the TV?
Sucker.

Nonetheless, I needed a few more deliveries from UPS and FedEx to
help me make up my mind about the trip. I wasn't even thinking about the
engagement, or his winking-ass diamond ring.

Bryce was whining again.

Rome called me several times a day. He sent the spare key to his condo.
His exact instructions were for me to stay there two nights out of the week.

I really couldn't think of a reason to decline his offer. After all, I *was* his girlfriend and I got a steady monthly allowance of $1,100 to assist me in paying for the $3 toll from Pennsylvania to New Jersey. Again, I really couldn't think of a reason to decline his offer.

Then Brand's sister, Bethany, called me.

I'd admit I felt a little weird about the initial phone call because I hadn't spoken to her since I asked her to be a bridesmaid at our wedding. I hadn't even called her to say that the wedding was off.

It was his sister. Let him tell his people, and I'd tell mine.

But Bethany wasn't the source of my resentment for her brother. She adored her older brother and would always be on his side, so I wasn't asking her to choose. Their older brother, Brighton, she was deathly afraid of, and rightly so. Every woman should have feared Brighton DeLoache. He was a woman beater, and did so without apology.

"Beth, I'm so glad you called me. I must admit, I've been reluctant to call you after Brand and I broke up. I felt awful about not calling you myself to say the wedding was off. You were, after all, one of my bridesmaids. Once we broke up, though, my loyalty should have been to you."

"Eva, I don't blame you for any part of the breakup with Brand. He's an asshole, and I guess it's better that you know now before you actually marry him. I would have hated for you to find out about the girls after you were legally married to him. At least this way, you can still walk away."

*Radar! Radar!*

She continued, "Plus, now he's being an asshole to everyone in the house. We are so glad he lives in Chestnut Hill and away from us. He only comes by to pick up the girls or to drop them off. Dad isn't even inviting him to Thanksgiving Dinner."

I felt bile rising in my throat. Beth wasn't done.

"Have you seen him lately? Probably not, so he wouldn't have to explain why his eye was black. Eva, you should have seen the fight! It was a mess. Bright beat him up like he was a girl. I thought about trying to stop them, but Brand got what he deserved."

I was about to spew forth chunks.

I caught myself.

"Beth, what are you talking about?"

"Eva, are you telling me that Brand hasn't talked to you about this?"

"Bethany, you're scaring me. What don't I know about Brand?"

"Eva, I don't know if I—"

"Beth, don't do this to me now. You called me to talk about something. Please finish what you were saying." I felt tears in my throat and I didn't like the tone of the conversation that Beth had started, and now wouldn't finish.

"Eva, I shouldn't have called you. Brand told us he would talk to you, would explain everything to you. I can't believe him! He never fails to be an asshole." She sighed and I could feel the tension in her words. "Eva, I'm sorry to have to do this to you, but I have to go. I should have checked with Brand before calling you. Eva, call Brand. Talk to him. Make him talk to you. I'll check back with you in a few days.'

"Beth, just tell me—"

"I'm sorry. I'll call you in a few days." *Click.*

Okay. Whatever it was, it wasn't good. What the fuck had Brand done now? I swore, if he got some bitch pregnant, I would kill all of them. I couldn't believe Beth would call me and then leave me hanging like that.

Why did I even bother with him? When was it going to become obvious to me that he was nothing but pain and heartache? When would I finally see the writing on the wall?

That nasty herpes bastard.

I ran scenarios around in my head all night. I couldn't think of what the issue could be, but I knew that whatever it was, I wouldn't be happy with it or him. He couldn't have had some kids on me. Could he?

When was I going to learn?

I thought about calling Brand right then and demanding the truth. Then I thought, maybe I didn't want to know. What if it was something that would change my feelings forever? What then?

When was I going to learn?

I turned off my cell phone. I didn't want to talk to anyone.

I curled up in Rome's bed and slept until it was night, day, and then night again.

# CHAPTER 39
*Taylor*

After he left, I sat on the couch, wondering why I had let that happen. He knew better than to come around here like that. Shit. I knew better than to let him come around here like that. I should've told that ass to leave.

I hated it when he asked me about her.

That nigga said he loved me, but I knew he loved her more.

When she called me to tell me she might be pregnant by him, I liked to have flipped the fuck out. I hated her for that. Yeah, I was surprised, all right. What I really wanted to know was how he managed to fuck her behind my back. How she managed to get him to fuck her, after she already had fucked his friend.

Why she got to fuck everybody? Why couldn't I have somebody to myself?

Why they always got to love her, too?

Shit. That damned phone was ringing. I didn't feel like talking to nobody, but it was probably Carlton.

What if he saw him leave or saw him come in?

"Hello."

"Babe, I'm gon' stay here at the studio tonight. Paul got the call from Rodney earlier today. They want us at the studio in New Jersey in two days." He was excited and talking so fast, I could barely hear him. "This might be the link we need to really get in on the music industry."

"Okay. That's great, Carlton! Have fun. I'm goin' to bed. I'll see you when you get back." I didn't want to talk. I wanted to go to sleep so I wouldn't have to think about what I was doing just a little while ago.

"Taylor, this might be it! Once the word gets out that I'm workin' wit' Rodney, I'll be able to sign more groups to the label. This small-time shit here in Philly will be some shit from the past."

He could see the dollars stacking. My internal cash register was steadily ringing.

"Okay, babe. I'll talk to you later.

"I love you, Taylor." He hung up.

And it was a good thing, too.

What was I supposed to say? I turned over and went to sleep.

"Tee, you told that dude you had to go, like he told you to?"

"What, I'm deaf now?" I hated it when he talked to me like I was stupid.

"All right, I'm around the corner. Be ready, 'cause I'm not gettin' out. I'mma beep the horn when I pull up in front of the door."

When I heard the horn, I ran outside to the Range Rover.

"Brandon."

"You take me out, Tee, callin' me Brandon, like we don't go way the fuck back." He pulled me closer to him. "Gimme a kiss and shut up."

I kissed Brand real quick, looking around the whole time. I looked at him again, real quick; he had a black eye.

"Evan told me he was here last night. Wassup wit' that? I thought you was wit' old dude now." Brand checked his mirror and drove off. "You know I can deal wit' you bein' with that lame-ass nigga you got stayin' here, but I thought you was done wit' Ev."

"What do *you* want, Brandon? I thought Evan was comin' back. He said he had to talk to me about somethin'. And what happened to your eye?" I was mad as shit that they both popped up on me like this. Too much stimulation, or too stimulating, or something.

"Nothing. Don't worry about it. I was goin' to have Evan tell you what I wanted, but then I changed my mind. Especially when he told me he was here last night." He stopped at a red light. "You know I don't like that shit, Tee. I was your first, and I don't like sharing my pussy wit' my boy. Not even wit' him, and I share everything wit' Evan."

*Please don't say it,* I thought.

"Even Eva."

"Brandon, I told you—"

"Tee, calm down, damn! I don't know why you always get like that when I mention her name." He was looking at me instead of where he was driving. "You know me and Eva are goin' to get married, Tee. That's just the way it is. We had our chance, you and me. It didn't work. You got to get over it."

Brand pulled in front of his apartment building on Sixty-fifth Street. Brand's apartment was on the fourth floor. He had the walls knocked out of two apartments to make what he called the penthouse. I couldn't lie, though, the penthouse was tricked out and I loved spending time there. But the best part was that Eva didn't even know he had it.

"What, Brandon?"

"Come on, we'll talk upstairs. You gonna make me somethin' to eat, like you always do? Come on, Tee, don't be like that." We got out and walked to the security gate.

I had helped Brand pick out the building. When tenants didn't pay on time, I was the one who called them. And if they moved out and owed him money, I reported them to credit agencies. I picked out the sixty-inch Sony plasma TV in the living room. I helped him pick out the Bose surround sound system. We picked out the furniture from Raymour and Flanigan—red leather, just because it was my favorite color.

"What do you want to eat, Brandon? And start talkin' right now, 'cause I want to be back before Carlton gets there." I opened cabinets and the floor freezer. I didn't see a lot of food. "You want shrimp and pasta?" I asked.

"Yeah, thanks. You know I can't remember the last time Eva cooked for me."

"You know, Brandon, you better start talkin', or I'm about to walk the fuck back home." I banged around some pots and snatched the colander from underneath the sink. "Talk, Brandon, or you won't be eatin', 'cause I won't be here to cook it."

"Tee, I gotta figure out how to tell Eva that Tasha and Angie are my daughters."

I had my back to Brand so he couldn't see me smiling. At first, I was disappointed that I wouldn't be able to have his first child. And now she wouldn't, either.

Still, I was shocked as shit.

"Babies by who, Brand? You never told me that you was that serious wit' anybody." I couldn't think of anybody Brand would fuck raw dog, and take the chance of some random chick trapping him with two kids.

"Christine. You remember her?"

"Christine? From high school? When did she pop back up? I didn't even know you still saw her." I ran the shrimp under warm water so they could thaw out faster.

*Wait a freakin' minute. Eva told me that Tasha and Angie were his dad's kids,* I remembered.

"Wait, you tellin' me you and your dad was fuckin' Christine at the same time?"

210

"Obviously. According to Brighton, Wayland was flying her up here from Miami every few weeks and on her breaks. You know he don't talk about his women, and we never saw her. Bright says he took her to hotels, and to the vacation house in Virginia Beach."

"Okay, Brandon, I got that. But didn't your dad remember that you and Christine went to the prom together? No disrespect, Brandon, but that's some real nasty, old geezer shit your dad is into."

"What's done is done now, Tee. Christine dropped the girls off with Dad and disappeared, claiming she had a scholarship to medical school. Wayland got a paternity test 'cause there was no way he was fathering kids at his age. You know how he feels about giving away his money and he had to know she was a whore. Once we figured out we were both fucking her, it was easy to figure out that I was their father, and the test proved it. Tee, I got to raise the girls and I got to figure out how to tell Eva about them." He corrected himself. "How to tell her that they're my daughters, and not my sisters. She's gonna flip the fuck out. She probably won't fuck wit' me after this. Tee, I can't keep doin' this shit to her."

I was trying to think and not let the shrimp burn in the olive oil. I dropped fettuccine into the boiling water.

"I don't know, Brandon. This is goin' to kill her." I didn't know if I should be mad or happy that Brand had two kids, and now Eva probably wouldn't marry him when she found out.

Part of me never wanted to let Eva meet Brand. Part of me wanted to keep what we had to us. But when Brand asked me to hook him up with Eva, I just did it. I knew I wasn't gonna like it, but we were over. Long over. Even though we weren't going to be like that no more, I still didn't like it.

And then there was Evan.

Brand came over to the stove.

"Tee, tell me how I'm gonna do this. You know her inside and out. How's she gonna take this? How can I do this, so that she will still love me?"

"I don't know what to tell you. I need to think about it. Let me talk to her, and I'll call you in a few days." I set the table for one. "Eat, Brandon. I'll be in the bedroom."

# CHAPTER 40

*Eva*

Bryce's ring, 112's "Cupid" awoke me at seven thirty-five Monday morning.

I let it ring. I wasn't in the mood.

I was stretched out in Roman's bed and consciousness was painful. I'd been able to delay the onset of depression while asleep. Surely my heart had broken, fallen from my chest, and was now on the pillow next to me.

I didn't want to think about what Bethany hadn't told me. I didn't want to think of what else Brand hadn't told me, and how it would play out in my life. How was Brand's next dark secret going to affect my life and health?

When was I going to learn?

"Cupid" again. I hit the ignore button. Straight to voicemail.

I called Sherry at Spring Meadows instead. Sherry was my supervisor/manager and the highest-ranked person in the Wraparound Department. She'd started out as a TSS ten years ago and kept moving up in rank with each degree she obtained. She was working on her second PhD in psychology. Raking in just under $120,000, even Sherry didn't get into the office before ten AM.

I left a message.

"Sherry, it's Eva LoDolce. I'm a little under the weather this morning and I don't think I'll be able to make it in for my meetings with my client, the parent, and the interagency at Shaw Elementary at eleven

AM." I cleared my throat and let the depression sink in. "I should be back by Wednesday, so can you have the secretary reschedule my meetings, please? Call me on my cell if you have any questions."

After that, I decided to call Rome and have him raise my spirits.

I didn't even have to read the numbers off the calling card anymore. I had been using the same one for three months. Roman put more money on the card each time I got close to the limit, or he had them take a certain amount off his credit card once I hit a limit. Or something. I didn't really know or care, as it was not coming out of my $1,100.

"Rome, baby, I miss you. Were you thinking about me?" I rolled over in his bed, onto his side. Well, it would be his side once he got back for Christmas. "Guess where I am, right this very instant?"

"Eva, sweetheart, I'd love to play guessing games with you, but I'm walking into the gym for our afternoon practice. Remember when I told you that I have two each day, so not to bother calling me till after three PM."

It was seven forty-five AM here. If they were six hours ahead of us, that meant it was . . . what time over there? I tried to do the math in my head, but it was hopeless. And Roman was making me feel like an idiot for not remembering what he told me.

Maybe I should mention to Rome that I was getting fucked doggy style by Bryce European style, his dick shaking hands with my spleen when I took Rome's call and he mentioned the times of his practices. I wondered if he would mind if I shared that tidbit of information with him.

"Darling, how silly of me to forget something so important! I was just calling you to remind you that I love you, and I can't wait to see you for Christmas." I plotted my Christmas wish list in my head as we spoke. I thought I might need the 2008 X5 to get over this slight.

"Eva . . ." I knew that was not impatience I detected in his tone.

"Roman, my apologies. I'll let you get back to practice. Call me after you've showered and pampered yourself. We'll have sex through the wires, and fall asleep dreaming of each other."

Wait, please. I was going to vomit from the bullshit spilling out of my mouth.

"It's a date then. Good-bye, Eva. I'll call you tonight."

Asshole. He probably had three sons I didn't know about. Fuck him. My spirits hadn't moved one inch upward. Next.

Call history. *Purposely missed calls.* Bryce.

*Send.* Five rings. Voicemail. No message left. *End.*

*Send.* Five more rings. Voicemail. No message left. *End.*

*Send.* Straight to voicemail. *End.*

Asshole. He probably had six daughters I didn't know about.

Fuck him, too. Next.

Brand? Hell no. Never mind. I just might vomit right on his nasty, herpes, cheating-ass, dark-secret dick. Asshole.

Call history. Missed calls. Shawn.

*Send.* Two rings.

"Eva! What a surprise."

That was more like it. Leave it to a chick to get it right.

Sexy, pure and simple. Damn.

"Shawn, you called?"

"Oh, you're ready to stop playing games finally?"

"I'm calling, aren't I? What's up, Shawn? The last time I spoke to you, you were fucking me at Taylor's house. You remember that? Do I need to refresh your memory?"

Silence.

"Oh, don't get quiet and shy now. Oh, what, that was then and this is now?"

"Eva, I can't—"

"Shawn, you just called me two days ago. I'm returning your call. What's up?"

"Eva, damn, can't a bitch take a minute to collect her thoughts? It's just a little awkward right now. I'm not alone, Eva. I'm at a friend's house, but I didn't want to miss your call since I didn't know, for sure, that you'd call me again."

"Yeah, well, whatever, Shawn. Tell him you gotta go. Tell him something better came up and his presence is no longer required."

"I see you're the same Eva you've always been: impatient, selfish, failing to see that the world does not revolve around you. Aggressive. I guess that's what has always turned me on about you. You know, Taylor could be really passive sometimes." She mumbled something in the background. "Hold on."

She put down the phone and apparently covered the mouthpiece, because I couldn't hear a damned thing. Maybe I should call someone else. I didn't have time for this and did I really want to eat pussy that had cum dripping out of it?

"Eva, where are you?"

"I'm in Palmyra, New Jersey."

"Hold on."

More mumbled conversation.

"Tell me how to get there, Eva. I'm bringing a friend with me."

"Where are you coming from?"

"Cherry Hill."

Damn, she was close, almost around the corner.

"I'm at Fox Hill Run, the condominium complex at the base of the Tacony-Palmyra Bridge. If your friend lives in Cherry Hill, he should know how to get here. How long is this going to take?"

"I'll see you in a minute, Eva."

*Click.*

Damn, that was a fine-ass, ballsy chick.

# CHAPTER 41

*Taylor*

That pain in the ass, Brand, dropped me off back at home. He was lucky Carlton didn't get there before I did. I was not trying to explain where I had been, and why a dude in a new Range Rover was dropping me off.

He got on my nerves when he came around, asking me to do him favors, especially if they included her. I should've never introduced them. I should've made him find somebody else to fuck around with.

But to men, there was no one else.

They had to have Eva and nothing else. Nothing less than.

Oh, yeah, they would fuck with me, but her, they loved. Wanted to marry her, take her home to meet Mother Dear, procreate with her. Have little Eva's with light skin and white people hair. They wanted to make sure their kids would be cute, and have soft curls instead of nappy kitchens.

Fuck her. Fuck Brand. Fuck Evan.

I should've killed Evan after Eva thought she was pregnant by him.

Evan was fuckin' around with me when he had sex with Eva in Atlantic City. Yeah, I knew about Lisa. She was a part of his harem, just one of the chicks he fucked when he got horny and I wasn't around, or said "not tonight."

And who did Evan come back here to, probably with Eva's pussy still on his face? Me, hat was who. Called me on my cell phone while I was out with my friends at Scooters.

*"No, Evan, I'm not goin' home right now. I'm out, I'm busy, and I'm havin' fun."*

Then he put that whine in his voice, telling me how much he missed me and wanted to see me. *"I miss you, Tee. Let me come see you for a little while. Nothin' funny, I promise. I just want to come get a hug and a little kiss."* I could hear him like it was yesterday, even though we had that conversation more than two years ago.

So I let his slick ass come in here. And did he mention that he had just come back from Atlantic City with Brand? And Lisa? And did he mention that he had fucked Eva while Brand and Lisa were doing somethin' else? Did he mention that he had fucked both of them in one night, that he made Lisa suck Eva's pussy off his dick?

I probably sucked both their pussies off his dick. But did I know that then? Hell no. I let him in and he talked me out of my panties, even though he said we were only going to hug and kiss. But I couldn't really say no to his fine ass, not since we first met at CCP. Not since now. I fucked him and fell more in love with him each time.

Fuck Evan. Fuck Brand.

But I loved both of them, so I did what they wanted.

I called Eva. Straight to voicemail. No message.

Called Eva again. Straight to voicemail. No message.

Called Eva for the last time. Straight to voicemail.

"Eva, it's Tee. Call me. I don't know if your phone is turned off or if the battery is dead, but it ain't even ringin', just goin' straight to voicemail. I miss you, girl, and I ain't talk to you in a minute. Don't be gettin' all new on me, Miss Thang. Just 'cause Carl's here don't mean you gotta get ghost. Call me back at home."

I wondered where she was. Knowing Eva, she could be anywhere—Philly, Jersey, Delaware, Barcelona. You couldn't put nothing past that li'l light-skinned ass.

Don't get me wrong, I loved Eva to death, like a friend. It was Brand's idea that I talk to her and get to know her, way back when. I should've known he wanted something out of it. I thought she was stuck-up and a bitch. Well she was a bitch, but she turned out to be a good friend, my best friend. And she was just a regular, 'round-the-way chick, even though she was pretty as shit. And the bitch was smart, too smart for her own good sometimes.

I wanted to hate her all the time, but I couldn't. I let her fuck my first love, Brand, and then my second love, Evan. But I fucked with them, too, so she didn't have every damned thing. She only got them some of the time.

And right now, she ain't got shit.

Well, maybe Bryce.

And how the fuck did Evan know that we had sex that night she broke up with Brand? Did he see something? Did she tell him? Were they fucking around again?

It was too much to think about.

I wondered what Shawna's fine ass was doin' right now. I missed her ass like crazy.

And while I was remembering how Shawna and I used to tear up the sheets, I called Carlton at the studio.

"Carlton, come home, baby. I miss you, and I'm horny as shit. Don't go out of town and leave me like this. Tell them you gotta leave for a few and get here. Make love to me like I'm the chick you want to marry, and then I'll let you get back to your fun."

I was practicing my horny dance as I walked upstairs.

"Okay, Taylor, but you better cum wit' me, 'cause I can't stay long."

"I got you." I laughed. "Frederick's of Hollywood or naked?"

# CHAPTER 42

*Eva*

I called security and put Shawn's name on the list of visitors. Not too long ago, Rome had gone through the same process for me. How things changed—sometimes for the good, but most times not.

"Miss LoDolce, your visitor has arrived," security called up through the intercom. "A Miss Shawna Williams and passenger are on the way to your door."

Damn, the bitch was good. It had only been twenty-two minutes. Luckily, I had jumped in the shower, washed my ass, brushed my teeth, and gargled with Listerine. I hoped she was ready for this sexual beating I was about to put on that ass—and in front of her friend, if I had to.

A light knock at the door announced their arrival.

I opened the front door and there stood Shawn, in all her sexy fineness. Her thick body was molded into pink fatigues, a pink Timberland hoodie, and pink, fur-lined Timbs. Her lips were glossy and almost the same color pink as her clothes, and her hair was longer than before, worn in a straight bob below her jaw line.

Her passenger was a back-in-the-day, Foxy Brown look-alike. She was taller than Shawn and slightly heavier. She was curvy with bowed legs. Her voluptuous body was camouflaged in a 76ers jersey, a pair of midnight blue jeans, and some throwback Jordans. She had a long, jet-black weave that hung down to her waist.

The pair was fucking gorgeous.

"Eva. Surprise," Shawn said.

I walked backward into the condo as the pair followed me inside. This crafty wench was too much for me. Never mind. Fuck that.

"Eva. This is Ebony, my friend. She's been taking care of me for a little while, since you never answer your cell phone. Oh, she knows all about you and Taylor. She's a nice girl, quite giving and an exceptional lover. She doesn't mind sharing me with you."

I was at a loss for words. Imagine that.

Ebony walked up to me while Shawn closed the door.

"Hi, Eva. It's nice to finally meet you, especially since Shawn talks about you all the time." She continued talking to me while she walked to my left, making a circle around my body and coming back around to my right.

I could feel her eyes groping me, undressing me, as I stood there motionless.

"Shawn, you were quite correct. She is beautiful! Eva, tell me, how do you feel about me coming here with Shawn?" Ebony looked over at Shawn for a brief moment, reaching out to caress her face as she spoke.

"Ebony, it's nice to meet—" I didn't finish.

Ebony was in my face in a flash, her hands on either side of my head, her mouth on mine. She was kissing me softly, pulling me into her space, holding my head still as she licked my tongue with her own.

Then Shawn was behind me, her breasts molded into my back. Her hands reached around to my breasts, pushing my wife beater up to knead them in her soft palms.

It was quite a sensation, one that was difficult to describe.

I heard Shawn whisper something and then, neither letting go of my body, they walked slowly around me and exchanged places. Shawn was now in front of me, her hands reaching down to my panties to lightly rub my clitoris. Her mouth was on mine, doing unbelievable things to the lips Ebony had just vacated.

Ebony, rubbing my ass from behind, moved her hand into my panties and rubbed my asshole with two fingers. Her fingers slowly crept forward until they met wetness and she dove in, finger-fucking me from behind.

Shawn's fingers slid into my panties from the front, sliding forward slowly until they met wetness and met Ebony's fingers inside my pussy. Their fingers fucked me from the front and back as Shawn's kiss deepened.

I heard Ebony whisper something and then Shawn's mouth left mine and I could hear them kissing each other to my right, as they continued their finger assault inside my pussy.

I felt my knees buckle when Ebony's fingers left my pussy and entered my asshole, moving in time with Shawn's fingers in my pussy. In and out, faster and then slower. Fingers in each orifice, stroking, slick, noisy.

Shawn kissed my lips again, briefly, and then left.

I could hear Ebony and Shawn kissing each other to my left and I felt left out.

We were still at the front door.

I turned, breaking them apart.

I could still feel their fingers moving in my pussy, even though their fingers were now in each other's mouths.

I took Shawn's fingers out of Ebony's mouth and put them in mine. I pulled Ebony to me and kissed her, Shawn's finger in our mouths, moving between our tongues. I alternately sucked Ebony's lips and Shawn's finger, and after a while I couldn't tell whose wetness was where.

Shawn was on her knees at my ass, pulling my cheeks apart, her small, pink tongue assaulting my asshole.

Then Ebony was on her knees at my pussy, opening my nether lips with her fingers. I bent forward, watching Ebony's soft, moist lips latch onto my clit and begin to suck. If possible, Ebony's tongue had surpassed Shawn's talented tongue as she licked and sucked in perfect rhythm.

Ebony turned her head to the side, and pushing me backward, pushed her tongue into my pussy, seeking my slippery walls. I came on her tongue, moving to the rhythm she put inside me.

As I cried out, knees buckling, threatening to leave me shivering on the floor, Shawn and Ebony walked me into the bedroom. They let me fall onto the bed, still unmade from my tumultuous night. They chuckled as my limp body hit the down-filled comforter.

Standing together, they slowly undressed each other. Their lips were fused together, only leaving one another long enough to pull shirts over their heads. Eyes half closed, I watched the show they put on for me. I saw hands caressing, tongues licking, mouths sucking on every available inch of skin visible.

Shawn's head bent as she took Ebony's breasts inside her mouth while one hand caressed the other breast. I saw Ebony's head fall back, her mouth open as she pushed her breast farther into Shawn's mouth. Shawn's mouth attacked Ebony's other breast, her free hands left to wander Ebony's body as she stroked and finally disappeared into Ebony's mound of dark curls above her clitoris.

Ebony's hands were groping and straining to reach anything and every inch of available skin on Shawn's body. Ebony's hands reached up to Shawn's shoulders and pushed her down until Shawn was face to face with Ebony's clit. Ebony turned her head turned to watch me as she pushed Shawn's head forward until her tongue disappeared into Ebony's dark curls, and her face almost vanished.

I watched Ebony grind her hips and pussy into Shawn's face and lips, her eyes never leaving mine. Her eyes would close in ecstasy for a short time and then snap open to continue to watch me as she gyrated harder and harder, until she was gripping Shawn's head fiercely, moving it right and left. She came in Shawn's mouth with a low moan.

My hands had found my soaking wet pussy, masturbating in time with Ebony's hips on Shawn's mouth. I watched Shawn stand and reach forward to hold Ebony's head in her hands as they kissed loudly, sucking and smacking loudly on Shawn's pussy-slicked, pretty face.

Then they were on the bed and all over me. Ebony alternated between tickling me under my ribs and kissing me. Shawn, who was bent over my face, rubbed Ebony's wetness on my face and hair. Ebony rested her head on my stomach, licking my breasts and then kissing me, and then Shawn.

Shawn moved over me until her pussy was on my mouth. She rested there, squatting over me until her engorged clitoris was slick on my lips and into my open, waiting mouth. I sucked her clitoris, finger-fucking her with both free hands, in and out of both of Shawn's holes. I could hear Ebony and Shawn kissing as Shawn gyrated her hips into my face.

Ebony left Shawn's face and kissed down my body until she reached my lonely, throbbing pussy. She attacked my clit, biting and sucking as she stroked herself, fingering her pussy and mine.

My hands gripped Shawn's ass, moving her hips around on my lips as I ate her pussy like I'd never eat again. I heard Shawn gasp loudly, and knew she was cumming. I pushed my clit farther into Ebony's mouth. I grabbed Ebony's head and rode her tongue until I gasped in time with Shawn's orgasmic moan and came in Ebony's mouth.

Mouth still wet from Shawn, I lay there, spent, as Shawn moved over and made room for Ebony, who was still masturbating. Shawn walked until she was standing over me and came above my face, cum dripping down onto my mouth.

Fuck that. Fuck men.

I could be gay.

# CHAPTER 43

*Taylor*

I met Carlton at the door in a Frederick's of Hollywood bustier, naked from the waist down. I had been masturbating and thinking about Shawna while I waited. I kissed him until I came on myself, and let him carry me upstairs.

I started out on my knees and let him fuck me from behind with his pants still on. I pulled his dick out of his zipper when we were downstairs, and he left it that way. I could feel the zipper digging into my ass while he pumped away, but I didn't care.

When I heard him moan, I pushed forward until his dick fell out of my pussy, and I crawled around on my knees until his hard dick hit my nose. I licked it for a few and then lay down, spread eagle, on the bed.

"Come get this pussy. You know you want it."

Carlton jumped on me, sliding right into my wet pussy. Now his zipper was cutting into my thigh but I wanted him, so I grabbed his tight ass and helped him fuck me until he told me he was cumming.

"Taylor, cum wit' me, baby."

He busted a nut in my pussy. I could feel it drip out of me and onto the sheets.

His body fell on me. I kissed his cheek and pushed him up.

"Thank you, baby. That's what I needed. Now go back to work and make me some money, 'cause I want to go on a cruise to Mexico this summer."

Carlton packed an overnight bag to take to the ATL.

"Taylor, babe, I'm outta here. I'll call you when we get to Atlanta. If we get to meet with JD, I'll have him autograph a shirt for you." He kissed me good-bye and dropped $300 on the bed.

"Thanks, baby." I yawned.

"Get out and go spend the money, Taylor. Do something fun while I'm gone. Call Eva and see what kind of mess she can get you into."

I lay there in the dark, watching the TV watching me.

I called Eva again.

No answer. No message.

I sent Brand a text message—*i clld her 4xs no ans*

Let him worry about her.

I had other shit on my mind.

Possibly a wedding to plan.

Shit.

# CHAPTER 44
*Eva*

I finally had to kick Ebony and Shawn's sexy asses out. They literally tried to fuck me to death!

They let me sleep for a few minutes, then they asked me if I wanted some more.

"No, please let me recuperate." I was serious.

They laughed and jumped on me.

*Officer, seriously, they attacked me. Stole my virginity. Made me eat two pussies at once. Shook their four titties in my face.*

*Shawn found a small dildo in Roman's side table. WTF?*

*They fucked me with it, sir.*

*And made me cum three times with that . . . fake . . . purple . . . penis.*

*I asked for a reprieve, officer. I advised them that I could not possibly take any more. I fully disclosed the fact that I could not take any more sexplay.*

*They laughed and attacked me again.*

*One of the women spanked me while the other licked my pussy and made me cum. Then they forced me to spank both of them and we all came again.*

*They ordered food and fed it to me. I still have four-cheese tortellini and marinara sauce to prove it. Well, when they left, I kept the leftovers as evidence.*

*Then they fucked each other and forced me to watch.*

*No, I didn't enjoy myself.*

*I only joined in once. Maybe twice.*

*You want me to come over to the station to file a report? In a thong?*

*Oh, and a trench coat?*

*No, sir, I can't describe them.*

*But they were cute as newborn puppies.*

I had to snap myself out of my dream.

Those two horny bitches had literally tried to fuck me to death. Everything except calling the cops had actually happened! I was sore and tired. And I needed to go back to work.

I turned my phone back on. Twenty-four events awaiting me: seven voicemails, nine text messages, and eight missed calls.

Damn, a bitch was popular.

Bryce: "Eva, where the fuck are you? This is some real foul shit you're into. I haven't heard from you in two days. Is that how it is now, Eva? Don't even bother calling me when you come to your senses." *Click.*

Roman: "Eva, love, are you still at the condo? I've been calling for a while. Not that I'm expecting you to answer the house phone, but you're not answering your cell either. Are you mad at me, love? Don't be. I just took a shower and pampered myself, like you said. I'm waiting so we can have phone sex. I'll try you back in a couple of minutes. Good-bye."

Bryce: "Eva, I'm sorry for hanging up and for cursing at you. I just haven't heard from you, and I'm worried. Don't do this, please. I'm sorry, again. I love you, Eva. I'll wait to hear from you. Either call or come home, please. Bye."

Roman: "Eva, I'm not sure if the time difference has you confused, but it should be eleven PM your time and I'm waiting to hear from you. I can't continue to wait up for you. I'm expecting a call from you soon, saying that you're at the condo and all is okay. *Silence.* I'm tired, Eva, and

I'm going to bed. I'll talk to you later. I just hope you have a good excuse for not getting back to me. Good-bye."

Taylor: "Eva, it's Tee. Call me. I don't know if your phone is turned off or if the battery is dead, but it ain't even ringin', just goin' straight to voicemail. I miss you, girl, and I ain't talk to you in a minute. Don't be gettin' all new on me, miss thang. Just 'cause Carl's here don't mean you gotta get ghost. Call me back at home."

Brand: "Eva, it's me. I love you. I miss you. Please go on the ski trip with me. I promise to make things right, if you give me the chance. I love you, Eva, and I want to marry you. Call me, and let me know what you decide to do. *Ciao*."

He was so corny. He got that *ciao* shit from me.

Sherry: "Eva, it's Sherry. I got your message. Sorry it took so long for me to call back. Were you aware that your client, Coco, has gone missing? Her mother seems to think she may be pregnant. Well, we'll talk about that later. I've rescheduled your meetings, and we are expecting to see you on Wednesday. Thank you, and see you then."

I was damn sure too tired to call back all these niggas, but I needed to do damage control.

Transatlantic call first. I checked the time. Great, Rome was in afternoon practice.

"Roman, darling, I'm so sorry I missed your calls. I drank a little too much last night from your bar. I'm afraid you'll have to replace the Belvedere. I had a hangover and have been sleeping off and on all day. I love you, babe. Call me back when you get in."

Bryce. Three rings. Voicemail. Somebody was still peeved.

"Damn, Bryce, I'm sorry! I didn't mean to appear to be so distant and uncaring. I'm just going through a lot right now. I've got a lot on my mind, especially you. I'm thinking we've been moving a little fast, and maybe we need to slow things down for a little while. I'll call you back later. Love you."

Brand. Of course, he answered on the first ring.

"Eva, I'm so glad you called me. Did you get my message? Did you make up your mind about the trip? Please say yes."

Someone was an eager little beaver.

I tried to keep my tone in check. I wanted to scream, *Asshole! What are you hiding from me now? What is your sister talking about?*

"Yeah, Brand, I got it." I didn't even know what my answer was to his question, or why I had even returned his call.

"So, have you made up your mind yet?"

"I don't know, Brand. I'm not even sure why I called you." I tried to keep it as honest as possible.

"Eva, just say yes. Make it easy and give us another try. We have so much to talk about. Eva, I just want to spend time with you, so we can focus on us."

"Okay, Brand, I'll go with you. But I'm not promising anything. Don't even think about sex. We'll talk, and that's it."

"Eva, you won't regret it. I'll get the details to you later."

"Great. I have to get myself together to go back to work. I'll talk to you later. I'll call you, not the other way around."

"I love you, Eva."

"Good-bye, Brand."

*Click.*

Damn, Shawna and Ebony. I wondered what they were doing for the New Year.

# CHAPTER 45

*Eva*

I met with Brand for lunch at Chambers 19 Bistro & Bar in Doyle-stown. He hadn't been calling, per my request, and I thought that if we were going to go on this ski trip, we might as well spend a little time together.

I got there first and tried to settle my nerves. I was righteously per-plexed by my actions in the recent past.

I had spent five straight days with Bryce, almost captive in his home. He didn't go to work and forced me to call in sick. He would not let me out of his sight. He cooked for me, baked cookies, and made love to me as if he hadn't seen me in a long time.

I was almost in love again.

Finally, I was able to sneak to the bathroom on the first floor of Bryce's place to call Rome from my cell phone. I didn't even want to see my Sprint bill.

Then I decided to let Brand take me out, and see what I could see.

He looked good, almost royal when he walked into the restaurant. He'd been working out and looked fit, as only wealthy people can. I wondered if we could get things back together, back to the way things used to be. I wanted to see if I could love Brand again.

"Brandon. It's good to see you." But until then, I was on my shit again.

"Eva, you look good, baby." He hugged me, held me for a moment, and leaned down to kiss me.

I kissed him back and felt warm fuzzies in my belly.

I had turned off my phone before I got to the restaurant because I didn't want to be disturbed by my legions of fans, male and female.

We ordered and ate. We talked civilly and laughed. Brand told me he loved me and missed me. We didn't talk about Jessica or the incident at the bar.

I told Brand I thought about him from time to time.

It was true. I did, although mostly when I was with another man.

I told Brand I looked forward to seeing him on the ski trip. I let him hold my hand and kiss each fingertip. We hugged good-bye.

Brand kissed me and I felt a jolt to my clit, remembering the orgasms he had given me.

I thought I might love him again.

But Roman was coming home for the holidays. Christmas was only four days away.

# CHAPTER 46

*Eva*

"Roman, what do you mean, you're not coming home? Christmas is right now! I'm here naked. You were supposed to be here hours ago. I've been waiting here for you all day. I have been cooking and cleaning. I have Christmas decorations up and down the walkway. I have friends coming over from two states to join us for holiday spirits."

"Eva, there's a storm warning at Heathrow Airport, and all planes from Spain are grounded until after Christmas. I'm sorry, love. Now, you know I don't want to be anywhere other than where you are."

I burst into tears. This was too much. Nothing ever worked out for me!

"Eva, don't cry. You know I would be there if I could."

"Rome," I wailed, "I don't want to be alone for Christmas!" And I was alone.

Bryce was in Virginia with family. Taylor was with Carlton's family in Willow Grove, PA. Brand was . . . who knew where Brand was, after I begged off spending time with him and his family? He was probably with Jessica and friends, having loud, raunchy sex at the wheel of the Range Rover!

It was too much.

I threw down Rome's cordless phone, kicking and screaming, wailing like a two-year-old. It was his dime, his phone, so I let the crying continue till the clock struck 12:52 a.m. Seven minutes was long enough for a tantrum. If I had to do Christmas by myself, I'd do it my way.

Sniffling, I picked up the handset.

"Rome," I whispered, nose running, "are you still there?" As if.

"Yes, Eva, I'm still here. Are you done now? That was quite a tantrum you put on for me. I must love you, 'cause you are such the petulant child wrapped up in that beautiful body."

"Rome . . ." I wailed again.

"Eva, calm down. Did you get the package from UPS today?"

"Yes."

"Did you open it?"

"No. It had your name on it."

"Okay, go get it and open it for me."

"Rome . . ." I absolutely dreaded sleeping alone tonight, and I didn't care about presents right then.

"Eva." His tone said, *Enough of that crying shit!*

"Okay, I'm going." I threw myself from the bed and dragged my feet to the closet, where I'd stashed the large box earlier that afternoon when UPS awoke me from my beauty nap.

Well, actually, the cute, blond-haired, blue-eyed UPS guy carried it in because I was lethargic and the box was much too heavy for a beautiful, delicate flower such as myself. I swear, that's what he said! I had never considered having sex with a pale or a pink, but things might have to change.

"It's here in the hall closet. What is it, Rome? Did you order something?"

"Just put the phone down and open it for me, Eva. Can you do that, or is my request just too taxing for you?"

Asshole.

I didn't even say hold on. I dropped the handset and ripped open the box. The word *furrier* caught my eye and then I worked that package open with much greater fervor.

A Giuliana Teso black/brown mid-length chinchilla coat was inside. We'd been looking at it online over the summer before he left for Europe. The price was . . . I didn't even know, because prospective customers needed to either call or come into a store in New York or Milan to discuss pricing. I figured that meant too much money.

"Oh my God, Roman!" I was breathless. I had forgotten about the phone.

I pulled it out and put it on. It was perfect. It came down to my knees and I didn't even find the clasps to close it. The high collar caressed my face and felt like heaven. I had never had anything so luxurious against my body.

I ran around, peering into mirrors, preening for my unseen audience.

Oh, God, Rome! The phone!

"Roman. I am speechless," I said after picking up the phone again. "You shouldn't have. No, you should have."

"Eva, don't you hear the doorbell ringing? Are you expecting someone?"

"No, I'm not." Still furred, I walked to the door, hoping it wasn't someone I didn't want to see, like Shawn and Ebony. Not that I didn't want to see them. Just not right now.

"Who is it, Eva?" Rome sounded concerned.

"I don't know. Hold on, Rome."

I opened the door and all six feet, seven inches of Roman stood in the doorway, shivering from the cold, while talking to me on his cell phone.

"Merry Christmas, Eva." He was still talking to me on his phone.

I was dumbfounded and continued to hold on to the handset.

"Are you going to invite me in or what?" That tall, sexy giant was there looking edible, with a cocky grin on his face. He had played me. He was here!

I was naked and appropriately furred.

I screamed and jumped on him, knocking his cell into the snow.

I burst into tears again.

"Oh, God, Rome. How could you do this to me?"

He left his cell outside and carried me into the house.

I was holding on for dear life, kissing him, sucking those full lips that brought me such pleasure. I couldn't get enough of him.

"Merry Christmas, Eva," he whispered into my ear as he held me and responded to my barrage of kisses and hugs. "Let me see you." He put me down finally.

I strutted around him, hugging my chinchilla to me and then flashing my nakedness to him alternately.

I stopped in front of him and reached up to kiss him once more.

"You shouldn't have done that to me, Roman! That was terrible, and you made me cry for nothing. How long have you been here, making me wait?"

He reached down to pick me up and hold me around his waist. I threw my legs around him, my arms around his neck, and stared into his eyes.

"I just got here, Eva, and I can't stay very long. I was going to bring the fur with me, but then I didn't think I'd make it here, so I sent it ahead, just in case the weather kept me in Europe." He kissed me long and hard, sending shivers through me, and I felt wetness pool in my middle. "I have to leave tomorrow morning."

"Stop playing, Rome. That's not funny."

"Eva, I'm serious. There are storms that shut down most of the airports in Europe. I only got to Heathrow because there were enough of us going abroad, so the conference flew us in our private plane. Then we were delayed for six hours until it was safe enough to fly out."

For a minute, I felt guilty for calling him an asshole. Never mind. He'd do something to deserve it later.

"I have to catch the eleven twenty-five AM British Airways out of Newark tomorrow morning, so tonight is it for us. Now show me how much you missed me, and how much you like your present."

I kissed him a little longer, squirming and enjoying myself immensely as he squeezed my ass and finger-fucked me while I was six feet up in the air in his arms. We stood at the door, where I'd been freaked by two women just days ago, and he loved me with his mouth until I came all over his fingers.

After I stopped shaking and regained my senses, he put me down and rubbed me on my lips.

"Eva, love, I'm starving and I need a shower. Can you make me a plate while I wash off sixteen hours of traveling grime, please?"

He could have whatever the fuck he wanted right now. I felt giving for once. It was, after all, the season for giving.

"Is that all, baby? I have your present, but I'm afraid that it pales in comparison to my gift. Now I feel like shit, Rome."

He kissed me and pushed me in the direction of the gourmet kitchen.

"You know being here with your fine ass is more than enough. Now, go do as I asked, please."

I had cooked an organic chicken and yams from Whole Foods, canned string beans, boxed mashed potatoes, and bought a sweet potato pie from ShopRite. I knew it was way too many calories, and too much starch, but those were the foods I liked, so he'd get over it. Plus, he'd only go back to Barcelona and run it all off in one practice.

I wanted to heat his food while still wearing my chinchilla. I just loved saying the word! But I was afraid of splatter so with much regret,

I draped it over a dining room chair and went about my work, naked as a newborn. I caught my reflection in the double oven doors and complimented myself on working my natural beauty for all it was worth.

I prepared a huge plate befitting of a six-foot-seven athlete as I watched the fourteen-inch Sony flat screen TV mounted under the oak cabinets. HGTV was counting down the top ten best-decorated homes for the holidays. Some rednecks in Galveston, Texas won a five-day, all expense paid trip to Maui.

*What a crock of shit*, I thought. Did they even have Christmas in Texas? They had no snow, ever. HGTV obviously hadn't come to New Jersey, because our walkway decorations put theirs to shame.

I cracked open a bottle of Alizé and added a little champagne for spice. I downed the first flute and then poured another. I then turned off HGTV because it was making me angry, and Texans obviously didn't have newer, updated anything, because they all looked like poor migrant workers who had found a few wreaths and thrown them on their doors.

Eight minutes later, with two flutes of champagne and one gigantic plate in hand, I made my way to the bedroom to feed my man like a king.

Great. Roman was naked from the waist up. The towel hid the rest. He was spread out all over the king-sized bed, snoring loudly. There were wet footprints leading from the master bathroom to the bed. I knew, from spending time with him in the summer, that it was useless to attempt to wake him.

I drank from his flute and nibbled his food. I downed my drink and went to brush my teeth. Asshole.

I spooned his long, naked back and fell asleep.

When I awoke the next morning, he was gone.

Damn, no sex, again. I was beginning to think that Roman was a very tall and muscular woman—hence, no dick. When was he going to spring it on me and fuck me senseless? But then again, what did I really care? With his $1,100 each month, I could buy whatever sex I needed.

# CHAPTER 47
*Eva*

I spent New Year's Eve with Bryce because, well, I technically was still homeless and needed to put down roots somewhere. Plus, he'd come back from Virginia with promises of presents and woes of how much he missed seeing me.

I was won over. I locked up Rome's condo tightly and sped across the bridge.

I made a stop in West Philly and had drinks with Taylor and Carlton. They looked so happy together, and Carlton appeared to be hanging in for the long haul. Maybe I'd been wrong about him in the past.

I tried not to think of my *ménage a trois* with Shawn and Ebony. Damn. They couldn't make it for New Year's Eve, so Bryce would have to do.

Guilt crept into my thoughts whenever I thought about how happy Taylor and Shawn used to be together, but I quickly banished those thoughts.

For Christmas, I gave Taylor a pair of 3/4-carat canary diamonds earrings set in platinum. *Thank you, Rome, baby.* For Carlton and Taylor, I purchased a gift card to *Outback Steakhouse.*

I got to Bryce's at approximately seven PM and pulled into the garage with my automatic garage door opener. Oh, hadn't I mentioned that? When I entered the house, I found Bryce napping on the family room sectional, looking his usual chocolate self in black linen pants and diamond jacquard sweater. I tiptoed over and kissed him awake. He acted like he didn't know I was there for a few, and then he pulled me down on top of him.

Soft lips kissed me hello. I molded myself on top of his firm, mountainous chest. Oh, I'd spent glorious hours on this chest, riding myself beyond orgasm after orgasm. He sat up with me still on his chest, as if I weighed no more than a newborn.

He removed my chinchilla and ran his hands up and down my spine, pulling me farther into his space. I'd forgotten how much I enjoyed being with Bryce and his sexy self. I felt him reaching for the buttons of my jeans and working them off my hips. I lifted my lower half, assisting him in removing my jeans and then my cashmere hoodie.

Once naked, I sat on his legs and removed his shirt, kissing him as I moved downward toward his wool pants. I ran my tongue around each nipple, biting and teasing as my hands massaged his bulging penis, pulling it through the opening in his boxers. I ground my hips on him through his underwear, leaving wetness in my wake.

When I reached his pubic hair, I kissed and sucked my way down his dick to the base of his shaft. His hands were in my hair, pulling and pushing, enjoying my talented mouth as I worked us into a frenzy.

I heard him mumble unintelligible words and then he was pulling me upward, caressing my breasts with the palms of his hands and fingertips. His mouth met my breasts, his hands squeezing them together, sucking both nipples at once. I was out of my mind and turned on as my hands worked underneath me, guiding his penis into my dripping pussy.

I felt him push his way into my sheath and I bucked as he worked my hips in time with his, sucking my nipples harder, one at a time. My hands were on Bryce, on his dick, and in my pussy. My hands were in my hair and his, leaving traces of wetness and fluids in their wake.

I sat still and let Bryce do the work, watching his face with fascination as veins and sweat beaded his forehead and face. His closed eyes popped open and locked onto mine, his body never losing contact with me as he drove his penis farther and harder until I felt pain mixed with undeniable pleasure.

I grabbed the back of his neck and joined in noisily as we fucked each other mindless. My legs were straining, sore, sweaty, and I leaned forward to increase the friction and kiss him. I felt the beginnings of an orgasm tingle through my limbs.

Eyes open, Bryce gripped my waist and drove himself forward until I thought I felt him meeting internal organs. His eyes bore into mine as he returned my kisses and yanked my hair from my head.

"Tell me you love me, Eva." I could see his eyes clouding and knew we were approaching the same intersection on Orgasm Highway.

"Bryce, I love you. Only you." I surrendered to the physical state of unknowing, no thoughts and no reason. I grabbed Bryce and felt him shudder as he, too, gave into a void of ecstasy.

I collapsed on his chest and licked the sweat from his forehead. Licking down over his eyes and down his nose, I finally kissed his lips and let my love flow from me into his mouth.

"Happy New Year, Ms. LoDolce. Do you want your other presents now?"

# CHAPTER 48
*Taylor*

Eva was MIA for, like, four days. Then she showed up at my door and didn't even bother to call first. I had called her too many damned days ago, and she never called back.

Then I wondered what would have happened if she was around when Evan or Brand came by. How would I have explained that shit?

But she did come past with a pair of yellow diamond earrings for me. For Carlton and I, she had a $100 gift card to Outback Steakhouse.

Eva was my friend and I was happy to see her, despite what I felt for the men who loved her. We made Absolut and cranberry drinks, drank shots of Cuervo, and then sat around laughing at the corny Christmas shows on TV.

Carlton was looking all glassy-eyed and goofy after she left.

"You know, I'd never noticed before, but she's real pretty," he said, as if he hadn't seen or been around Eva before.

"What?" I knew that shit didn't just come out of his mouth. I knew that his mouth wasn't hanging open, about to catch flies.

"Eva. She's nicer than I remembered. I can see why she's your best friend. I knew she didn't like me before, but she barely knows me, and she gave both of us nice gifts."

"Yeah, well, the li'l bit of money she spent on us ain't shit to her. Them niggas spottin' her somethin' like two grand a month." I snorted. "This little one-hundred-dollar gift card ain't hurt her pocket. Trust me."

"Maybe so, but she didn't have to do it." He came across the room and hugged me around my hips. "What's wrong wit' you? It's the holiday season, and your best friend just left you with a bangin' pair of diamond earrings that have to be worth at least a grand."

Maybe I was just in a pissy mood right then and wouldn't be happy with anything at all. Those fucking assholes—Evan and Brandon. Why did both of them have to show up now? I was doin' okay with just me and Carlton. Now I was mad at the entire world, not wanting to speak to my best friend, and not being appreciative of the gifts she gave us.

Carlton kissed me on my neck.

"Smile, 'cause none of my boys gave me shit for Christmas. You should be happy you got a friend like her."

I pulled away from him and stomped up the steps. What the fuck did he know? All caught up in her shit. Smiling and cheesing because she came in with gifts worth less than one percent of what she was wearing.

I yanked my T-shirt over my head, catching my new earrings and pulling on my ears.

And shit. Fuck it.

*Why they all got to be so fascinated wit' everything she do? Why she got to be so special? Why is everything she do so fuckin' great?* I wondered.

First Evan came by after I ain't seen him since . . . I didn't even know when.

Then Brand with his bullshit, needing favors and shit.

Now Carlton acting all in love, bamboozled by Eva's looks and fake kindness and money she was fuckin' niggas for.

Why couldn't she ever let me have nothing?

Niggas just fucked up everything. If Evan hadn't fucked me that night and Brand hadn't come to get me and make me fix him something to eat like old times, asking me to do favors for him so he wouldn't hurt her feelings . . . well, what about me?

I wondered what Shawna was doing right then.

I wondered when I was supposed to tell Eva about Brand's kids. Why couldn't his punk ass tell her? Why did I have to be mixed up all in their shit?

Fuck it. If he didn't tell her, she'd find out when I was ready to tell her.

Maybe I'd just wait for a while before I told her. Maybe I'd let her get married to him first. That would put a serious cramp in her pretty-ass style.

Whatever.

Then here come Carlton in the room, looking at me while he took off his clothes.

I guess he wanted to fuck now.

He probably wanted to fuck her. Yeah, well, he wasn't touching me tonight. He wasn't gonna ram his dick all up in me because he couldn't have her. Wasn't gonna be fucking me and thinking about her.

He'd better masturbate with that gift card she gave him.

That was about close as to some pussy he was going to get tonight—hers or mine.

# CHAPTER 49

## *Eva*

Brand had a present for me, or so he said. It was January 2 of the new year, and I was determined to figure out where I was going and with whom. He called while I was out browsing the mall, tearing up the Fendi shop and contemplating my life.

I didn't really want to see him. I'd see enough of him next week, when we went on the ski trip. I had been thinking about how I would get the secret information out of him.

I was dressed as fiercely as possible, in clothes bought with Roman's monthly allowance. I had gone on a shopping spree to the King of Prussia Mall and did serious damage to my savings account. My new favorite shopping jaunt was Neiman Marcus. I finally shopped without peering at the price tag before I checked the size.

Okay, I admit it. I still perused the clearance items first. I was trying to break myself out of it, though. But I found a Michael Kors belted shirtdress in mocha brown and brown Christian Louboutin "Melissandre" suede knee boots to match. My quilted tights completed the ensemble, and I looked like a snow angel covered in chocolate.

I'd been doing everything I could to take my mind off the mess of my non-existent relationship with Brand. Could I ever trust him again? Would I ever love him the same again? What was his secret? How would it affect me? How would it affect us?

Brand was waiting at the front door when I drove up. I had heavy thoughts and I wondered what I was doing there, and why I kept giving

Brand more and more chances to break my heart.

"Eva, I'm glad you came to see me."

Brand looked *okay*. Maybe his jacked-up behavior had dimmed his shine just a tad. Oh, don't get me wrong, the brother was dressed to the nines as usual. Every item of clothing screamed of expensive, tailored finery. He had bigger diamonds in each ear than he'd had the last time I saw him, and there was some new trinket twinkling on his left wrist.

I offered him my cheek and moved quickly into the foyer.

Brand took my hand and walked me into the family room, leading me to my favorite comfy wingback chair. He was trying to show that he knew me, and was willing to do what it took to get me back.

Not.

Walking to the stairs, Brand looked back over his shoulder.

"Eva, I have to run upstairs to my rooms and get the itinerary for the ski trip. Someone wants to say hello to you."

He turned and jogged up the steps.

I heard squeals and laughter, then thumps and giggling. Four little feet raced down the stairs and into the kitchen.

"Miss Eva, where are you? We s'posed to find you and give you kisses."

Angie, followed by Tasha, raced back through the foyer and into the family room. They flew across the room and tackled me in the chair. They were so goddamned cute. And heavy. They had grown since I last saw them here, the day I bought my truck.

Bethany had them dressed like twins, as always. Ever since their mother ran off to Vegas when they were kids, Beth had taken over as the matriarch of the family. The girls wore Children's Place dresses in different colors, but matching styles. Their hair was braided into different styles and hung just past their shoulders. They looked just like

Brand's father, Wayland, if you asked me. I guessed that meant they looked like Brand and the rest of the DeLoache clan as well.

I wondered what Christine, the girls' mother, looked like. The girls obviously didn't get their genes from her side of the family, and their hair looked to be the same grade as Bethany's.

As usual, I didn't know what to say to them. I accepted their kisses and hugs and patted their little heads. Cute, but usually dirty, and I didn't need the grime today.

"Oh my, look at how big you two are, and how absolutely adorable," was all I could come up with.

Brand's voice boomed from up above. I wondered where the girls slept when they were here.

"Tasha, Angelique, bring yourselves upstairs right now. We're not going anywhere until this room is cleaned and shoes are put away."

Giggling, they promptly ran from the room and upstairs to do their brother's bidding. I heard them squealing and laughing as they ran.

I almost smiled at their cute selves. This might not be so bad after all. Then I caught myself and wondered if Brand would use this opportunity to come clean and confess his dark, dastardly secret.

*Oh, God, Brand. Please do the right thing for once. Just tell me the truth and let us move on. Give me the opportunity to get over this, so we can move on together.*

"Eva." Brand was suddenly back in the room while I was in the middle of daydreaming about Brand turning into the knight I once believed him to be.

"Did the girls find you? I told them to come say hello, like proper young ladies. Yeah, right. Those little tomboys should be on the football team. Forget cheerleading and cute little uniforms and pompoms." He sighed and shook his head. "Can you believe how big they've gotten since the last time you saw them?

"So anyway, Eva, these are the brochures for Smugglers' Notch Ski Resort in Vermont. We're leaving Friday evening and returning Tuesday morning. This explains everything." He started walking toward me with a knowing grin on his face and handed me a colorful brochure. I caught the look.

"What do you want, Brand? What's that look for?" I wasn't in the mood for his shit.

"I'm just glad you're here, Eva. Can't I be glad to see you again under amicable conditions?" He was standing in front of me, caressing my hair. He always did love my hair. Not as much as Bryce, though.

I didn't say anything.

"Come with me into the library for a second. We had a portrait taken and I want you to see it." He pulled me to my feet and across the foyer in another direction.

Red lights flashed and smoke alarms blared inside my head.

I walked in front of Brand into the library and immediately saw the family portrait. It was breathtaking, and obviously the best money could buy. Up close, the portrait appeared to be transposed onto a leather canvas. The entire DeLoache clan was dressed to complement one another in muted grays, blacks, and browns.

Only Tasha and Angelique were in Juicy Couture velvet-trimmed dresses, their tiny, pretty, brown faces beaming. One of them was missing teeth and they were holding hands. Wayland, Brighton, Brand, and Bethany surrounded the girls, smiling as only the wealthy could—assertive, all knowing, and confident. I'm sure Brand's mom was in still in Vegas, devastated that she had abandoned the family when he was a child and was now missing out on the family riches.

I heard the door lock.

And then I felt Brand behind me, standing close so that his lips were in my hair and on my neck. His strong arms reached around me and pulled my body onto his.

I leaned back and closed my eyes. This felt so good and so right. If I could only pretend that he hadn't fucked Jessica in AC. If only he didn't have secrets and other hidden drama that always reared its ugly head and usually fucked up my life.

But I couldn't forget our past, damn it!

Brand, feeling the change in my posture, let me go and moved around to face me.

"Eva, I love you. I want you to be my wife. I want to make a new start on this trip. Let's start over for the new year. Can you do that with me?" I wanted to so badly. He kissed me and I felt myself responding to his kiss.

"I wanted you to see the portrait, Eva, because it's missing something. It's missing you, Eva." His kiss deepened and I couldn't stop it. Wouldn't stop it.

His hands were on my breasts. And moving downward. I felt the first hint of apprehension.

"My intentions are to have the portrait redone after our wedding."

Brand was on his knees in front of me. I pushed the hint away.

"I love you, Eva. Don't you understand that?"

He put my hands on top of his head. The hint was trying to sneak into my head again.

"Give me another chance, please."

My tights were rolling down my legs. I demanded that the hint leave.

"I want to marry you, Eva LoDolce."

His hands pushed my thong aside and his mouth latched onto my clitoris.

"I want to make you Mrs. Brandon DeLoache, finally."

Bastard. He knew that shit turned me on.

Like a virginal novice at this sex thing, I came within a few seconds. Brand stayed there, licking and murmuring soothing love sounds.

Like a sucker, I was falling for it. All over again.

A light knock sounded at the door.

"Mr. DeLoache, the young ladies are requesting your presence upstairs in their bedroom." That damned butler. I was wondering where he had been hiding the entire time.

Brand got up from his knees, wiping his mouth.

"Eva, I've got to go. I promised the girls I'd take them to the Please Touch Museum if they cleaned their room. You know they won't let me back out now. Would you like to go with us?"

"No, Brand, I've got to start packing for the trip. I need to pick up a few things and make sure I can find appropriate snow gear. I'll take a rain check. Call me tomorrow." I moved away, pulling up my tights, unsure of my emotions and not wanting to say something that I might regret.

"Eva, I love you. Do you need money to get anything? I can see you're doing okay without me, but don't spend your own money when you're doing me a favor." He pulled out a stack of hundreds, peeled off $1,200, and handed it to me.

I didn't want to take it, but my mind was screaming, *Fool! Take that money. Are you stupid?* I waited for him to walk over and place the money in my hand. He kissed me once more.

"Thank you, Brand. I'll show myself out."

He never once mentioned the possibility of a secret, or any information he needed or wanted to share. He had every opportunity to confess his secret, yet he chose to continue his deceit. I was too much of a punk to ask. Wasn't this how I got into his shit in the first place?

Whatever. I had shopping to do.

# CHAPTER 50
*Taylor*

I couldn't believe Eva's simple ass! I couldn't even believe she was going on that ski trip with Brand. And I had to find out from Evan! Yeah, when a nigga found out Eva was going with Brand, then all of a sudden he wanted to take me with him. Not the hell hardly, Evan. Please. He was lucky for what he got the last time I saw him.

I just wouldn't let that ass in the next time.

But Eva. That chick didn't know whether she coming or going. Plus, I knew for a fact I could've fucked Brand in the apartment that day. But I had just fucked Evan the previous night, and I didn't do nasty shit like that no more.

Speakin' of Brand . . . I still didn't get the chance to talk to Eva and figure out what was up with her. I knew she didn't know about Brand's kids, and part of me didn't even want to tell her. Part of me wanted her to get married to him and then find out, after she was all in love and the honeymoon was over.

But then again, if it were me, I would want to know. If Carlton had more kids that I didn't know about, and we got married, I would be ready to commit a homicide. I might kill him and those kids. Their mom could catch it, too.

Shit. Maybe I should tell Brand I talked to her and she'd be cool with it. Maybe I should tell her myself.

*Would she tell me if she knew something I didn't?* I wondered.

Part of me wanted only the best for Eva. The other half wanted her to feel what she kept making me feel.

Like I wasn't shit. Well, maybe she wasn't shit.

Why all my niggas gotta be in love with her? How come I wasn't good enough for none of them? How was I going to do this?

Carlton called me from the road. Him and Rappin' Papers were on their way to New York to an underground rapping contest at some club. The contest didn't start until three AM, and they figured they'd crash overnight somewhere in the Bronx. They wouldn't be home until the next day.

I was pissed off and stressed out from Eva, Brand, and Evan.

I wasn't in the mood for nothing or nobody, so I quickly ended the call with Carlton.

I picked up the phone to call Eva, and then hung up.

I picked it up again and pressed redial, and then hung up.

I picked up the phone again, and the doorbell rang.

It was Shawna.

I said fast prayer to myself before I opened the door—for what and to whom, I still don't know. I think I was asking for the strength to get through whatever Shawna was about to whip on me. I could see it in her eyes. Something told me to feel guilty about my relationship—but for a minute, I couldn't even remember Carlton's name. I felt our relationship sliding out of me when Shawna stepped in the door and kissed me before I could close it.

I kissed her back. I loved this bitch, and it wasn't no use in denying it.

Shawna pulled back and smiled at me. "Tee, we need to talk. I got something to tell you, and I think it's gonna piss you off."

Fuck talking. I didn't want to talk. We could do that later.

I wanted to fuck this pretty bitch and make her mine again. The rest of it could wait.

"Tee," she started.

I kissed her to shut her up and closed the door. One hand was in her bra, pulling her tits out. The other one was digging in her jeans, sliding into her thong to feel the wetness that would prove she missed me too.

"Tee, I gotta tell you something and I need to get this off my chest."

My fingers were slipping and sliding around inside of her wet pussy, and I ain't want to hear shit. "Shhh, don't talk right now, baby." I didn't even know I missed pussy like this. Carlton had me dick whipped lately and I thought I forgot about this shit. I thought I was straight again and repulsed by pussy.

Shit, I thought wrong.

I dragged Shawna over to the sofa while she kept trying to talk to me. On my knees, I had her jeans down around her knees and I was fighting to get my mouth inside her. Her legs wouldn't open far enough, so I pushed her legs over her head and dove in headfirst.

As soon as I licked her pussy and ran my tongue from asshole to clit, I knew what I had with Carlton was over. I didn't even care. I used my fingers to pull her lips apart and fucked her with my tongue—it was just like old times. I felt her shaking and heard her moaning my name, and I knew I was home again. I tasted the change of her slickness in my mouth and as I slurped up her first orgasm. Then I asked my first question.

"Who was she?" I fucked her with two fingers and rubbed her clit with my thumb.

"Who was who?" Shawna was squirming and getting wetter.

"Whoever you want to confess about." My tongue followed my fingers.

"What makes you think it was a 'she,' Taylor?"

Shawna pushed me away from her and sat up on the couch. Shit, it was the same place I had been with Evan.

"I know it was a 'she' cause you love pussy, Shawna. You wouldn't even bother tellin' me about some nigga." I watched her stand up and start to pull the rest of her clothes off. She stopped before she was naked and sat down. I pulled her boots and jeans the rest of the way off.

"Okay, yeah, it was a chick."

"So what, Shawn? I ain't been sittin' here by myself all this time either, you know."

"Don't you want to know who it was, Taylor?" She reached out, pushed me from my knees, and started pulling my jeans down. My panties were soaked and shit was pooled on my thighs. She moved forward and licked the wetness.

"No, not really." I could barely think and hell no, I didn't want to know who else she had been with. Or did I? She pushed my panties aside and sucked on my clit. I felt horny and turned on in a way I never was with Carlton.

"Really, Tee? I think you might be interested in knowing who else had been in this pussy like this." She continued to suck my clit and I was about to bust in her mouth. Thinking about other bitches doing this shit to Shawna was turning me on.

I let go of my orgasm and she ate it up. Fuck whoever else she did this with. She was doing it with me now.

"Fuck her, Shawna. Fuck it. Was she pretty? If the bitch was pretty and was eatin' pussy like this, we could invite her ass over."

"Oh, it's like that, Tee? You might be interested to know who it was."